Bucket of Frogs

(NEW WRITING SCOTLAND 26)

Edited by

Liz Niven
and
Brian Whittingham
with **Michel Byrne (Gaelic Adviser)**

Association for Scottish Literary Studies

Association for Scottish Literary Studies
Department of Scottish Literature, 7 University Gardens
University of Glasgow, Glasgow G12 8QH
www.asls.org.uk

ASLS is a registered charity no. SC006535

First published 2008

British Library Cataloguing in Publication Data

A CIP record for this book is available
from the British Library

ISBN: 978-0-948877-87-2

The Association for Scottish Literary Studies
acknowledges the support of the Scottish Arts Council
towards the publication of this book

 Scottish
Arts Council

Typeset by AFS Image Setters Ltd, Glasgow

Printed by Bell & Bain Ltd, Glasgow

CONTENTS

INTRODUCTION

Whether it's gulls, lichen or magpies, ice cream, brickyards or playgrounds, or perhaps, art, death, or war, this vibrant new collection of prose and poetry is indeed just like a bucket of frogs. As editors we scooped into the brimming mix of manuscripts, a more than healthy number of submissions once again, there's no fear of a drought from Scotland's writers. And, like wee weans collecting tadpoles in those non-PC days when you could get up to all sorts of activities and parents actually encouraged you, it's been a fascinating pursuit. And here we have not merely tadpoles but fully developed frogs.

The range of content is wide and sometimes astonishing. And locations? We shift from Seville to Connecticut, flit from Dufton to Mexico. While submission guidelines require writers to have Scottish connections, their imaginative land-scapes can be without/outwith boundaries.

The submitting writers' anonymity has continued, we're delighted to say. It means we're never sure who to avoid because we've rejected a weel kent author; it also means an occasional bear hug from a brand new first time writer. And that's a great moment for us, for them, for the world of Scottish writing – the ASLS anthology is still often the first important point of publication for a new writer. The moment the tadpole becomes a frog. Kiss the frog and we might have a Booker or a Costa prizewinner one day.

The three year remit of one of the editors has come to an end. The rotating process lets a fresh perspective arrive, like a draught blowing in through an opening door. New preferences, subjectivity take a new direction. There's an inevitability that personal preferences of subject matter or voice might inform an editor's selection but the main thing is that the poem or story has been carefully crafted. And whether the subject matter is rural or urban, Scots or English language, exotic or local location, the work selected must be well written. Carefully constructed. It's also important, at a very basic level, and to give your work its best start in life, that *New Writing Scotland* receives pristine sheets of non-crumpled, non-folded, non-put-in-a-drawer-for-years manuscripts. After all, there's a wheen o competition out there waiting to fight for its right to life in print.

As Fleur Adcock states, in the humorous but perceptive 'The Prize Winning Poem', 'dawn will not herald another bright new day, nor dew sparkle like diamonds in a dell'. In this year's anthology, clichés do not clutter and croak from the works: a fresh originality and vitality kept the editors riveted as we followed imaginations through experiences of death and war, love and voyaging both literal and metaphysical.

We hope readers will enjoy scooping out handfuls of stories and poems from this hopping good *New Writing Scotland* 26.

Liz Niven
Brian Whittingham

NEW WRITING SCOTLAND 27

The twenty-seventh volume of *New Writing Scotland* will be published in summer 2009. Submissions are invited from writers resident in Scotland or Scots by birth or upbringing. All forms of writing are invited: autobiography and memoirs; creative responses to events and experiences; drama; graphic artwork (monochrome only); poetry; political and cultural commentary and satire; short fiction; travel writing; or any other creative prose may be submitted, but not full-length plays or novels, though self-contained extracts are acceptable. The work must be neither previously published nor accepted for publication and may be in any of the languages of Scotland.

Submissions should be typed, double-spaced, on one side of the paper only and the sheets secured at the top-left corner. Prose pieces should carry an approximate word-count. **You should provide a covering letter, clearly marked with your name and address. Please do not put your name or other details on the individual works**. If you would like to receive an acknowledgement of receipt of your manuscript, please enclose a stamped addressed postcard. If you would like to be informed if your submission is unsuccessful, or if you would like your submissions returned, you should enclose a stamped addressed envelope with sufficient postage. Submissions should be sent by **30 September 2008**, in an A4 envelope, to the address below. We are sorry but we cannot accept submissions by fax or e-mail.

Please be aware that we have limited space in each edition, and therefore shorter pieces are more suitable – although longer items of exceptional quality may still be included. A maximum length of 3,500 words is suggested. Please send no more than a single prose work and no more than four poems.

ASLS
Department of Scottish Literature
7 University Gardens
University of Glasgow
Glasgow G12 8QH, Scotland

Tel +44 (0)141 330 5309
www.asls.org.uk

Keith Aitchison

REVOLUTION

We had said goodbye to the little flat on the edge of Maryhill
and moved to London as requested – or as instructed, any
difference being obscure within the ranks of those committed
to making revolution. I went with some apprehension,
Martin with enthusiasm fired by unspotted certainty, finding
beyond the spread of luxury studios and apartments a pair
of sparsely furnished rooms to rent in a row of dingy
buildings where the pavements were cracked and grubby and
traffic noise roared from the High Road to burst relentlessly
against our windows throughout the night.

I had work as a supply teacher, bringing long hours
among the sluggish crowds crossing the city at the worst
times: exhausting journeys to the poorest schools and their
exhausting, bored and uneducated children waiting only for
their release to low-paid jobs, or the dole, even prison. Then
there were the International's committee meetings –
organisation, action on immediate issues, study, long-term
agitation. It all took up two, sometimes three evenings each
week, and every weekend I volunteered several hours for
proofreading, correcting typos and punctuation in draft
Party documents and articles for next week's paper.

'You've impressed a lot of people,' Martin commented
approvingly. 'You'd have support for a position – Branch
Treasurer, maybe?'

'Great,' I said, rather too mechanically for his comfort.

I had not complained, not at first. My wish for a life
changing a rotten world had been granted, and I had always
known it would leave little to spare for the young woman
who still wanted to dance and go to the cinema, must put off
having children for ... how long?

And the years were passing.

Martin worked full-time for the International, organising
newspaper sales in Greater London. It paid almost nothing
for twelve-hour days, but he loved it. And loved the
opportunities which came with it – drink and political
discussion next door to the International's offices in the
green-tiled pub whose jukebox secreted rebel songs among
the rock and pop; Party events with local London branches

in the back rooms of other pubs; meeting clever theorists he'd been reading for years.

Meeting other women.

We'd told Iain he must visit once we were settled, and though we never did seem to reach that stage, he did come at last, in the schools' Easter holiday, arriving on his second-hand motorbike with that battered old rucksack strapped to the pillion and a bottle of malt whisky in the side pocket. He was grinning, face shining with the sweat of frantically navigating North London in the evening rush hour, still with the beard, his hair a bit longer.

It was good to see him, not only because he was our friend – I'd known him since school, of course – but in hope that his simply being here might help bring back the Martin I'd married. By then, I knew Martin had been unfaithful – some woman in one of the South London branches. He was ashamed, and confessed, it hadn't been anything serious, only casual, promised it would never happen again. But it did, and I was hurt and wondering how many others there'd been I didn't know about, how many more to come. Still, I wasn't going to give him up without a fight.

When Iain came, the three of us were together once more, just as in what I was already thinking of as the good years. Perhaps my relationship with Martin might be wound back to something nearer that day we met and found, within hours if not minutes, that we could not wait to go to bed together. The only man I'd ever been to bed with, and the only one I wanted, even now.

Iain seemed really happy, glad to be with us again, cracking jokes in his old style as if we were still meeting in town every week for a couple of pints and a band thumping out new music. He opened the whisky, poured us all a drink, then offered seconds, helped himself to one when Martin and I demurred.

With some muted grumbling, Martin had postponed a meeting that first evening, and we ate in a small Turkish restaurant with a handful of tables in what once had been a shop, sat beside the bay window with the High Road at our elbows and Turkish songs urging us to imagine their warm and colourful world had closed around to take us far from our drab North London street. Pictures of Istanbul hung on the walls: ferries crossing the Bosphorus, a gleaming stretch of gold-filled windows in the Grand Bazaar, slender minarets flying above great and graceful mosques. Iain ordered for us, dishes he remembered from a month travelling the Turkish coast – I had aubergine stuffed with currants, minced lamb and nuts. We shared a bottle of dry and peppery Turkish red, and then, as the rich flavours of the food gave us the taste for it, Iain called for another, at least half of which he drank himself.

'Decided what you're going to do yet?' Martin asked. 'Work, I mean, something with a bit of a future?'

'Not sure,' Iain shrugged. 'I'm still at the bakery. Doesn't pay particularly well, but with overtime there's enough for the bike and something for the summer trip. Good crowd of people. All the rolls you'd ever want. Practically my staple diet.'

'Why don't you come down here?' I suggested. 'Lots of jobs, different types of work – you'd find something you liked, I'm sure.'

'Maybe. It's an idea, but how are you two getting on down here? What's married life like in the Great Wen?'

'Fine,' Martin turned to me for support, for silence on our troubles, and I saw from Iain's quick eyes that he had noticed. 'We're very busy, of course. Not so much time together as we'd like.'

'It's quite the test, really.' I spoke as neutrally as an uninvolved commentator. 'Not quite what we'd expected. So busy with work, travel, meetings and so on. We can go days without really seeing each other.'

'Come home, then,' Iain faced us in turn. 'Nothing's more important than what you two have together. Nothing.'

'That's not possible,' Martin came back quickly, before I could say a word. 'This is where the real action is, where revolution is being made. We couldn't retreat to a backwater like Glasgow – we'd never forgive ourselves.'

And he looked to me for agreement.

'You feel that as much as I do, don't you?'

'I suppose you're right.' Reluctantly, I supported him, but then couldn't hold back the discontent. 'But we've got to get off the treadmill, get some space for ourselves now and again – you do realise we hardly ever have an evening for just the two of us?'

'Come on,' Martin frowned at me, 'we were out only last Friday night.'

'With your pals from the editorial board. In that bloody old pub again! And we were only together because I travelled across London after work rather than wait alone in an empty room. Again.'

Music fading, I heard the bellicose roar of traffic grinding down the dark and cluttered street beyond the window.

Not the best start to Iain's week with us. He watched with worry crinkling around his mouth, but said nothing. What could he say? This was not sortable except by Martin and me, or rather, by Martin.

But then Iain asked for raki, and drank mine too eagerly when I didn't care for it, ordered more, seeming happy to sit and drink that aniseed spirit till the restaurant closed.

We dragged him to a club on the High Road and drank and danced till the small hours. Iain danced with me beneath swirling lights, then with other girls, and there came a moment when I thought – hoped – he might be getting off with a pretty young blonde. But no, he'd had too much to drink and between his broadened accent and slurring words the poor kid couldn't make out what he was saying and had to give it up as useless.

'I'm on holiday,' he said defiantly when I taxed him with it. 'Can't have a drink on holiday? I've seen you knock back a few.'

I glowered, just about ready to tell him off. But right then, I needed to focus on reminding Martin how good we could be together, what he risked losing by cheating on me, and so I left Iain sitting at our table, drinking whisky, took Martin on the floor for a slow and smoochy number, pressing my thigh between his and feeling the answer of his rising erection.

We made love later, mouths jammed in the tightest kiss to stifle our cries, Iain being on our sofa just through the plasterboard wall, and afterwards Martin held me and whispered that he loved me and, for a little while, I could let myself believe that everything would be all right.

Martin was working that week, of course, so Iain and I spent time alone, visited the Victoria and Albert Museum – where we seemed to spend a *very* long time in galleries devoted to the Middle East and Orient – and the second-hand bookshops in Tottenham Court Road, where he bought a well-thumbed history of Arabia. He wanted to see the house of John Keats in Hampstead, and I went too, quietly through the small rooms, then out into the garden, where Iain stood silent for some minutes, lost in thought.

The second day, when the sun shone and the air was warm as a Glasgow summer, he bought another helmet and took me out into the country on his pillion. I hung on grimly, arms tight around his waist, trying not to yell in alarm the first times we leaned into the curves of the road. It took around half-an-hour for me to relax even a little, but once I realised I was not going to be thrown off, I actually began to enjoy swooping down tree-lined roads with little traffic and the wind plucking at my jacket like a living creature wanting to play.

Lunch was at an old stone-built pub in the pretty Chilterns with dark wooden panelling and beer poured from earthenware jugs; we sat outside on a bench in a sheltered, sunlit corner beneath an elm tree with birdsong in our ears. Iain had just one pint of bitter, something of a relief, as he had been drunk both nights with us, finishing that bottle he'd brought and speaking of buying another.

'Listen,' I said firmly. 'You do know you're drinking too much?'

'Holiday, remember?'

'And when you get home, you're on the wagon?'

'No,' he admitted. 'Okay. I know, Lesley. But it's just a phase. I'll get fed up with it.'

'You have to, or you'll be just another drunk, and you're better than that.'

Iain looked up at the blackbird singing in the tree.

'If this is the day for personal stuff,' he faced me again, very serious, 'can I ask something? Kind of difficult.'

'No secrets, Iain,' I spoke breezily. 'Ask away.'

'You and Martin, everything okay?' He was awkward, grimacing. 'You know ...'

Anyone else, maybe even my sister, I'd have told them to mind their own business, but Iain, well, in a way it was his business. He'd brought us together, me, his old friend, and Martin, his new. I could still see his face filling with delight the night we told him we were going to live together, remember how he hugged us both and swore we were made

one for the other. And I believed, lived that, made sacrifices
for my life with Martin. Gave up Glasgow and my friends to
be with him, but now hardly ever was.

'It's fine, Iain, we're fine. Don't worry about us.'

I wondered at the lie, wondered for which of us it had
been, saw from Iain's eyes that he did not believe me.

Then it was no longer possible to pretend everything
was fine.

News from Iraq that Sunday lunchtime – Scots soldiers
ambushed in a roadside bombing, two killed and one
described as very seriously injured, which, after all the deaths
and wounds everyone now knows meant he'd probably been
burned, maybe lost his legs. In the photographs, the two dead
soldiers looked school age. I thought of the bored and
hopeless teenagers I worked with, wondered how many of
them would end bleeding into some dirty gutter far from
home.

'Jesus,' Iain said bitterly. 'Poor wee boys, dying to save
that lying bastard Blair's face. Jesus. Why doesn't he go and
fucking fight, he thinks it's such a good idea?'

Then he saw Martin watching the report and nodding
approval.

'Jesus!' Iain exclaimed. 'Show some pity, man!'

'Don't be weak,' Martin was controlled, calm. 'It's
necessary. The resistance have to kill the occupier, you know
that. Their duty.'

'But you don't need to celebrate it!'

'We're on their side, aren't we?' Martin's logic was
remorseless. 'We support resistance to imperialism, don't
we? The acid test – do you put country above the fight
against imperialism? Or do you support the killing of your
country's soldiers acting in imperialism's interest? The acid
test, Iain – what's your position?'

'Obviously not yours!'

'Obviously!' And now Martin too was angry. 'I'm a
revolutionary – you're a political piss artist – and you always
have been!'

Iain glared at him, opened his mouth, glanced at me
and closed it, picked up his jacket, stalked out of the flat. I
stared at Martin, he looked back defiantly, then swore and
shook his head regretfully.

'Didn't mean that to happen. But you see how he allows

sentiment to cloud his thinking? And who ever made a revolution like that?'

'So he's got a heart, how unforgivable of him.'

'Not unforgivable, just dangerous – for us, too.'

'You go after him, now! Make it up with him! Go on!'

And after a muttered protest, Martin came slowly to his feet and went out.

I waited, cleaned the tight little bathroom, working mechanically, simply keeping myself busy. An hour passed; finally, I could wait patiently no more, followed into the evening street.

Stood in the last sunlight sliding over the roofs and thought it through. Pretty easy – where would two Glasgow men go to make up after an argument? Exactly.

I began down the High Road pubs, peering into their twilight and cigarette smoke, listening for Scots voices among the London accents. Found them in the old-fashioned bar with scarred linoleum floor and shaky furniture, seated together at a table in one of the small booths, came quietly up and sat the other side of the wooden partition so as not to join in until I knew it was going well.

They weren't speaking about the war.

'Lesley needs more than you're giving her,' Iain was solemn. 'You've got to make her happy, man, don't you see that?'

'It's not your business,' Martin was patient, controlled. 'It's between us.'

'She's my friend. But anyone can see she's unhappy.'

'Yeah? Well, maybe you should have married her, not me.'

His words were cold, cut like frozen rain. I was suddenly afraid.

'Hey!' Iain's voice was alarmed. 'This isn't something to mess with!'

'Look,' Martin's voice rose in that way it had when he was irritated. 'Tell you what, you get yourself a relationship and try to deal with it before giving anyone advice – you might learn something.'

'Don't let's fight again,' Iain pleaded. 'Come on, you know you've got to find time for you both. She's lonely, Martin. In this god-awful town you brought her to, she's nobody but you and you're always busy. Martin?'

'You,' Martin said decisively, 'you can just keep the guilt trip to yourself and shut the fuck up. Why don't you get pissed out your head – that's all you're good for anymore.'

I heard the scrape of a chair being pushed back, cowered in the booth corner as Martin walked past and out the door, face tight with anger. Iain made no sound. We sat noiselessly either side of the partition.

I should have gone round to him, I know I should have gone round to him, but I was still shocked by Martin's brutal words, didn't have the courage, and after some minutes, I slipped away without Iain noticing.

He came back to the flat later, as darkness fell, packed his rucksack, saying something about having phoned home and now must get back early, wouldn't listen to me telling him to at least spend the night. He glanced at Martin, both of them stiff and unbending, barely a word exchanged. Maybe I should have said something more, brought it all out in the open, but I was afraid, feared where Martin might take things, that he might be driven to say what could never be unsaid.

I hugged Iain, felt his hand stroke my hair, just once.

'Keep in touch, folks,' he said to us both with forced brightness, but looking the longer at me, 'you know where I am.'

We watched him leave, the motorbike light slipping past the queue of cars at the end of the dark street, curling into the High Road. Gone.

Martin made a phone call, went off to a meeting. Clapham, he said, newspaper sales were falling in Clapham and he needed to discuss that urgently with the local branch.

The same branch that woman had joined.

I was in bed when Martin returned, lay silent as he came in beside me.

'You awake?' He whispered.

'Yes.'

'Something I've got to say,' he took my hand and squeezed it, and my heart rose.

I turned towards him, gazed at his handsome face, street-light filtering through the thin curtains and accentuating his cheekbones, put my other hand on his, wanted to kiss him, to hold him, to make everything all right.

'Iain,' Martin said slowly, staring up at the patterns of light and dark across the ceiling. 'Iain. I don't want us to see him again.'

'What!' I shook, couldn't believe I'd heard right. 'No!'

'It's not easy,' Martin's arguments were measured, logical. 'And it's painful. But it's necessary. He's not with us anymore on what matters. He doesn't have the commitment, the discipline – his drinking's enough to tell us that, leave alone his position on Iraq – whatever that is! He's become a problem, and next he'll be a risk. So, there can't be a next time.'

I said nothing at first, couldn't speak through the hollow ache growing inside, closed my eyes. In our silence, the perpetual growl of the High Road pressed close on the glass. Finally, I breathed very deep, held my voice firm.

'There's no other reason? You haven't argued about anything else?'

'What else could there be?' Certainty rang in every word. 'What else could be important enough?'

Slowly, scarcely breathing, I released Martin's hands, looked at his face once more, saw he still watched the slow shadows above our bed.

Turned my back to him.

Ruth Aylett

PICTURES AT AN EXHIBITION

What do you think of this one then? That's us you know, me and the lads. 'The constructors', that Frenchie painter called it. Bloody typical though – he got it wrong. See, we wasn't constructors, we was erectors. And before you start, I do know the jokes. All of them.

What we did was erect scaffolding so the constructors could construct. That's what we're doing there. In the picture. We each put a few bob in for it – well the families did for Jeff, Rick and Den. Commemoration. Then a 'grateful city and populace', so we was told, added the rest. That's why we're here tonight and why I've got me best togs on. Sort of guests of honour you might say. Funny thing, bad conscience, ain't it? It don't bring no-one back though.

We was all London lads. But the bird flu plague put a stopper on construction and erection both. Bit of a ghost city, was London. So we hit the road like a lot of others. Though I say it myself, we was a bit more far-sighted, didn't want to join the refugees. We stuck together. No scrabbling round the Midlands for us: got our passports together, got the medical clearances and off up here to Scotland. Immigration was a doddle with our skills because after all that ethnic cleansing stuff there was a load of rebuilding to do. Not enough erectors for all those big tenements, specially not with even worse problems over in Glasgow.

We fancied Edinburgh though, thought it had a bit more class. Capital city and that. Don't believe it when they say all Scotties sound the same. Edinburgh accents are a lot easier to get your head round than Glasgow ones. Well, if you don't mind me saying so, you don't sound like much of a Scottie. No offence. You think it's a bit daft London lads like us rebuilding stuff trashed by anti-English riots? Can't argue with that. Still, they was shorthanded and pretty ashamed of themselves too. Not a good start for a new country – they just wanted to get the evidence cleared up pronto.

Good money. Had to keep your head down a bit in the evenings and watch what pubs you went into, but we stuck together. Anyone got a bit of lip the rest of us'd be there. Just

looking ready if needed shut most things down before they
got started. The fuel shortage was a bit of a bummer until we
got a set of bikes to whack around on – enough of us for a
right little cycling club.

Our main problem was the Noxies. You must have come
across them. The Knox Army of God they call themselves,
but noxious by name, noxious by nature we reckoned. As far
as we could see they had the whole town shut on a Sunday,
specially the pubs and offies. We had to stock up on a
Saturday and play cards in the digs. Weekdays we'd be up on
the erection (look mate, we really do know all the jokes)
and we'd see a crowd of them down on the street. They'd be
chivvying people – put a hat on, cut your hair, go home
and change your clothes, read the Bible. Gone a bit quieter
now, haven't they? Course, we knew they was nutters, but it
was still a surprise, what happened.

Yeah, he's painted us on a lovely day. He was right about
the weather too, though you wouldn't think so on a day like
this with all that clammy mist in from the sea. Even before
the bird flu, London wasn't a right laugh in the summer. It
would hit 40 degrees and the sky'd sort of vanish into the
smog. Here it never went above 30 that June, and the fuel
rationing cleared off most of the traffic. Lovely blue sky for
weeks, nice bit of a breeze off the sea. Den was ever so proud
of his tan. We had him painted with his shirt off just to
remind us how proud he'd been.

Where we was erecting used to be a school named after
some dead geezer, George Heriot. Big Gothic pile near the
centre of town, great view from the erection (yeah, yeah).
Don't know what they'd been throwing at the outside, but
lots of stonework damage as well as paint and stuff all over
it. Trouble was they couldn't empty it – full of refugees from
when the floods washed that chunk off Leith. Still haven't
managed to rehouse them all yet have they? Anyway, lots of
families holed up inside, had been for months. Long enough
for the Noxies to get onto them. Later it turned out there'd
been all kinds of wild stories put round – drugs, violence,
sex. Real Sodom and Gomorrah stuff, the Noxies reckoned.

So it was another lovely day, not a cloud in the
proverbial. Not so lovely was the huge mob of Noxies who
turned up mid-morning. Brian saw them first, way before
they got to the front door, and gave us a shout. The three of

us down the bottom hauling poles up – we was only two-thirds done – nipped up the erection sharpish. Safer out the way we reckoned. We saw the big red jerries right off. Like we told the inquiry, smelt a rat. See, with the rationing it was hard to get your hands on fuel. Had to be an inside job from one of the depots, all those identical red jerries. Didn't want to hear that though, did they?

Front door smashed, in they went. Shouting, then screaming from inside. What do you do? Eleven of us against how many of them? We stayed put – even now don't think we could have done any good. Then smelt the fuel from right up top. Noxies surging out again. A bloody big bang. Vapour going off – someone had tossed a match.

None of us'd ever been in a huge fire like that. Heads out the windows high up, women, kids, screaming. Bastards had poured fuel at the bottom of the stairs, first floor upwards people couldn't get out. Well, what do you do? 999 on the mobile. Got the lads into a chain, pulling people onto the erection, passing them down. Smoke everywhere, noise, chaos. Everything got hot. Fire engines finally arrived, their lads came up top too, hosing it all down, but it had well took by then.

Course, we'd been only two-thirds done. That top end of the erection, not properly secured. Or maybe it was just the fire burned it through at the wall. Not sure. Came down, didn't it. So did the poor sods on it. And Jeff, Rick and Den.

Anyway, turned out we was heroes. Trouble is, three of us was dead heroes.

I like the picture myself. Me and the lads. That's how I like to remember us, all together on a nice sunny day.

Colin Begg

SIERRA NEVADA DREAMING

I dreamt that in North Ayrshire
arose a great mountain range
a Cunninghame Cordillera:
above Kilbirnie earth's crust thrust
skyward in snow frosted folds,
jagged and bright
to corrugate clouds
against the brassy sun

night fell
and we began to climb
and by morning we would scale
the highest peak –
Mulhacén of the Garnock
and tiptoe over cornices
fluting the abyss
of the East face

glaring and glinting
snow grips the heels
of our new-waxed skis
as we speed Southwest to the ravines
of the Three Toun Alpujarras
their white walls reflecting
yachts that dance in Irvine Bay

and soon the heat will thaw our trail
and tiring knees in slush will fail
we'll stagger last miles to an old cortijo
in the sandhills of Ardeer
to feast on bread and oil, and be carried in a rustic cart
to the shining coast, to bounce north to Puerto Largs
where speedboat-envious Glasgueños stroll in evening blush

how this occurred is pure conjecture
blame Nobel's dump beneath the Clyde –
one day in the West grew a great disruption
a fracture split and drained the tide –
Goatfell's glory faded, melting
as magma pulled the chasm wide –
shining summits steeply rising
as on tectonic folds they ride

Arran dropped slow below the sunset
and no-one missed her granite charms
for we had kissed the Costa climate
embraced her dusty Spanish arms

Liam Murray Bell

THE PIANO

'You shall do no such thing!'

'Why not?'

'Because I shall tell Father.'

Silence. Therese paced around, glaring at the impassive Mary, who sat in the armchair with her arms folded across her chest.

'I must go,' Therese stated. 'Patrick will be waiting.'

'You can't go though.'

'Why not?'

'Because I shall tell.'

'Please let me go, Mary.'

'I cannot.'

'You can!'

Therese stamped her foot against the soft carpet. It made no sound. A single tear appeared in the corner of her eye and slid down her cheek. The tear caught the light from the fire and glistened.

'Mary, Father is in his study, if you just let me go, he would never –'

'I cannot.'

'You can. You know you can,' Therese stifled a sob. 'If you would just let me, then Father would never know.'

'It's not right.'

'It is right, Mary.'

'A young girl of seventeen out on her own.'

'Patrick will be there.'

Therese whimpered slightly as she spoke his name. Mary, instinctively, stood up and placed a protecting arm around her sister. Therese looked up into the brown eyes she knew so well. They were weakening.

'Don't come crying to me if you get found out,' Mary said.

'Oh, Mary. Thank you.'

*

The piano came bouncing up the gravel driveway. It strained and bucked against the thick, black straps. Therese watched its approach from the living room window. The pickup truck

shuddered and came to a stop. Discord rang through the
air. She blinked and focused on the piano. It would be
getting wet, she thought. She turned and shuffled to the door.
Her breath was short.

'Mickey, is that yourself?'

'Afternoon, Aunt Therese, you see what I've brought
ye?'

'Sure Mickey, it'll get wet.'

Her eyes travelled past Mickey to rest on his son, Peter,
who was fumbling awkwardly with the black straps. The
piano rocked slightly. Therese held her breath, thinking it
was going to fall. Peter continued regardless. The piano
steadied itself.

'You'll have a cup of tea before you do anything.'

'That would be nice now.'

'Will Peter take a tea as well?'

'Sure he will. Peter, come over and say hello to your
Great-Aunt.'

Peter lifted his eyes away from their fierce contemplation
of a troublesome knot and scuffed his feet across the gravel.
The rain was scarring his grey hooded jumper and plastering
his dark hair to his forehead. Therese felt his rough lips
brush against her cheek.

'You taste of talcum powder, Great-Aunt Therese.'

Mickey reached across and lightly clipped Peter across
the ear.

'Get you inside,' he said. 'You recognise the piano,
Auntie?'

'It's my piano.'

'That it is.'

Therese felt her eyes well with tears. She turned back
into the house.

'Where did you find it?' she asked.

'Down in the spare room in my mother's house. Covered
with dust.'

*

'Therese? Therese!'

She heard Mary's voice on the other side of the thick
wooden door. There was the muffled clatter of breakfast
dishes from downstairs. Therese continued to stare into the
mirror. Her cheeks were flushed.

'Therese, breakfast is ready.'

Therese wiped a tear away from below her eye and took a deep breath. Her dark hair was tangled into a bun on top of her head. Hurriedly she snatched up a brush and tugged at the greasy mass.

'Therese, what are you doing in there?'

Therese took another deep breath. Her blue eyes seemed to stare through the mirror, beyond her own reflection. Her hair was tidier, but she still looked dishevelled. Flustered.

'Really, Therese, you have been behaving very oddly this week, will you not tell me what's wrong?'

Therese moved across to the door and traced the intricate grain of the wood with her finger. She could feel her sister's presence on the other side. Her eyes burnt and stung. She couldn't open the door.

'You used to tell me everything, Therese.'

There was a note of hurt in Mary's voice. Therese opened the door, just a crack. She could see a thin strip of Mary's face. It wore a worried frown. Therese's words were soft and laboured.

'I think I might be pregnant.'

*

Therese found Peter a sheet to cover the piano with. It had embroidered yellow carnations along the edge. She trailed it through her fingers. The persistent ache of arthritis in her stiff joints stopped her. Peter took the sheet from her and disappeared back outside. Therese shuffled through to the kitchen.

'You'll have a cup of tea, Mickey?'

'If it's not too much bother, Auntie.'

'No bother, no bother.'

Mickey had aged since his mother's death. The shadow of wrinkled skin lingered around his eyes and mouth, and silver hairs appeared intermittently amongst the brown. Therese's hand went up to her own cheek. It was ridged and leathery.

'You played that piano as a girl, Auntie?' Mickey asked.

'It was mine, yes.'

'And you played it as a girl did you?'

'Yes. It was an eighteenth birthday present.'

'From Grandpa?'

Therese plucked teabags into three mugs. She nodded to herself. The kettle began to hiss.

'From my father, yes,' she said.

*

'Play your scales, Therese.'

Her father's voice in her ear. She had been staring at the polished black-painted wood, in silence, with her long fingers caressing the cold ivory keys. She looked up at her father. He replied with a nod and a thin smile. That was as demonstrative as he got.

'Go on, Therese, play your scales.'

His voice was softer now, toned down in gratitude at her appreciation of the present. He coughed. The sheet that had covered the piano, embroidered with dainty yellow flowers, was still clutched in his rough fingers. It billowed as he waved his hand impatiently.

'Yes, Father,' she said.

Therese's breath was short and heavy in her excitement. She felt her protruding belly straining at the tight corset. She smoothed her cotton dress with her hands and checked that the bump wasn't visible. She was five months pregnant. It was getting harder and harder to conceal.

'Go on, then, Therese.'

Therese placed one slender finger gently down on the middle C. A note, sharp and clear, sounded through the room. She raised her eyes to her father. He nodded. Falteringly, she played the next two notes in the scale. The vibrations filled the small drawing room.

'Well?' her father said.

'I do not know the rest.'

'Well, you shall soon learn. I've arranged more lessons with Miss Fordham. She was impressed by how much you picked up in that one session with her, and with a piano of your own you will be a virtuoso in no time.'

Her father, suddenly aware of his own volubility, lapsed into silence. Therese, with tearful eyes, gazed up at him. All her worries about the pregnancy had been forgotten, all her tension and anxiety eased by the polished black piano in front of her.

'What do you think of the piano, then?' Her father asked.

'It's wonderful, Papa!'

Therese leapt up and threw her arms around her father. He did not move, but patted her twice on the back. As she drew away, Therese felt the string on her corset break and the fabric give way. There was a distinct snap. Quickly, she threw herself back down onto the piano stool and began pressing keys furiously. Her face had flushed and her breathing came in gasps. Tuneless chords merged into each other as she stabbed at keys from beneath a film of unshed tears.

'Therese –'

Her father began, but he was interrupted by the chime of the front door.

'Ah, that'll be Mr Shaw.'

Therese, her back to her father, continued to hammer hurriedly at the keys. She could feel her father's eyes upon her. Her fingertips were sweating, sliding across the ivory.

'Posture, Therese.'

She straightened. Automatically. Her father paused for a moment.

'You're sure you like your present, Therese?' he asked.

'Very much, thank you, Papa.'

Therese spoke softly and with a cracked tone. Her father grunted. Therese focused on the white ivory keys. Her hands were still now. Silence. Then, the soft click of the door.

'I don't deserve it,' she said to the empty room.

*

Mickey cradled the mug of tea in his hands. Peter sat beside him, staring sullenly into his own mug. Therese watched the steam rise slowly towards the ceiling. Her mug lay on the table to her right hand side, untouched.

'You alright, Auntie?'

Therese had to drag her thoughts back to the present. She couldn't remember moving from the kitchen to the living room. For a moment she was confused. Then she remembered.

'Fine, Mickey, fine.'

'How did the piano end up in my mother's house then?'

'Sorry?' Therese said, looking up.

'The piano.'

'You know I moved to Scotland when I was eighteen.'

'Yes,' Mickey nodded.

'I left the piano behind. With my father and Mary.'

The clock on the mantelpiece ticked through the silence. Peter's eyes raised themselves from his mug to gaze intently at her. She groped around on the table for her mug. Tea slopped over the side.

'Great-Aunt Therese?'

'Yes, Peter?'

'Why did you move to Scotland?'

*

'Mary, are you asleep?'

'No.'

'What do you think I should call her?'

'How do you know it will be a girl?'

'She will be. I just know.'

Enough moonlight seeped in at the window to let Therese see Mary twist her head round to look across. Mary's face was pale in the half-light.

'Therese?'

'Yes?'

'When will you tell Father?'

Silence. The shadows seemed to lengthen until they consumed Mary's face. A cloud must have drifted across the moon. Therese stared into the darkness.

'I cannot tell him, Mary.'

'He must notice though. In fact –'

Therese's bed was suddenly uncomfortably warm. She pulled her legs out from underneath the covers. The breeze from the open window bathed her with cool air.

'In fact what, Mary?' she asked.

'I was just going to say –'

'Yes?'

'Father was asking Collette the other day if she had noticed you spending a lot of time in the bathroom in the mornings.'

'And what did Collette say?'

'Nothing really. She said she hadn't noticed.'

'Good.'

Therese breathed again. It was a great relief to lie in bed without the restriction of the corset. The cotton nightdress was soft against her skin. Suddenly, she felt a lurch in her belly. She leapt into a sitting position.

'Therese,' Mary hissed. 'What's wrong?'

'Oh, come here quickly, Mary!'

Mary jumped from her bed and clasped at Therese's clammy hand. Therese could feel her own hand shake.

'What is it, Therese?'

Therese could hear the panic in her sister's hushed tone. She lifted her sister's hand from her own and placed it on top of the cotton nightdress.

'It's kicking,' Mary gasped.

'*She's* kicking,' Therese corrected her.

Silence. They could both feel the baby's convulsive movements inside Therese's belly. Mary's brown eyes glittered. Therese smiled.

'Is she indeed?'

The voice boomed from the doorway. The sisters froze. Neither dared to look. Then Mary snatched her hand away from the swollen belly, and Therese hurriedly clutched the sheets up to her neck. Her eyes swivelled around. Their father stood, silhouetted, in the doorway. He advanced into the room. The moonlight angled onto his face, exposing the ugly grimace of disgust on his lips.

'I think you should come to my study, Therese,' he said.

*

Therese's tea was cold. A congealing puddle of milk floated at its centre. She stared vacantly at the fire. It danced, flickered, and swam with her tears.

'My mother would have wanted you to have the piano, Auntie.'

'Mary,' Therese whispered.

'Yes. You were a great comfort to her at the end, you know.'

'Poor Mary.'

'She often talked of you when I was young.'

Therese nodded and smiled at Mickey.

'I loved her very much, you know,' she said.

'I know. She was very grateful that you came back.'

'I came back too late.'

'You came as soon as you could. Grandpa made it difficult.'

Therese sighed. The clock ticked loudly. Mickey glanced at it and nudged Peter. They both began to rise from their seats.

'All those years, Mickey.'

'Your letters were a great comfort to her.'

'I didn't come to see her. I didn't −'

Therese trailed off. Her eyes had reverted back to the fire. Peter, without a word, moved across and placed another log onto the heaped coals. They all watched intently for a moment, as the flames began to lick up the side of the wood.

'C'mon son,' Mickey said. 'Let's get this piano inside.'

Peter nodded.

'You'll be alright here for a minute, Auntie?' Mickey asked.

There was no answer.

*

'Bless me father, for I have sinned. It has been eleven months since my last confession.'

The confessional box was dark and draughty. The priest, a vague shadow on the other side of the dividing screen, was breathing heavily. She avoided looking at him, staring instead at her tightly clasped hands.

'What troubles you, child?'

'I gave birth to an illegitimate child. A baby.'

The musky incense burnt her nostrils. Her eyes filled with tears. Her mind rang with the echoes of a scream; the darkness flashed an image of the tiny reddened cheeks; and, just for an instant, she could feel his insistent grip around her finger. Then it was broken.

'And where is the child now?'

'It is in an orphanage. A Protestant orphanage.'

Silence. Therese heard the small gasping breaths of her baby as she held him in her arms. Her baby. She had not named him. Her father had allowed the matron to do that. Neil. She detested the name.

'And the father?'

'He lives in Cushendun.'

'Is he a Catholic, though?'

'He is.'

The priest was silent. Patrick had offered to marry her,

to care for their son. Her father had laughed — a short
sardonic cackle. She envisaged Patrick's face, crestfallen, as
he was told that the baby was to go to the orphanage. She
saw his tears as he was told that she was to go to Scotland.
He must have cried.

'And have you mended your ways?'

'I am to go to Scotland. To Ayr. To live with my cousin
Katy.'

'I see.'

'She is my father's sister.'

'And you repent your sin?'

Therese stumbled from the confessional box with tears
streaming down her cheeks. The chapel swam and faded
before her eyes. She collapsed against a pew and pressed her
forehead against the cold, smooth wood. She gulped in the
thick air, trying to fill her lungs. She tasted bile.

Hail Mary, full of grace, the Lord is with thee.

*Blessed art thou among women and blessed is the fruit of
thy womb, Jesus.*

She saw the long, dark room with the stone-clad walls.
A succession of wooden cots, spaced at regular intervals
along the tiled floor. Murmurs and soft breaths rose from
them and dispersed into the cold air. She felt his shallow
breath. His head was nestled comfortably against her breast.
She held him closer.

Hail Mary, the Lord is with thee.

Blessed art thou and the fruit of thy womb, Jesus.

The matron prised him from her grip. She could feel
her father's hand upon her shoulder. The matron lowered
him into a cot. The rough, grey sheets lay stiff against his soft
skin.

Hail Mary, with thee.

Blessed art the fruit of thy womb, Jesus.

He awoke. Blue eyes, large and bright, frantically
searching for his mother. She heard his screams.

Hail Mary, Blessed art the fruit of thy womb.

He screams.

*

Mickey and Peter struggled into the room at one end of the
piano, pushing with all their might against its weight.
Therese's eyes shifted across to them.

'Neil,' she said.

'Sorry, Auntie?'

'That's his name.'

'Whose name?'

Peter was pushing against the piano with his shoulder. Mickey had paused to listen to Therese but now he resumed shoving and pulling. They moved it, by degrees, until it sat at an angle against the far wall. Then they looked round at Therese, beads of sweat erupting across their foreheads. Therese's eyes stared straight through them.

'He wouldn't want to know me now, though.'

'Who, Auntie?'

'He was adopted by a Protestant couple named Roberts.'

'Who?' Peter asked.

Mickey shrugged. Therese's eyes slowly focused on them and a spark of recognition lit within her. She shook her head slightly.

'It's too late,' she said softly.

Slowly, painfully, she levered herself from the armchair.

'You'll have a cup of tea,' she said.

'No really, Auntie, we must be off.'

'I must give you a cup of tea before you go.'

She shuffled over to the piano and reached a stiff, crabbed hand out towards the yellowed ivory keys. Her index finger gradually straightened and pressed down gently on the middle C. The note sounded, sharp, clear, and out of tune.

Tom Bryan

GARDENS, STRANGE AND COLD

He has only just stepped from the bus and his wife is shouting at him. In front of everyone. More than an hour on a crowded bus, just home, and in front of everyone she is shouting at him. She is not angry though.

'Come quickly,' she says, grabbing his hand like a child would do. 'Hurry.'

'Have you ever seen anything like this?' she asks, pointing to the gable wall of their house. He looks. He hasn't.

The gable end of the council house is white harl, set against the blue June sky. The yellow broom is ablaze on the green hill, looking like blisters on the sloping back of the land. He bends down to look more closely at what he thinks he has seen. To make sure.

The creature is bigger than his big working-man's hand.

'A butterfly?' she says.

'No, I think it's a moth.'

It is shivering and distressed, beating its wings against the wall.

She looks at the moth, then at him.

'We can't leave it here. The neighbourhood cats will kill it. We'll bring it inside, poor wee soul.'

He thinks. *She is like that. Everything in the world is her poor wee soul.* He has always liked that kindness about her.

'Fetch my cigar box. It's nearly empty anyway.'

The cigar box has a picture of Prince Edward on it. With his big hands he guides, nearly scoops, the moth into the box and closes the lid. They put the box near the gas fire while they have their tea.

'Yon creature is a wonder.' She speaks over the soft sound of chewing and working forks.

'Not a wonder from here. Not by a long way. There is no creature like that in these islands.'

'Will it live?'

He's not sure. 'I don't think they have mouth parts for feeding. It's the caterpillars that feed. Adults mate and die.'

After a cup of tea, he lifts the lid of the box. The creature is dead. They marvel at the size of it and the colour of the wings. In their combined century of Scottish life, they have never seen so many colours as are on the wing of the moth.

He takes the bus to work in Edinburgh only three days a week now, working in a dying trade. He makes miniature furniture for exhibitions and displays. He carves the wood and paints the intricate detail. More and more of the work is mass-produced and made in man-made materials. He admits some of it looks better than his work. It costs less too. On the bus he puts his leather tool bag on the net rack above the seat and carries the cigar box on his knee.

The museum is not far from his work and he has an hour for lunch.

The young man at the museum is sniffy at first.

'A moth. Yes, we have many moths already.' He opens the box impatiently, expecting something that it isn't there. He changes his tone, like an engine moving up a gear.

'Where did you find this?'

'Yesterday. Teatime. It was clinging to the gable end of my council house. It was still alive.'

The young man clears his throat.

'May I keep this until Dr Wilson comes back this afternoon?'

'You may keep it forever if you like. Display it so others can see it. It is a wonder, right enough.'

He goes back and finishes his afternoon's work, a copy of a Duncan Phyfe chair.

He rides the bus home having been told his firm will fold in a month's time. Something he has been expecting since his work week was cut from five days to three. He will be given handsome severance pay.

The bus moves through the June countryside, sun, green hills, cobalt sky, cold enough to let all the colours blend in a vibrant way. The grass shivers on the hill, the way the moth shivered.

He goes back to the museum the following week.

The same young man greets him.

'Dr Wilson said your moth was a long way from home. It comes from the Atlas Mountains of Morocco. It may have been a stowaway with fruit or vegetables but chances are the southern winds blew it here. With your permission, we will display it in our cases adding your name to the information.'

'No, keep the moth but leave my name out. My name is not important.'

He has a relative in New York who will sponsor him. He will go out alone, leaving his wife with their grown son in Scotland. Being an old merchant navy man, he will sail to New York.

He goes through immigration with his tool bag. It being morning, he decides he will walk to his nephew's apartment. He will ask directions.

The moth is in his head, even in New York. He thinks of its shivering, its colours. He remembers a line from an old poem. 'To sleep in gardens, strange and cold.' Both man and moth. He crosses the busy street and keeps walking.

BRICKYARD, ASSEMBLY LINE

Raccoon-eyed in clay,
splattered up to the elbows.
Blue-grey mud slapped, coaxed,
readied for the kiln today.

We sort the finished brick,
clanging them together like healthy bells
or else crumpling, ill-fired,
hollow and sick.

Laughing, comparing tattoos
glowering as the mood takes.
Pop pills or salt tablets
washed down with hip-flask booze.

Out of kilter tango is what we feel.
In the bad light of the factory
to the beat of juddering machines,
grinding gears, as old metal peels.

My mind is here, at dawn.
Two hours until morning break,
but I've run out of mental tricks
to get from now to then.

But we leap clear when the cogwheel crashes,
run down into our precious time.
Wage slave or saboteur,
we all bolt together outside, to the sun.

Eliza Chan

SUBTEXT

Patriarchy murders the dream of a better tomorrow. The misogyny of Raymond Briggs' *The Snowman.*
By A. Bowman (Senior Lecturer at the University of Ashwood)

In the ever-popular children's picture book *The Snowman* by Raymond Briggs, misogyny is rife,[1] continuing the tradition of A. A. Milne[1] amongst others to create an atmosphere of hate between the sexes.[2] The Snowman of the title, or should I say snowperson, is given the masculine role of friend and replacement patriarch. The boy's mother helps him in his creation of this frigid substitute, a physical representation of the love he has never received from his father.[3]

Telling is that the boy, James, gives the Snowman legs. Legs are not a normal feature of childhood snowmen. Circular balls of snow normally suffice.[4] In this case however, even before the Snowman begins to move, he is provided with proportional limbs for arms and legs. The boy shows by this creation, a need for physical contact. The Snowman later uses these arms and legs to take the boy on

[1] Those who deny chauvinism in *Winnie the Pooh* are blinded by false loyalty to a childhood memory. The alteration of honey to 'hunny' alone shows the extent Milne is willing to subvert female power for his own gains. What is more, the only female character of any merit is Kanga, who is little more than a receptacle for her male child Roo. See my forthcoming article *'Winnie the Pooh: Lord of the Flies* in the Hundred Acre Wood?'

[2] This is not to be confused with 'hate of the other' as shown in my article 'Why was Spot the Dog always hiding? Racist lynching masquerading as children's games'; or even a 'social class hate' as seen in my article 'The nightmare of Victorian chimney-sweeps revived: Sooty Heights and the social order of puppet animals'. Both can be found in my forthcoming book, *Children's Literature and the Secret Voice of Hate: A Feminist Review of the Ladybird Books.*

[3] Of course this was the polar opposite of my childhood. I was brought up in a loving and stable household with my brothers Julian and Richard. My what adventures we had! We always seemed to stumble across foul play but Timmy, our loyal collie, was sure to pluck us from any dangerous gypsies.

[4] Once we were snowed in on the mountains. Luckily Grandpa and I did not mind sharing the cabin with the goats, and our neighbour Peter would regularly come by. He was the goatherd and constantly fretted over the health of his wards. Not much chance of them getting lost or eaten by wolves whilst they frolicked indoors, leaping over the tables and knocking over everything in sight.

an adventure: dance, walk,[5] hold his hand and hug him before he ultimately becomes a slushy pile of failed dreams at the novel's end.

I have, for deliberate reasons, fallen into the trap of calling the Snowman a *man*. Of course as a non-reproductive object he is not a man.[ii] He has more feminine traits than critics have often envisaged. Take, for example, the replacement of the stereotype carrot for a tangerine nose. The phallus of the carrot is substituted for a feminised seeded fruit, multilayered and round.[6] This is taken further in the short film inspired by the book wherein the Snowman takes James to a party at the North Pole.[7] During the dance there is only one female snowman[8] as denoted by her floral hat, dress and apron. The presence of an apron puts the female in an automatically subservient position. Yet she is not discriminated against. The other snowmen treat her equally during the dancing, many of them taking on the female role by dancing with each other as well as with James.[9] They, in fact, emulate female behaviour with their courtship dancing

[5] As well as Clara and Katy, I knew another child who learned, under my tutelage, how to walk. Or rather, in his case, run. Colin was a petulant and selfish thing who needed little more than a sprinkle of sunshine and a temper more snapdragon than his own to prevail upon him.

[6] If I was a bra-burning feminist, I'm sure I'd make much of that. Luckily for my readers, I retain a balanced opinion of things.

[7] Critics have debated whether it is the North or South Pole they travel to, as the existence of penguins indicates the South. However, conclusive evidence indicates it is definitely the North Pole: everyone knows Santa Claus does not winter in the South.

[8] Female snowperson? Or snowwoman? Either alternative is acceptable but for the sake of continuity I shall continue to use the more familiar terminology of 'snowman'. We can expect a gender-neutral version of the word to appear much as air host/hostess have become flight attendant and waiter/waitress have become servers (although in my opinion 'servers' is a much more derogatory word with connotations of servitude and slavery). 'Snow-individual' or 'snow-non-gendered-humanoid creation', as put forth by an esteemed colleague, are regretfully not succinct enough to have a popular usage.

[9] My first dance was not as exquisitely enchanting as those Jane Austen novels would pretend possible. I spent the whole night with my back to the wall, much to the chagrin of my sister and any would-be dance partners. Truth of the matter is, there was a gaping tear in the russet taffeta skirts which was a mortifying embarrassment.

and jollities rather than the masculine bravado[10] that often prevails.

Where are the other female snowmen? Like Tolkien's Ents, they are a long-forgotten sex.[11] More than that, they are an unimagined sex. If all snowmen are the creations of the imagination of children, then the absence of female snowmen is an indicator of absent female role-models for British children.[iii] Women are present in these children's lives, but they are not respected or idolised the way men are.[12]

In the film, the only other child is a blonde girl[13] who spies the flying pair out of her window. This child is similarly awake at the magical time when snowmen can fly and yet she is trapped with the private sphere of her house.[14] She lacks both the creativity and the insight to either make a snowman or perceive its supernatural powers. Moreover her miscomprehension of the Snowman and James as Santa Claus shows that women are inferior intellectually to men also.[15]

Yet all of this did not exist in Raymond Briggs's novel. His picture book shows a world populated with men, with

[10] Despite being of the wrong gender, I have often been a great proponent of activities which could be termed as falling under the auspices of 'masculine bravado'. After my best friend tricked me into white-washing a fence for him, I decided I'd had enough of those attempts to sivilize or unsivilize me. I took up on that raft with Jim and we ended up in a right pickle with robbers and drunkards and all them others.

[11] Actually I am inclined to think Tolkien was the forefather of misogyny as well as fantasy. His only sympathetic female character spends most of her time emulating men, even as far as going into battle in drag. Peter Jackson fared little better in padding out Liv Tyler's Arwen in a ridiculous array of costume changes and arbitrary husky elvish.

[12] Let's be honest, film directors, CEOs, MPs, Nobel Prize winners are all prevalently male despite sexual discrimination supposedly ending in the 1960s.

[13] Swedish? Or just to oppose the hero's startlingly ginger hair. A boy once called me 'Carrot-top' in school so I smacked him one. Precocious thing that Gilbert.

[14] Actually her bedroom. And there is another child sleeping in her bed, showing that women are not even given the luxury of privacy.

[15] How exactly you mistake a snowman and a ginger boy for nine reindeer and a sleigh, complete with red-nosed leadership and a plethora of 'ho ho ho's', I don't know. Benefit of the doubt would assume she needed glasses. A possible ignorant orphan at the most extreme. However, pretty female orphans have a tendency to be adopted by, or marry, rich benefactors. The disturbing thing is when both happens, as in *Daddy-Long-Legs* by Jean Webster.

James's mother playing the part of domestic aid and housewife only.[16] James clearly yearns for male attention; even his pyjamas are a miniature version of his father's sleeping clothes. Affection has to be provided by a six-foot lump of frozen water.[17] The tragic fashion in which James devotes his love to the Snowman is shown by the removal of his mitts in order to fix the Snowman's face, a face complete with a loving smile.[18] The need for physical contact, the obsession with detail, shows that Briggs is compensating for something missing in the boy's life.[iv] Later James holds the Snowman's hand during their walk in the air, their relationship having progressed from that of creator and creation to equals.

These connotations are obvious to see for anyone with the sense to look past the whimsical pencil drawings and altar boy solos.[19] In *The Snowman Story Book*, words[v] have been added by Briggs to his celebrated pictures. The repetition of the words 'he', 'him' and 'his' emasculate the entire text to a degree that the pictures alone did not emphasise.[20] Furthermore the letters themselves can be interpreted as attempted male domination over any female expression.[21] 'I's, 'L's and 'J's punctuate the text in sentences

[16] Marmee was more than the ideal mother and housewife. She didn't just look after us but also the local poor families. Amy was the vain one, would rather have ribbons for her hair than food for a sick child. It's rather suspect that she ended up marrying the boy next door who had been in love with me, but I don't think she'd appreciate me bandying that around. Possible material for my next novel all the same.

[17] Never give a horse cold water to drink after he has been out all night. I learned this the hard way when I nearly gave our horse, Black Auster, colic.

[18] In the film version James doesn't even start out wearing mitts, causing outrage in houses across Britain. More than that, parents were appalled to find the rate of childhood hypothermia and pneumonia had increased dramatically around the film's release year of 1982. The children of the nation standing in the snow at midnight was a scene from a Hitchcockian nightmare.

[19] Boy sopranos themselves are heavily connected with castration. Freud did not live to see *The Snowman* but an educated guess at his reaction to it would have involved the words 'phallus' and 'psychological projection'.

[20] See Ursula Le Guin's *The Left Hand of Darkness* for a study of gender perceptions and the personal pronoun in narrative. Or learn a language such as Japanese, wherein the personal pronoun is androgynous.

[21] Russell Hoban's attempts to alter this in his post-nuclear *Riddley Walker* fails abysmally, to the extent that he later claimed this was not his intent. Daniel Keyes similarly made patronising claims that a female language was somehow retarded in his otherwise beautiful *Flowers for Algernon*. Of James Joyce, the less said the better (unfortunately academics tend to disagree with me on this and many other points).

like 'In the morning James woke to see snow falling.'[22] In contrast female phrases such as 'James gave the Snowman a hug and said good night'[23] are very rare.[24]

Female power is blanketed in a suffocating carpet of snow.[25] James ties a scarf in a tight knot around the Snowman's neck, later to be replaced with his father's tie, a symbol of authority. He bends to the will of the male machine and institutionalised uniforms.[26] Even the gift given to him by Santa Claus,[27] a scarf spotted with miniature snowmen, is less innocuous than it first appears. This is a device for tying, throttling the boy soprano's larynx so that he cannot speak out against the powers,[28] nor can he mature to surpass them.[29] He is instead invited in his tragic loss, to substitute the Snowman with a hangman's noose.[30]

People have always assumed that the fantastical journey of James and the Snowman was only the delusions[vi] of a childhood imagination.[31] The Snowman must melt to a pile of slush by the novel's end to ensure that James moves from adolescence into maturity and accepts his position in the world. Nonetheless, this view assumes that it was the natural

---

[22] Briggs, R., *The Snowman Story Book* (Penguin: London, 1992), p4.

[23] Briggs, p18.

[24] What I mean by 'female phrases' is a domination of yonic letters such as 'A's, 'O's and 'W's.

[25] Need I make the link between the words 'snow' and 'white powder'?

[26] The school story has been undermining individualism for years from Chalet School to Malory Towers. Some good old fashioned jingoism runs riot in *Goodbye, Mr. Chips*. I had taught as a school mistress in the Marcia Blaine School at Edinburgh and knew that the realities were less focused on teamwork and camaraderie, and more on getting ahead. That was back in my hey-day.

[27] The Santa Claus of the film disguises himself under a feminine apron to gain James's trust leading to the question: where was Mrs Claus?

[28] By recent government figures, thoughtcrime will be impossible given the utter domination by doubleplusgoodthinkingful Newspeak by 2050.

[29] Stunting natural ability can often have unusual consequences. Being able to levitate pencils and headmistresses was one of my earliest tricks.

[30] I've never understood why the prize turkey in the butcher's window was unsold on Christmas Day. Nor why Tiny Tim mattered so much when the rest of the unnamed Crotchet family shivered under the dual disadvantage of poverty and reasonable health.

[31] They make similar arguments against Narnia, Pern and Krynn: however I am yet to see conclusive evidence that they don't exist. Unfortunately the Pernese immigration services refused to stamp my passport due to my one-quarter citizenship.

actions of the 'bright sunlight shining'[32] that results in the Snowman's demise. Sunrise in British winters is preceded by dawn. The Snowman would have had more than adequate time to shelter himself within the chest freezer in the garage, shown to him previously by James. There is no reason that a snowman with newfound emotions, movements and attached personality, would be willing to stand and wait for his death.[33] It must be concluded, therefore, that it was not a suicide or act of nature, but a murder.[vii]

As the only two candidates are his parents, we can quickly narrow the perpetrator down to his father. Who else would have noticed his trousers were wet from the Snowman's borrowing? Not to mention the wet armchair when James allowed the Snowman to recline by the fire. The father, knowing he is to be replaced, can only wreak his revenge by destroying the one thing his son loves. This in effect renders James to a lump of cold snow.

Any hope for a future where boys grow up into men empathetic with women's plight has been massacred by this supposedly delightful Christmas tale. Children the world over and generations apart have watched and read Raymond Briggs's *The Snowman*, little understanding the damning damage it has done to their gendered perceptions of the world. Give in and hope melts under that glaring light of interrogating dominance.

---

[32] Briggs, p19.

[33] Some people would point to characters such as Johnny 5, Robocop or the Terminator but a snowman has a vastly superior intellect to constructs of steel and microchips. Certainly all are man-made but a snowman is an individual creation without the factory-line aspects of technology. In Sapporo, Japan, armies of snowmen annually attack the city under the guise of the Yuki-matsuri (Snow Festival). They learned the technique of infiltration from Ambergris' gray caps.

Endnotes

[i] I first came in contact with the picture book when I was ten and my Da was in a rare mood of good humour. His face, when not down-turned with sooking at a smouldering pipe, was a road map of wrinkles moving across his flaccid features like river tributaries flowing into that opened mouth. A voice gruff with the slick of stout Irish pints would demand: 'Look! What's that? A snawman. What's he doin?' Timpani drums hammered in my head and stammering a twitched reply my garden bird voice was eaten whole by his harrier. My eyes remained evermore averted during our story time, pouring over each sketched drawing, fascinated by the changing direction of lines, the production process

lying vulnerable under the surgery lights. You could almost hear the pencil rustling still across the paper to finish each image just as he turned the page. Hear it behind the cacophony of jackdaws in my head.

ii In inclement weather his boots hammered upon their own anvil, forcing the air to yield before his tread. My Da's red hands would be tightly squeezed into sausages of mixed meat, banging at the doors, the walls, the faces that stood in his way. We could hide but there were too many of us, and not enough dens, clubhouses and secret passages to conceal all. Tables were no good. However much you thought yourself hidden, a snag – a patent shoe like a polished apple, or a sneeze from under a lace veil – gave you away. Dragged to some ritual sacrifice, the last of the Mohicans would feign no weakness until tears slithered like guilty pleasures down both cheeks. The ivory teeth gave way to discordant gnashing, and thumping, and crying, until it was off the end of the keyboard ... the end of the scale.

iii The smell of lavender and soap suds, mixed like watercolours on a chipped plate. Fingering the puckered ends of aprons strings, slickly squelching as I pressed my face into her back. Let her absorb my trembling frame, let her absorb his every blow. My Ma was no rock, no anchor and no sail. She was a mop of flailing indecision, soaking up the dirty water with the clean.

iv Gingerbread men make good voodoo dolls. You can bite off their heads and crumb up their arms and their icing faces remain in an upturned crescent moon. Da saw us as much of the same. Physical contact was something never lacking in our childhood. Things that can be thrown without breaking: cutlery, clattering like cymbals if properly timed; books, a well-placed corner of a paperback can cause substantial injury, especially when followed by its sequel. Collecting long sagas is ill-advised. The hardback is often preferable but less readily available. Also, small children. Remarkably flexible. Although like elastic there is only so far they will stretch before the inevitable smell of rubber lingers like mould on your fingers and the backlash stings the palms.

v 'The boy who never grew up,' was the nurse's reply when she swaddled me in the yellowing blanket. I could feel the scabs and vomit of past victims in a lingering sediment about my bed. To be stuck here, forever, in this state of helplessness. Floundering in a green sea. At school they said we could never understand wartime trauma. I looked again at the gaudy pixie figure upon the ward wall: his green tights and tunic like a leprechaun stretched on a rack. He brandished a sword, he could fly, he never had to see his parents again. Candyfloss for the mind, it melted inconspicuously into the gloom, sugar-coating my witch's house. 'Is there a book?' My eyes demolished every word that was put before me and every story became a bead to drape around me in a necklace of plastic pearls.

vi Can you build a house of paper? Windows of plastic covers and doors that creak in unyielding spines. The wallpaper embossed in immortal names, dazzling in the torchlight. Lock the door and swallow the key. Eat me. Drink me. Which will make you small? A bookworm luxuriating in the inside pocket, warm there where a heart still beats. An index intersects a pouting chasm. The universal gesture for mutism. Oh haven of bibliophiles, six days a week you are my refuge. Then the day of rest when the Devil knocks upon my door. Forty days and forty nights endured in arid sands. Aslan breathes me back to life and Merlin tells me I am king. There is no test that the Green Knight may set that I am not equal to.

vii Da told me constantly, persistently, that I was good for nothing. God forbid that I dreamed of adventure in the great wide somewhere. To make-believe you are a little princess when the puddle water through fifth-hand and foot shoes tells you otherwise. You need life experience to write, they say. Well it rained on me like gobstopper hailstones on the roof of my sanity. I've read them all. These people that have the answers: hysteria, the Electra complex, madwomen in attics, the other, the strange ... But it is not alien, dear Steerpike. You wanted to be one of us, where you belong. A stone falls bruised but unbroken into the ink of that well. We are stained now, you and I. It was not suicide or an act of nature, but a murder.

Ian Crockatt

WASHING THE CORPSE
After Rilke

Of course we are accustomed to death. But when
the kitchen lamp splutters and smokes in a draught,
and darkness throws itself about the room, and a waft
from the unknown corpse washes over you, your mouth, your
   skin ...

They scoured the stranger's neck, coarsely laughing
at the farce-life they invented
to contain him, hamming it up on his breast till one mock-
   fainted.
The other, doubled up and coughing,

propping her vinegar-sponge against the nose,
couldn't go on. They paused. Some water-drops
from her stiff brush pooled at the base
of his chest. They saw his contorted hand's crass
last grasp at words – a cramped gesture that croaked 'stop,

I no longer thirst.' They heard. Uneasily now,
clearing their throats, they got on with it,
stooping beneath their own monstrous shadows
which reeled on the patterned walls as if they were caught,
frightened and thrashing, in a net.

We sponged and scrubbed till his numb limbs gleamed.
Implacable night bloomed through the window-frame.
Suddenly the naked nameless one's loom
pulsed, then swept like a lighthouse's round the room.

Tracey Emerson

OUT WITH THE OLD

'That's weird, me too,' I say.

'Seriously?' my sister says.

'I can't think what else to do.'

I'm standing on a chair in my kitchen, removing sticky-bottomed jars and bottles from a cupboard. Two hundred miles away, on the other end of the phone, Lucy is on her knees, cleaning out the shelves beneath her sink. She's counting now, silently she thinks but I hear the whispered numbers.

'I've got six bottles of kitchen cleaner,' she announces.

That makes me snigger.

'Your kitchen's a dump.'

'Cheeky bitch. You try keeping a house tidy with three kids.'

I notice we've managed five minutes without mentioning it.

'Did you check out the website?' she says. I knew it was too good to last. I keep up the distractions.

'Guess what I've found? Instant hot chocolate, November, two thousand and one. That's repulsive.' I turn and face the red plastic bin, which sits ready and waiting, lid removed in anticipation. I launch the hot chocolate skywards. 'Shit.'

It's a poor throw. The purple tub hits the floor, its top shoots off and my white tiles are marbled with piles and streaks of brown sugary powder.

My sister calls me a twat. My little sister. On her knees in low-cut denim probably, one of her sequinned thongs visible to anyone standing behind her, a gel-filled bra spreading out an obscene slogan on a tight T-shirt.

Her cupboard continues to surprise her.

'Brillo pads. I never use Brillo pads.' A pause. 'Did you look at it?'

I did check the website. Briefly. Entered the Universe of Cancer with its list of bodily organs. Human parts displayed out of context, grisly and glistening in alphabetical order. Bowel, Breasts, Liver, Lymph. Liver didn't look good.

'Most liver cancer is secondary, indicating a primary cancer has ...'

'There's no point doing all that until Monday,' I tell her, with older sibling authority.

'Where do you think the primary cancer is?'

'Stop it.'

'I reckon the stomach. She always says she feels sick.'

'Not always.'

My cupboard is empty. All the pastes, spreads, dips and sauces, designed to make the bland bearable, stand in front of the kettle. It's like a reality TV contest. Who will stay and who will go? It's not a decision I'll take lightly.

'I don't think I can wait till Monday,' Lucy says.

I'm not sure I can either.

'You'll have to.' I use my sternest voice.

'Christ,' she says, 'I've got three boxes of J cloths.'

We spend several minutes discussing J cloths. I'm all for them but Lucy claims they're unhygienic.

'They just sit around the sink, stinking.'

A tiny silence and we have to say goodbye to end the strain of not talking about what we need to talk about.

I'm alone now. Virulent fear divides and reproduces, making me fight hard to breathe deep. I soak a piece of kitchen paper and wipe down the jars and bottles. Peanut butter, best before 08/04. Sweet chilli sauce, best before 03/02. Mango chutney, best before 03/05. Best before. Best do that before ...

It's too late for the mango chutney. The jar, half full of furred fruit and stale spices, arcs across the room and lands in the bin, its weight pulling the black binliner down with it.

Fear is replaced by the thoughts I shouldn't have. I rehearse what I'll say to people if it happens, practising my expressions of strength and serenity.

'My mother died quite recently. Cancer. She was only fifty-two.'

I will be tinged with the glory of the too-soon bereaved.

The phone rings.

'Only me.'

My mother's catchphrase. Words to uplift or irritate, depending on my mood, her tone of voice.

'What you up to?' I ask. My super-strength kitchen towel dissolves into twisted shreds.

'I'm doing out the glory-hole.'

'Really?' I explain my feng-shui of congealing condiments and Lucy's cleaning of The Cupboard Under the Sink.

'Oh well ... great minds.' Her voice echoes round the glory-hole, she's obviously in quite deep.

The Glory-Hole. The Cupboard Under the Stairs. You won't find glory in a glory-hole. There are walking boots, old newspapers, piles of ironing, vegetables seeking shade and ...

'I've found your Nana's button box.'

... and ancestral memorabilia from glory-holes long gone.

'Don't throw it.'

'I'm not going to throw it.' Her voice stretched martyr-thin. Then I remember.

'Shouldn't you be resting or something?'

'Don't you start. Plenty of time for that later.'

Not according to the Universe of Cancer. Best rest before ...

'Where's Dad?'

'In the garage ... sorting some bits.'

We're all at it, mucking out the past to avoid the present, making space for an uncertain future.

'Hang on love, your Dad's calling me.' She oohs and aahs her way out of the cupboard, her skinny legs cracking as she stands up. 'Okay,' she shouts into the distance. She sighs before returning to me. 'Your Dad says can he bin those bloody books?'

'No.'

'They're in the way.'

'Tell him I'll sort them at the weekend.'

She tells him. Then she tells me I don't have to come at the weekend.

'I want to.'

I want to go home and soak her all up. I need to make the most of her. I need to check how long I can keep cooked chicken in the fridge and how many times should I reheat it and I've got pus coming out of my belly button, do I go to the doctor or should cream from the chemist do it?

'Well if you're coming,' she says, 'we'd better get organised.'

We make plans for the weekend, then say goodbye so she can return to the glory-hole. I call Lucy.

'I feel guilty,' she confesses, 'I'm always giving her a right slagging.'

'Don't feel bad,' I giggle, 'she drives me mental sometimes. Especially with the singing.'

Mum sings while she cooks and cleans. High-pitched la la las of anything from Frank Sinatra to Kylie Minogue.

'It's even worse when she does her own words to the tune.' My sister laughs but I've crawled beneath her words and what I see scares me and I think that she might break apart before I do.

Then I remember.

'Oh my God, she did the best double entendre ever when I spoke to her just now.'

That's the reason I had to speak to Lucy, to pass on one of our mother's gems.

'Tell me, tell me,' she says.

Before saying goodbye, Mum and I had discussed the meals for next weekend's visit. Even if Monday's test results bring a prognosis of three months to live, it's unlikely to deter her from following the pre-planned menu.

'It'll be fish on Friday, then takeaway Saturday. Indian I think. Sunday we'll have a roast. Pauline's found this fantastic butcher in town that does organic so I'm going to get myself down there and give his meat a go.'

'Do you get it?' I ask her. 'Give his meat a go.'

It isn't that funny but Lucy and I are hysterical. The kitchen spins around me. I lie down on the floor, my back against the cold tiles, dragging my hand through the dark mountain ranges of cocoa dust, which I suppose I'll have to clean up later.

Graham Fulton

COFFEE MORNING

In the hall beyond
            the yard of graves
the Dunblane children happily wait
to have their faces brushed with paint
by a girl who's almost
            twice the age
she would have been ten years ago.

A butterfly for a little lass.
Spider Man for a little lad.

It's gone 9:30, the stalls are set.
A spark in a Barcelona top
is jamming a home-baked cake
                        in his gob.
Cubs are offering raffle tickets,
tablet squares and pots of tea.

The sun plays hide and seek on the floor
that's marked out for a netball court.
The three foot Ronaldinho sprints
the length of the hall and
                        back again,
remains of icing, web on his skin.

Mothers chat, remember, together,
not to look at the clock and cry.
Strangers receive a second glance;
a man with a woggle collects
the token fee in a tub, it's 50p.

REVOLUTIONS PER MINUTE

An Old Man of Hoy of 45s
and stacked-up LPs, mostly The Stranglers,
forged in the mists before CDs,
the dreadnought of punk, Atlantic of spit.

As *Down in the Sewer* ground through the speakers
The Dekester brought out his Falklands medal.
Thatcherite disc, Elizabeth hair.
It gleamed in the moonlight, I was impressed.

He told me how his mum and dad
believed he was dead when the *Plymouth* was hit.
They cried when they thought that he had died.
They cried when they heard he was still alive.
He had to clean the limbs from the deck.

He told me of a jolly jack tar
who spanked the monkey nine times a day,
another who used a special sock.
The Government kept us in the dark.

They can stick their medal up their arse
he said as he turned up *No More Heroes*,
this is what's real, this is what counts.

Peaches, Duchess, Jean-Jacques, Hugh.
The moon and Earth go round the sun,
the sun goes round what it goes round.
This is what this is all about.

Mark Gallacher

HARTMAN RUNNING

Hartman hit the ground running.

Reed cried down to him from the high window but it was too late to do anything. A stun-gun crackled. Reed tumbled though the window, cartwheeling as he fell.

Hartman cornered the building, saw his face reflected in a window, realised he'd never shown such terror, never looked back with so much life.

*

The first time Hartman met Reed was in the back room of an Information Café. 'Writing Class' written on the poster outside. Hartman had expected some sort of propaganda experiment, followed by free food.

Instead there were sheets of paper on shabby desks and bright plastic pens. Reed told them to write, anything they wanted. They looked around, bewildered, afraid to meet each others' gaze.

'What will you do with it when we're finished?' Hartman asked.

'Nothing. Keep it. Put it under your pillows and read it again in a year from now.'

'It's illegal,' one of them said, a gaunt man with watchful eyes.

Reed shook his head. 'You are still allowed to own the thoughts inside your head.'

A sick-looking woman at the back of the room began to cry. She pushed the single sheet of paper away and stood up and fled. The man who'd challenged Reed left too. They all left. Apart from one.

Hartman lifted the pen. He hadn't seen one since he was a boy. His father had refused to throw anything away. His mother had handled all of his father's things like they were diseased. 'Soiled technology!' she'd screamed once after an argument. 'It's perverse to keep such things! They'll arrest us!'

His father became a recluse. Then one day he disappeared. 'He brought it on himself,' his mother liked to say in moments of remorse. Then she disappeared too. A lot of people disappeared. Barricades went up. People whispered the names of countries like they were ghosts.

Hartman leaned over the paper and began to write about his father. When he finished and looked up Reed was watching.

They became friends of a kind. Reed telling stories as they walked through the decay of the city. Hundreds of stories. Reed naming the old names of places. The forgotten histories.

Once Reed told Hartman a story about a man who was arrested because he went out for a walk. 'That's how people disappear,' Reed explained. 'They go out for a walk and don't come back. Because they can't explain why they do what they do. These times are for quiet terror and blind obedience.'

*

They went to the Midsummer Day Book Burnings on the main hill above the city. Ashes and flames from the house-high heaps of banned books crackled and dizzied the air. Each bonfire of books had a single white witch impaled on the top. The children had little pocketbooks to throw onto the pyres. There were dozens of fires burning along the coastline in the twilight. People laughed.

Reed swayed and stared into the terrible conflagration. Reed closed his eyes as the children played and the books burned in their thousands.

Hartman felt it too. The loss.

They walked back down the hill followed by a cohort of Librarians on their way to a party. Hartman recognised one of the Librarians as the man who'd challenged Reed in the café. Hartman looked away but they'd been seen.

*

Sometimes Reed wasn't himself — ill-weathered, sullen. Hartman sensed some kind of decline in the old man.

'Bad to worse. Worse to evil,' Reed whispered once in an Information Café as they looked across the road at a fleeing young boy set upon by three Librarians. The boy howled as they pinned him to the ground. A stack of brightly coloured comics spilled out onto the pavement from the inside of his jacket.

The boy lifted his head and his eyes saw Reed and
Hartman. Hartman choked but Reed told him not to look
away. 'Because you must bear witness. You cannot turn away
from the beauty and you cannot turn away from the horror.
One day people will ask how we let it happen. It's not the
police who make the missing disappeared. Not the
Librarians. It's the rest of us who refuse to see.'

'Come on,' Reed told Hartman and they left the café.

They turned a corner. Reed stopped and leaned his head
against a café window. Reed whispered and Hartman, fearful,
leaned close, tried to catch the words. Neither prayer nor
poetry, curse or lamentation, the words issued out of Reed's
trembling mouth like a shiver of icy vapour.

Reed turned and held out his hand. A key. He gave it
to Hartman. 'For the books.'

*

A forgotten tunnel in the huge granite ruins of a once
grand building. Its entrance hidden by man-high heaps of
broken masonry and brickwork, rods of tangled and twisted
steel.

'There is a sack of glass tubes with a chemical in them,'
Reed explained. 'Shake them and they will radiate light. If
they're still there. I haven't been inside in a long time.'

'Why not?'

'I grew afraid,' Reed said. 'No. Worse. I dreamed I
burned the books myself just to be free of the agony. You're
on your own now. I'm being sent away.'

'Where?'

'The Centre for Corrective Thinking,' Reed said and
smiled weakly. 'They're onto me. Go on now. It's what you
want.'

Hartman shuffled through the tight dank darkness until
his hands touched the cold metal. He felt for the lock hole,
turned the key and pulled the door open and slipped inside
and pushed the door back and locked it.

He found the sack by his feet and took out a light tube
and shook it; green spectra spilled out across his hand, like a
ghostly dance of ether in the darkness.

He held his hand up. There were the books, all around
him. He just stood there. He didn't have the words. He
didn't have the experience to describe what he was seeing for

the first time. For some absurd reason he was sure his father had stood in this room, had touched the books.

*

Reed gone. A year passed. Hartman was ordered to help mend the border fences across the hills southwest of the city. Beyond the fences and pig wire he sometimes saw corpses dotting the landscape, crowned with crows, twisted and frozen, like fallen pilgrims in a shrineless world.

*

One day in an Information Café a young girl with soft grey eyes and short dark hair shook the greasy rain from her coat and sat down next to Hartman. He watched the city news on the café's single info screen. A bumper harvest, the newscaster said. Hartman ground his teeth together. He was hungry. Council elections were coming up for two vacant positions. Despite the hardships of everyday existence the Council was committed to open government. 'We are after all,' the newscaster said, eyes glistening with pride, 'the last surviving city democracy in the world. We believe in the freedom of legal information.'

The newscast finished. A series of graphics stacked up on the screen like multi-coloured toy bricks and a list of the candidates and their pictures, each with their own banal quotation. Hartman doubted they were real people at all. But then he recognised the man who'd challenged Reed all that time ago. Hartman read the man's quote: 'A world without books.' He wondered what kind of brutality it had taken to rise so fast up the ranks.

The girl was staring. She held her hand out over the table, palm upwards. Hartman recognised the key.

'Not here,' she whispered. 'Outside.'

They stood on the street and the girl talked. She told Hartman Reed was stealing books from the library and leaving them around the city. 'He doesn't know what he's doing,' she whispered. 'It's only luck they haven't caught him or found the library. But it's not just him. It's everything. It's getting worse. People are dying before they disappear. Even the Council is scared.'

'What do you want to do?'

The girl looked away, afraid to say it. She drew a breath in. 'I want to get across the water. To the islands.'

'Dead Land,' Hartman countered.

'How do you know? Stupid lies. Come on. I want to show you something.'

'I don't want to.'

The girl leaned forward, her grey eyes wide; Hartman saw his own twin reflection in her pupils. 'You're not alone,' she whispered and the way she said it made Hartman feel as though his heart was broken. 'You think you've been alone your whole life. That's what they want you to think. You're not alone. Not yet.' The girl looked around. 'We have a boat.'

'We?'

*

Hartman followed the girl across the city, into a district he didn't even know existed. The old industries, the broken machineries, the rust of another age. Occasionally a building was half-repaired and they could hear hollow hammering or the thrum of a single machine inside.

There was a canal. They walked alongside the tar-black water. The canal went under a bridge and then it disappeared into a tunnel.

'Don't tell me,' Hartman stopped. 'That way.'

The girl took his hand. Her touch surprised him.

Eventually the tunnel widened out, the cobbled path they walked on gave way to flagstones. The ceiling of the tunnel swept upwards in a huge dome. The girl let go of Hartman's hand and stooped down over a box shape. He heard her fiddle with something and dull lights came on along the arch of the ceiling.

The girl stood up. 'A battery,' she said and pointed at the metal box and the wires leading away from it. 'I learned how to make that from one of the books.'

Hartman wasn't paying attention. He was looking ahead at the warped wooden berth built along the side of the canal. A sailboat was tied up at the berth, the mast just clear of the tunnel's ceiling. 'How did it get here?'

'We don't know,' the girl said. 'We found it. Whoever brought it here didn't get out again. I think they came for someone. We've been watching this place for a while. It's a forgotten place. It has a name. Look,' she said and pointed at the hull. 'Nova Scotia. I don't know what it means. Do you?'

Hartman shook his head. 'Where does this canal go?'

The girl pointed. 'The open sea. We sail tonight. We meet here at midnight. There's enough food for three weeks' sailing. We have a chart and a compass.' She saw how Hartman frowned. 'We know which direction to sail the boat,' she explained.

'What about the books? What about Reed?' Hartman asked but he knew what she would say.

'Reed's finished. We've some books on the boat. Not many. But enough.'

Hartman came back over to the girl. They stood close and Hartman could see how beautiful she was. He wanted to kiss her. The girl sensed it, did not retreat.

'If I can get him here without being followed will you take him with us?'

'What use is he?'

'He can remember stories. He's like a library.'

The girl bit her lip, a little frightened of Hartman. 'We won't wait. This is our last chance.'

Hartman nodded. He asked the girl her name but it felt as though he was asking something else.

'Clarissa,' she answered and walked back along the tunnel.

'How old are you?' he asked and a terrible regret lay at the end of that question.

She turned, points of light swam in her eyes. 'I'm sixteen,' she said and stooped over the battery box. 'I'm fertile. You know what they'll do to me.'

Hartman thought there wasn't one piece of innocence left in the world. And that was something even the books couldn't mend.

She pulled the wires in the box and there was darkness.

*

There was a summons pinned on Hartman's door. He'd seen such pieces of paper before. People never came back.

He went inside and pulled his father's ancient rucksack out from under the single bed and packed some clothes in a hurry.

The neighbour across the hall opened her door a fraction. Hartman couldn't see her face. 'They came for you,' she said. 'I won't tell them I saw you. You'd better run.'

Hartman's anguish broke through his words. 'Come with me. Come with me.'

The woman sobbed and closed her door and bolted it.

*

Reed lived on the South Side. Hartman found the street and hid in the doorway of an abandoned church and waited. He was about to give up when Reed passed on the other side of the road. The old man shuffled in a strange way. His head was shaved and there were scars on his skull. He wore an old tweed jacket and Hartman could see the top of a book jutting out from a pocket.

Reed went into a building. Hartman crossed the road and followed him inside.

He heard Reed climb the stairs and called out his name – a sort of desperate whisper but Reed didn't turn. Hartman climbed the stairs two at a time and saw Reed disappear inside a flat. Hartman glanced back. Shadows and the drip of water somewhere, an organic rankness clung to the crumbling walls.

He went to the door. He opened it and walked into a huge apartment, almost entirely in darkness apart from the open windows on the far side. And there stood Reed half-silhouetted in the fading light, holding the book in his hands. Hartman said his name. Reed turned; a misshapen smile of recognition on his slack face. Hartman came forward, smiling himself.

Two Librarians stepped out of a doorway in the full darkness of the other side of the room. Hartman didn't even turn. Reed's bright wet irises beheld them. Reed took a half-step to the side. The book held out in his withered hand.

'I knew I'd get both of you,' one of Librarians said and Hartman recognised his voice.

Hartman leapt through the open window, taking the book with him.

*

Running blind through the backstreets he heard the sirens

announcing the hunt. People began to open windows along the buildings to watch.

In one street a group had gathered outside an Information Café to watch for him. They said nothing as he ran past; just lifted their arms and pointed in the direction he was running in, so the Librarians would know which way to go.

Hartman stopped and came back and hurled the book at them. They scattered as if he had lobbed something diseased among them.

The Librarians had gained on him by the time he reached the canal. He ran inside the tunnel and kept going. A single bullet whined through the tunnel. He tripped and fell sideways and his head stuck the wall and he clattered to the ground. He got up again and staggered forward. The air stunk of oil and the fumes and it made him gag.

When he reached the boat there was only the girl on the deck. He scrambled onboard and she slipped the rope from the mooring and started the engine up. The boat moved forward.

'The others?' he gasped and she pointed a finger at the deck. 'They're sick,' she said. She didn't ask about Reed. She went down below and came back up with a flare gun in her hand and told him to duck.

He saw four Librarians moving along the tunnel. They grinned, strangely silent. He saw the one who'd killed Reed.

The girl fired the flare gun. The flare struck the tunnel wall, deflecting into the canal. Flames spread out over the water and then suddenly the tunnel was full of fire. Hartman held his hand up as if he could hold the heat and glare away.

The girl dropped the flare gun onto the deck and turned and took the helm and throttled the boat's engine. They moved forward faster, the hull of the boat scraping against the canal sides. They moved away from the flames.

*

It took them a week to reach the first island. But there were bodies all along the raised beaches, some of them tied to wooden pillars, adorned with coloured rags and feathers. Warnings.

They sailed on for another four days and came to a

smaller island. There were trees in the valleys going up from the cliffs and there were some high hills in the north cloaked in rags of mist.

The other two were old and sick. Hartman and the girl managed to get them over to the beach on the dinghy. They just lay down and died right there. Hartman had never seen such sickness. They buried them behind some sand dunes. They didn't even know their names.

Hartman felt like they were coming to the end of things and not the beginning. But the girl was stronger than him. She walked up and down the strip of beach and when she came back she even smiled. 'If there's people on this island, they're hiding like us.'

They sailed the boat around the north point of the island and found a cove that was sheltered by high cliffs. They anchored the boat in shallow water near the beach.

The girl pointed to a wooded hill flanking the mountain. 'We'll find cover in there,' she said. 'That's where we'll start.'

The first things they carried from the boat were the books.

Alan Gay

PORTOBELLO BLUES

Outside Arnold Clark the flags hang lank. The car service executive tells me that it will take several hours for my car to be repaired. So, I'm picking my way down Portobello High Street round flattened chewing gum and the remains of last night's splattered fish suppers. A peeling sign on Semi-Chem says UNDER NEW MAN_GEMENT. It's been there several years and catches the mood.

I buy a lukewarm cup of tea at a kiosk outside Sunnyside Rest Home and talk to an old man wearing a baseball cap and trainers as he squirts tomato sauce over his hot dog. He tells me that the dual carriageway that now slices through the town celebrates the name of Sir Harry Lauder who performed in Portobello in its heyday. Fishwives' Causeway survives encased in concrete.

A shop on the corner advertises BLIND CLEANING. I shrink at the implications and move on when men arrive with pneumatic drills to dig up the drains. Further along the street there's a dog-grooming salon with photographs displaying dog hair-dos, right next door to a ladies' hairdresser. The irony is not lost. It is too early for queues outside the Social Security, optimistically named Phoenix House.

Attempts to escape the growing roar of traffic lead me to the beach; a miniature Siberia stretching into the distance, where the sea lies hidden under a blanket. A bald man kneels building a sandcastle watched by a girl and boy who hold mobile phones to their ears. I can only guess at the family circumstances that brought them here on this bleak March day.

Thus Portobello rolls open its shutters indifferent to the Baptist Church shop window's dictum that '150,000 people will die today. The vast majority are entering Hell'. I spend the rest of the morning watching dogs drag reluctant owners along the beach; until the haar turns to drizzle, driving me behind the closed indoor bowling pavilion, where I crouch listening to gulls that cry for answers that no one can give.

CEILIDH

Morris dancers from Leicester on cricket pitches:
men dressed in black satin breeches
with tiny bells fixed with bows
waving handkerchiefs and sticks.

Freeze them.
Turn off the accordion band:

two lines of dancers, hands on hips
knees raised just the right amount,
sticks about to touch.

Now go to village halls
at the end of a long Scottish glen.

Follow the wheeze of squeezebox,
and the squeal of fiddles competing
with whooping men in kilts
thundering up and down in boots.

Flushed girls with skinned wrists
locked behind brawny backs spin in reels
that swing their legs free of the floor.

No amount of fiddling with a freeze button
can hide the need
to make more of the dance
than the music asks.

Behind all the booze and noise
a ceilidh tries to shape its own course,
determined *not* to be in step;
not to follow the caller.

PRISONER'S ESCAPE KIT

Prerequisite
A desperate wish to escape
smell of stale sweat, cellmates,
shouts in the night, lights, constant din.

Kit
File to cut through bars in cell window
       smuggled in a cake.
Sheets to knot into a rope.
Soap to make mould of prison door key.
Mirror to look down corridor for approaching warders.
       Other prisoners will bang mugs
       on pipes as a distraction.
Rolled blanket to simulate sleeping prisoner.
       Photograph of family must not be removed.

Unobtrusive clothes.
Spectacles
       if not normally worn.
Forged visa.
Passport with new name.
Aeroplane ticket.
US dollars for bribes.

On-the-run
Dye hair or wear wig.
       Hairstyles should reflect
       what you are not.
       Beards are always suspect.
Use remaining dollars for plastic surgery.
Cultivate squint or uncharacteristic tic.
Never hold another's eyes for more than two seconds.
Never slouch along a wall.
Do not contact wife.
       She will be watched.

Make for Bangkok or similar.
Share safe house with fellow escapees
deep in shantytown.
Try not to notice
smell of stale sweat,
shouts in the night, lights, constant din.

Diana Hendry

OTHER MOTHERS

Sarah's I'd have liked. Elegant,
cultured, a film and art buff,
at ninety taking a glass of champagne
as a pick-me-up.

Or Henry's. Nifty stitcher of patchwork quilts,
sender of perfectly chosen post-cards,
knitter of multi-coloured mittens, dedicated
to the art of being useful.

Or maybe Di's. A sea-captain's wife,
sex on stilettos, rosy and risqué,
bobbing up behind her cocktail bar
plump on sherry and joie de vivre.

Ah but there was mine
with her cool upper arms, her wedding band
that could heal a stye and her perpetual question –
What's the point? What's the point?

Mother I'm still asking.

Kate Hendry

WHEN GORDON RAN AWAY

Annie waited for them to leave. She woke herself up early, so she could listen out for them getting ready. First Mum, then Joel, leaving her alone, the house to herself. Mum was driving to Heathrow. She was a useless driver – she said so herself. She'd wanted Joel, the lodger, to drive her, but he couldn't, he was working, so she'd be going at forty miles an hour all the way along the M4 and leaving hours more time than she really needed, if she'd been a normal driver. 'You're useless,' she'd said to Joel. Annie had tried to soothe things between them. 'You wouldn't let him drive fast anyway,' she'd pointed out. Mum always had her foot on an imaginary brake, it used to drive Dad mad. Joel had laughed. 'In my car, she lets me.' Mum had given him a look. 'I'm better off going alone,' she'd said, 'you *are* only the lodger,' and she'd walked off, more angry than before.

Mum was flying to Paris to collect Gordon. To fetch him home again. It wasn't just Gordon she'd gone to get, there was Melody Hunt too. They'd run away together. Nobody thought it was romantic. Mum was angry. Annie felt cross too, because Gordon had got Mum going again and nobody had talked about anything else for weeks. Even teachers at school had been asking her, when she was trying to get a break from it all. She was glad it was half term. Dad thought Mum was over-reacting. 'About time the boy got his leg over,' he'd said. 'He *is* seventeen.' Everyone seemed to get her going.

They'd been gone for almost a month, at the coldest time of the year. Every time they woke up to frost Mum said 'I hope his balls shrivel up with the cold.' Then she'd tracked them down. They were stuck in a tiny room in a huge hotel on the outskirts of Paris. Mum said it was soulless. She seemed glad.

*

When Mum came in to say goodbye she stroked Annie's hair and kissed her forehead. Annie pretended to be asleep. She could hear Mum breathing loudly through her mouth. She dozed after that, waking to hear the regular noises of

Joel getting up for work. The sounds from his room; the
creak from his mattress, the hollow dunt of the loose
floorboard by his bed as he stood up. He never missed it. His
yawn as he stretched, it was so loud, like it took over his
body. Then the latch lifting on his door and for a moment he
was outside her room. He'd be in the kitchen for a while,
but Annie couldn't make out any sounds. She imagined the
toast crumbs at the corners of his mouth, she liked to think
of him lonely at the table and with nothing to read. Finally
the front door, clicked shut. He'd pulled it to gently, so as
not to wake her.

She lay in bed still, stretching out so her feet touched
the sides. She had the whole day to herself. Joel would be
home first, at six. Mum wouldn't be back until ten, eleven
even, at night. She wasn't to wait up. She didn't want to
anyway, seeing Gordon all pale from living in empty hotels
and only white bread to eat.

There was no need to get dressed straight away, she
didn't even have to eat breakfast. She could just eat toast,
there was no one to check. She got up and stood at the top
of the stairs wondering what she'd like to do first. Joel's door
was open, by at least a foot. She edged it open another few
inches so she could see in. Just to make sure he really had
gone to work, that she'd heard the sounds right.

His bed was unmade, the curtains half shut, his bedside
light still on. His room was always a mess. Mum complained
about it but Joel laughed and teased her, said she loved it,
didn't she, being the stern landlady. Then Mum would laugh
too, she didn't want to be stern with him at all. She'd come
and do it herself, she said, when he was asleep. Joel said he
wouldn't mind. She hadn't done it last night though, judging
by the heaps of clothes on the floor.

There wasn't much to look at – a record player on the
floor and a pile of LPs. She didn't recognise the name of
the top one. *Jethro Tull*; a picture of a man in a wood sitting
by a fire. What would it be like to listen to the records
together? To like them as much as he did, to sit together
saying nothing, just listening. If it was what they did together
in the evenings – him choosing one then her. Maybe they'd
sit on the bed. She sat on the edge of the mattress, but it was
awkward, still having her feet on the floor. She brought her
legs under the duvet, they'd be right next to each other now,

probably with their legs touching; it was a narrow bed after
all.

She couldn't work out whether to have her hands under
the duvet or on top. Underneath she felt like a little girl,
waiting for a night-night kiss. On top and she was like a
patient in a hospital bed. Maybe it was because her hands
didn't have anything to do. Maybe it was because of the frilly
nightie she had on. Mum liked to buy them for her even
though she wanted pyjamas. It wasn't the sort of thing she'd
be wearing with Joel, sitting in bed, listening to his LPs.

She pulled the nightie over her head. She wouldn't be
naked of course, she'd have on something silky with ribbons
for straps. In cream. He wouldn't be wearing anything on
top, men didn't have to. Without her nightie her breasts and
belly, both rounder than she'd like, were out. She'd rather
have had them under the blankets, but then she'd have to be
practically lying down and they wouldn't be lying down, to
listen to his LPs. There was nothing for it but to have them
out and just pretend they weren't there. She closed her eyes,
which helped, and pictured him next to her. The sound of
his breath, his hands near hers, doing something ordinary,
because this was their habit, especially on Saturday
mornings. They couldn't stay there for ever, of course. She
got herself back into the nightie, rearranged the bedding how
she'd found it and started into the empty house.

*

It hadn't been any quieter without Gordon. They hadn't even
noticed he'd gone to begin with. He was always hiding in
his room. Mum went in with some clean, ironed clothes and
he wasn't there. His window was open and a rope was
hanging from it. Annie thought this was stupid – Gordon
and his fancy knots. Why couldn't he have just sneaked out
through the garden like any normal person? Gone outside to
fetch something and then just left through the garage. That's
what she'd have done. Gordon just wanted to make a great
escape, as if he'd been imprisoned in a tower.

Mum had freaked out. When she'd screamed Annie had
come running and found her with the rope in one hand and
a note in the other. 'I thought he'd tried to hang himself,'
she sobbed. Joel had come in and comforted her; she'd cried
with all her face hidden in his chest. Then she'd begun to

read out the note and Annie could tell she was going to be angry. 'We're really sorry but we have to get away. We need some space to ourselves. We'll be okay, don't worry about us. We've got some money.' That was when she'd really started yelling. 'What does he mean, space?' Annie hadn't said anything, it wasn't a real question. Joel hadn't answered either. 'Why does that boy have to talk in clichés? I've no idea what he means. Doesn't he have enough space from us, shut away in here all day? We hardly ever see him. That bloody girl.' She'd meant Melody: Mum had never liked her. Annie didn't much either, though she was pretty. Melody only wanted to be Gordon's girl*friend*. She was going out with someone else. Someone stupid called Dave who wore leather clothes. Gordon pretended not to mind, though he wasn't friends with Dave.

Annie had to go past Gordon's room on her way down to the kitchen so she had a look in. It was a mess too and it was beginning to smell. Mum had refused to tidy it. Sometimes Mum had been so angry she didn't even want to look for him. But then she didn't want him to get away with it either. And it *was* February. He'd be cold, even in France.

It wasn't the first time Gordon and Melody had tried to run away. Mum had caught them at the bus stop, trying to get to London. It was just after Joel had moved in. Annie had been away visiting Dad. Gordon had refused to come. Annie had felt annoyed when she found out why. She'd wanted to stay at home too, what with Joel being so new. But she'd gone because of Dad – she'd felt bad for Dad, sorry for him. He must have thought Gordon didn't want to see him. She'd made up an excuse for him about school work. Dad would want to believe that – Gordon never usually did any. She'd gone to all that effort and it wasn't that he didn't want to come at all. It was just an excuse. She'd been glad they'd been caught. She wished she'd seen the shouting after.

By the time she'd got home, Mum had stopped shouting and had started worrying instead. She'd got a theory about Gordon and Melody. Gordon only wanted her *because* he couldn't have her. She was unobtainable. It was a thing people did, she said, 'love hopelessly.' Mum was worried because Melody was his third hopeless love since he'd turned sixteen. Mum said Gordon was like her when she was in love.

Vernon had been the most recent. 'Some people need to love in vain,' she said, 'it's safer.'

'What about Dad? You didn't love him in vain.'

'No,' Mum sighed, 'and look what happened there.'

Gordon still had a photo of the first on his bookshelf. Theresa. Annie picked it up and rubbed the dust off with her nightie. There wasn't a photo of Justine: Mum wouldn't have allowed that. There were two of Melody though, one even had Gordon in it and they almost looked like a couple. Gordon was gazing at her and she was smiling back. It wasn't fair, Melody being so friendly with Gordon when she didn't want him. Though Annie could see why. He never came out of his room for a start and he never said much. He would be boring to go out with. Annie looked round the room trying to feel like she'd missed him. Gordon's metal bed, the red paint chipped. She had one the same only hers was blue. Gordon wouldn't want to be back at home. Especially with Mum being angry. That would go on for days, maybe even a week. Annie wondered what she'd do while Mum was being angry. She couldn't side with Gordon. She didn't want to, it was all his fault in the first place. Not that siding with Gordon would stop the anger anyway. It would probably make it go on for longer. There'd be two of them getting it.

Once they'd run away together. Gordon had packed Annie's rucksack for her and woken her up when it was time to leave. She'd been pleased he'd wanted her to come though she'd not had any real reason to leave. She'd only been nine. What had been Gordon's reason? It had been before Dad had left. They hadn't even managed to get out of the front door. It should have been late enough but Mum and Dad had been still up, talking. There'd been double the shouting – most for Gordon but Annie had got her share too. She couldn't remember Dad saying anything. He'd taken her back to bed though and carried their bags back upstairs. That was the sort of thing he did.

'I needed someone practical,' Mum would say when she was trying to work out why she'd gone for Dad in the first place. But then other days she'd say, 'I was such a fool, you should never pick a man for his DIY skills.' Maybe Melody would go out with Gordon if he was more practical. But then knots *were* a practical kind of thing, especially if you had a

knot for all situations, like Gordon did. Melody obviously
didn't need any knots tying. Annie turned the radiator back
on as she left the room.

*

As she had the house to herself Annie thought she'd use
Mum's bathroom. It had black and white tiles up to the
ceiling. You could see your face in the black ones. She liked
it when the door was ajar and she could see Mum in her
bedroom, folding clothes, putting them away. The sound of
the wardrobe door opening and shutting.

The first phone call had come like that, when Annie
was in the bathroom and Mum was in the bedroom,
changing the sheets. The phone was right by the bed but
Mum had pounced on it. She'd been doing that for weeks;
waiting for the phone to ring, then pouncing. Occasionally,
when she was feeling really angry, she'd ignore the phone: 'A
woman's whole life is about waiting,' she'd say, 'waiting for
men and jumping to their every call. I refuse to do it.' The
phone would ring and ring and ring and then stop. Then
she'd feel terrible and she'd ring the operator to ask who had
phoned and it'd be Susan Carey from across the road, or
someone from the library and she'd be angry with them then,
for hogging the line. Didn't they know about Gordon?

This time Mum did answer and it was him. It wasn't a
clear line. Annie, in the bath, could hear Mum shouting
'Gordon? Gordon? Is that you?' Annie flattened the water
very gently with her hands and watched the bubbles
disappear. Then, when Mum knew it was him, 'Where the
hell are you?' A pause. 'Just tell me where you are and I'll
send the money.' Another pause, Annie rested her hands on
top of the water and listened harder. 'Darling, I need to
know where you are, that you're safe. I can't give you money
without knowing that. Okay, I'll write it down. What? Yes,
got it. 34971. Sweetheart, I love you. We miss you. Can't you
just come home?' Annie paddled the water with her knees
to make it feel warmer. 'Just tell me where you are.' Mum
was shouting again. 'Oh God, why are you doing this to me?
Gordon? Gordon? Are you there? I hate you!' And then
Annie heard the phone falling to the floor and her mother in
tears.

She went to her, still wet, with the towel half round her

and comforted her. She wished they could forget all about
Gordon. That it could be just the two of them, looking after
each other. Though Joel could live upstairs. 'It's okay,' she
said, stroking Mum's hair and kissing her forehead.

Out of the bath, she sat at Mum's dressing table with
an orange towel wrapped round her. It was one of her games,
sitting on the round three-footed stool in front of the mirror.
You could spin it to get to the right height. Annie was almost
as tall as Mum now; she only needed one spin. Mum's
earrings were in boxes on either side of the mirror. She laid
them out, putting the pairs together, and chose the heaviest,
to feel how they stretched her earlobes down. Three gold
balls with green feathers in between. Then she went to
mum's wardrobe and took out the fur coat. It had been a
present from Vernon. It was made from sixty rabbits. Mum
said Vernon was good at 'grand gestures.' She didn't really
like it, but she wanted it in her wardrobe. After Vernon,
she'd got it out again and tried to wear it but it had just
made her cry. Then Joel had tried to get her to wear it too.
He liked it, he said it was glamorous and that he'd like to
take her out it in, her arm hooked round his elbow. Mum
had managed to get to the front door with it on. Joel had his
cowboy boots on with the heels so he was taller than usual.
He was taking her out in his car. They weren't going to be
back late. Then at the last moment she said she couldn't do
it. It was making her uncomfortable, it was too hot. Joel had
just laughed. 'Stop it,' Mum had said, 'you're just the lodger.'
Annie had taken it upstairs and hung it up back inside the
wardrobe.

Annie took it out and tried it on. She got some of Mum's
heels out of the wardrobe. Mum never wore them either. Joel
had been encouraging her but she refused. She'd tell him he
was just the lodger and to stop commenting on her clothes
but Joel just laughed and said somebody had to. Annie
walked up and down in a black pair, looking at them in the
mirror from all angles. They didn't look like her feet. Her
body had disappeared under the coat. She looked like she
had too much skin. Or fur. The earrings made her look
foreign.

She wondered about Gordon, living in a foreign country
for all these weeks. Mum had got the operator to trace the
phone call, that's how she'd found out they were hiding in

Paris. She had wanted to go straight away but Joel had
persuaded her to stay. 'Paris is vast,' he'd said, 'you'll never
find them.' Mum had cried and ranted for hours after the
phone call, well into the evening. Firstly in the bedroom with
Annie, then at the kitchen table, then into Joel's chest, again.
She'd stop for a bit and Annie would think it was over. So
did Joel and he went off to his room. But then she started
again. Annie could never work out how long it would go on
for. There weren't any signs. The best thing was to just wait
and not expect anything. It always stopped suddenly, just
when she'd settled in for a night of it.

*

Annie was hungry so she got into her own clothes and went
downstairs to the kitchen. It was lunchtime but she had her
breakfast, with an extra slice of toast. There was still the
whole afternoon to wait, until Joel came home. He'd said
he'd bring back fish and chips for them both. Just the two of
them eating together. By the fire would have been perfect
but she didn't know how to light it. The table would have to
do. Maybe they could light a candle. That's what Mum
always did at tea time. It would be hours till Mum got back,
with Gordon. They could sit at the table for hours, watching
the candle burn down. She must remember not to play with
the dripping wax.

The second phone call had come a week after the first.
This time it had been from the British Embassy in Paris.
Gordon and Melody had come in looking for money. The
British Embassy had found out where they were staying.
Mum spun around the house packing her bag, phoning the
travel agent, phoning Dad and everyone else. Everyone
who'd left her on her own to cope, shouting at them, crying
with relief on Joel's shoulders, hugging Annie, kissing her
lots of times on the head, playing Nina Simone very loudly
on her stereo, making chicken soup for Gordon. It seemed
she'd forgiven him already. Joel went out after a while, he
had things to do. Annie tried to help, but mostly she sat – at
the kitchen table, on Mum's bed, on the sitting room floor
– watching. Mum was to fly to Paris to get them. Annie held
her breath for most of the day waiting for Mum to leave.

She could breathe properly once she'd gone, once the
house was empty. But by the time she'd finished eating she

was waiting again. Hanging on. Waiting at the window seat for Joel to come home. Waiting for their hours alone. Waiting for Mum to ring, waiting for her to come home, waiting to see Gordon again. Waiting for it all to begin again, for it all to be going on around her.

Angela Howard

THE TABLE

There was a man who loved wood. He loved feeling the grain, the smoothness under his fingers when he planed and sandpapered it. He'd watch how it drank the beeswax and shined with the polish he rubbed into it.

His wife was a scriptwriter, and she asked him to make her a table large enough to sit all her friends round. She wanted to invite them on a regular basis when they could all try their hand at writing because that way perhaps she could get more ideas for her dialogues: she'd always had difficulty with dialogue.

He chose mahogany for the table, African mahogany, and planned the shape and size, calculated the angles and the length of the legs. He sawed the surfaces, which he fitted together by carving thin indented lines along the edges, tapering the other sides to slide in together. Then he carved in the curves and made one large oval shaped surface. She asked for drawers where her friends would keep their papers and pencils, and he fitted the corners with dovetail precision.

The hardness of the African mahogany made it easy to plane the surface smooth. But it wasn't the same touch under his fingers as with the cedar wood he'd known as a boy. Cedar was soft and porous and absorbed everything around it, whereas mahogany reminded him of his wife: firm and hard. His hands would skim up and down her sculpted body and he'd feel her curves, sublimely subtle, a slight change of line inwards then out to another lithe stretch of the thigh down to her calves, like the branch of a tree. When he planed the wood into its final smoothness, he thought of her.

But he also thought of his woods back home, the berries he used to pick, their liquid freshness and the sweet smell they left on his fingers. The next day he went to the supermarket and bought raspberries and redcurrants, and when he arrived home he rubbed their juice into the mahogany, using it as a dye.

Later, he heated up a pot of beeswax with linseed oil on his fire, and mixed it until it melted into a warm, thick creamy substance which he kneaded into the surface of the table with the flesh of his palm, buffing it up with a thick cotton wad which he tied to his forearm for extra pushing pressure.

But now he couldn't smell. He couldn't smell the wood, or indeed any of the ingredients he was kneading into it. Yet, as a young boy, the smell of the trees had been overpowering, especially when he prised the bark off the trunks, releasing the pungent odour of resin. The wood responded well to his penknife then, and it wasn't long after that that he took up carpentry, choosing soft, pliant cedar and carving pieces into things like picture frames and miniature Swiss chalets which let out the odour of his forest.

Then he met and married her, and his sense of smell vanished.

There were no cedars in the new neighbourhood where they lived; there were willows and birch. Perhaps willows and birch just didn't have a smell, he thought at first. Perhaps only cedars have a strong smell. But then there were other things he couldn't smell, like her perfume. She'd ask him if he liked it, stretching her neck so he could catch the smell. He leaned in. Then he said yes, because he didn't want to admit he could smell nothing.

He loved his wife though, and she loved him too, even if it was in another kind of way – a hard kind, like this mahogany.

She watched him knead the layers of beeswax slowly, rhythmically into the surface with his forearm.

'You don't need to do all that,' she said. 'It's fine. Leave it like that. Time's running out – they're coming on Friday.'

He looked up and saw her face flushed, like the wood with the berry juice rubbed into it. She was agitated; she just wanted it done, finished, and it didn't matter to her whether it was perfect. He waited for her to leave the room and continued, applying more juice, adding more beeswax, heating the linseed oil, and from time to time he'd sniff closely at the curled bits of shaved wood leftovers, trying to recapture his sense of smell. Because he never gave up.

He finally finished the table on the Thursday evening, the day before her friends were due to come, and he took her in to look at it.

'It's very accomplished, beautiful,' she said, smiling up at him, relieved he'd finished it.

'Here, smell it,' he said, putting his arm round her, drawing her up and then running his hands over the finished surface.

But she pulled away. 'Oh, I don't need to smell it,' she said. 'That's not important, really. It's the surface that counts.'

She didn't want to broach that subject of smell; she knew it upset him, and it upset her, too. There was nothing they could do about it, anyway. At first she'd tried hard to console him, but all he'd said was that he'd started losing his sense of smell when they got married. That made her clam up. He had seemed indifferent to her perfume, so she'd stopped using it. He was more bothered about the smells missing at his workbench. She'd stopped making any reference to smell or perfume or odour when he was around. She'd tried saying it didn't matter that he couldn't smell, but that had made him mad. Then she'd explained that she'd meant it didn't matter *to her* that he couldn't smell, that she loved him for what he was, not what he couldn't smell. That made him even more angry. She often saw him secretly sniffing the bark of the trees, the sawdust at his workbench: always wood and his trees, and he'd have that look of questioning anguish on his face.

Now, to please him, she came up near to him and his table and ran her hands across the smoothness, just as he had done. 'It's lovely,' she tried.

He wanted to take her right there, on his table, but he saw she wasn't ready to thank him in that kind of way, even though she knew that he liked her taut and nervous like that.

'Go on, tell me what it smells like,' he coaxed her.

She sighed, and he caught the expression of annoyance brush over her face, her lips tight.

It was impossible to read her thoughts. 'Go on,' he insisted, trying to soften her.

'You're really not missing much,' she'd tried to console him one night. They were lying in bed. He was wondering what secrets she was hiding; whether her skin smelt of sap, or apples, or berry juice, or even something acrid, whether her odour changed with the days of the month. When she left the bed with what seemed to him a dismissive wave of her hand he buried his head in the sheet where she'd been lying, trying to recapture her.

It was Friday evening, and the friends arrived. They were all women. One had dark hair with a flushed complexion, soft as a peach, and another had red freckles which reminded him of the grain in his wood. There was a younger woman, too, who was very thin, with hands like little maple leaves. She laid them on his table and stroked the surface.

'Don't forget to show them the drawers underneath,' he whispered to his wife before they started.

She looked up. 'It would be nice to have keys for the drawers,' she said.

Because, she explained, their ideas and thoughts, which they'd jot down each evening, should be kept locked up until they matured.

Locked up and matured, he thought, lingering on the words and then looked at her breasts; saw them apple-tight under her blouse. He thought yes, she kept everything to herself. All seemed to have hardened inside her, and wouldn't come out.

While the group was writing he sat in his workshop thinking back to when he was a boy. At home he used to watch the mist rise in the mornings. It was as if the earth was secreting all its juices, and as it rose it gradually dissipated to reveal the splendid cedars. He'd imagined them as real people, gathered together to discuss the day, just as his wife was doing in the other room with her friends, opening up to each other, discussing how to approach their scenarios while he sat out of earshot.

The trees back then, he thought, gave out their scent mostly when it was damp, or raining, and it was when he cut into the bark with his penknife, scarring the trunks, that the smell came out most strongly – he could almost recapture the smell now. Yes, trees kept their perfume to themselves unless you really worked on them. That's why he'd taken to carpentry, carving into the wood to find out more.

He could hear his wife's words, but they were mottled through the walls.

That night, after the scriptwriters had gone, when his wife was sleeping, he crept downstairs to his table and went to her drawer. But it was locked. Every drawer was locked. He'd only made locks because she'd asked for them, and he'd given her the keys. But he hadn't thought they would actually use them. So how was he going to know what she was writing? He didn't feel he could ask; and she never volunteered to tell him.

The group gathered round his table each week for a month, and at the end of the fourth session she told him that each one had written a scenario.

'They're not very interesting, but at least they've managed to complete them,' she said.

At last she had spoken about it, so he dared followed up with his question.

'What's yours about?' He was hoping that perhaps the smell of the berries or even just the mahogany with the vibrancy of African dance and song in it could somehow have crept into her story.

'Oh, mine wasn't very good. I didn't write much, nothing worth taking up,' she said, turning away to the window.

That was when he saw her mind as a knot, a knot in the branch of a very hard tree: beautiful, but refusing to be unravelled, and he realised there was no point in asking again.

The scriptwriters came one more time to discuss possible future sessions, and they wrote on his table, and when they left he was alone with her and the knot in her head.

'I don't think the group will meet again,' she said one morning over breakfast. He was finishing his bowl of coffee and she was clearing the table.

'Why not?'

'Oh, we didn't really "gel". Somehow the atmospherics were wrong. Don't know what it was – perhaps the table?' She caught herself, but it was too late.

He looked up. 'What do you mean, the table?'

'Oh, I didn't really mean that.'

'But you said it. The table.'

'Yes, I don't know. Well, perhaps it's too big – or too ... I don't know. What am I saying? I don't mean that at all. It's a wonderful table. But you know, oh, I really don't know.' She was fumbling for words.

He put down his coffee bowl and pushed back his chair.

'How can you say that my table wasn't good enough? I made it for you!'

She was standing stiff by the window. He walked over, took her arm. He felt quite stiff himself but controlled his gestures. He felt the hardness of her muscles in her arm as he pulled her round and when they were face to face he saw her lips hard shut so that her mouth reminded him of his chisel.

'Come with me,' he said, loosening his hold and leading her through to the drawing room where the table stood. 'Tell me what's wrong with it.'

'Nothing, it's not the table, really,' she pulled away from him.

'Please, don't lie to me!' His voice was loud. He pushed her back towards the table. 'Don't tell lies!' he took her by each arm and started to shake her. Then he thrust her onto the table and leaned over her. 'What is the matter with you?' he yelled.

Her eyes looked like bright black berries staring up helplessly. He pulled back and let her go. She leaped up and ran out of the house.

He ran out after her, but she had vanished. He stood in the garden, hesitating. What was he doing? He didn't know, and ended up running to his shed where he pulled out the sledgehammer and rushed back into the house with it, ran to his table, lifted the sledgehammer high above it and brought it down in a swift parabolic movement so that it landed smash on the table. He hacked into the surface, into the sides, into the drawers. There were still bits of paper in the drawers and he ripped them up, picked up the sledgehammer again and hacked at the legs until the table fell at an angle, an easy angle for him to take one more swipe and split the surface in two. He fell back to the floor, out of breath, heart beating fast. He was lying next to a piece of broken wood with a streak of bright red running through the grain. He looked at it closely, brought his face up to it and sniffed.

He could smell it: a kind of dry sweetness, a faint metallic odour mixed with honey, a soft perfume which must be the beeswax mixed with the resinous linseed oil. He sat up, held it close to his nose, sniffed further along where the red streak had vanished, where the wood had no polish. There he could smell, too: it smelt dry and ungiving, the mute hardness of mahogany. Then he saw at his feet a piece of paper torn up, but there was writing on it: handwriting. 'The Table,' it said, and underneath it said: 'There was once a woman who loved her husband. But he only loved wood ...'

Ian Hunter

MR MURDOCH COMES TO TOWN

Donald Murdoch took the sonic dart from Stornoway to Edinburgh airport, then a slingshot pod into the city centre. He quickly found the MSP hover lane and set the controls for New Holyrood.

It was a beautiful day, although chaotic down below, as usual. The snarl-up headed back towards Livingston. Still, that was the reason he was here, he supposed. To make things better. Elected to represent the Highlands and Islands Coalition Against Road Charges. To be honest, Murdoch hadn't thought much of his chances, but he'd been helped by the Government's new policy of extending road charges to owners of private single-track roads. Talk about shooting yourself in the foot. Those roads had only been created due to the incentives and tax reliefs on offer and were self-financing once built, generating money from tourists who wanted to get about the isles. They were all over the place. Everyone on Uist now had their own road and were expected to pay for using it. The Government wasn't interested in improving infrastructure, Murdoch fumed, they just wanted to make money.

The public certainly agreed. He could hear them on his media-cap, phoning Sir Robin Galloway on *Good Morning Scotland*. Gently he touched the cap with his finger, not quite believing he owned one. This certainly was a bonus. No sooner had he been elected than the free subscriptions started flooding in: BBC Spectrum, BBC Hyperbeam, Sky Hyperbeam, MacDonald's Hypervision and Pepsi Digihype. It certainly beat being back home, on an island where the use of technology was strictly controlled by the Free Kirk. There, they would huddle in the village hall watching early twenty-first century digital TV programmes on an old-fashioned giant plasma screen.

As he hovered closer to his destination, Murdoch chewed on his lower lip, and nodded determinedly, thinking he would have to wangle a way to get the hyper channels beamed into the villages, give his constituents some modern programmes to watch for a change. After all, he wouldn't have been elected if it hadn't been for their help. All the other parties used zipverts, holobites and virtual canvassing to get their message across, but because of Free Kirk decrees he could use none of those things. Although it had been a masterstroke to go door-to-door, even if there had been a few nasty incidents with sheepdogs and one near fatality involving an old woman on an organicroft, who got a nasty shock when someone actually knocked on her door for the first time in years.

'You're tuned into the zeitgeist of the moment. The pivotal points in Scotland's agenda with Sir Robin Galloway. We'll take some more calls after this classic practical joke.'

God, it was the exploding pacemaker at the cremation one again. He knew it backwards. Murdoch closed his eyes and concentrated on his cap, telling it to change stations.

'Pull over.'

Keep going, he told the cap.

'Pull over.'

What was this? Some rap song? On every channel? Maybe it was an advert.

'Pull over. NOW!'

Murdoch looked round. It was a traffic sphere, like a hovering beach-ball made of metal. A flashing arrow appeared on one of its visi-screens, indicating the rooftop below. Murdoch trained the pod's navi-camera on to the building and let the controls take him down.

The sphere was waiting for him. Light danced across his features, scanning him in, and an approximation of his face appeared on a screen, looking stern. He was the law, or something that looked like him, wearing the hat and uniform of a policeman. 'Do you know what lane you were flying in, sir?'

He smiled. They might have his face, but they didn't have his voice. 'The MSP hover lane.'

'Correct, and do you know the fine for hacking into their flight code?'

Murdoch smiled again. 'I didn't. I am an MSP.'

'Really, sir?'

'Honest.'

Murdoch reached into the pod and took out his briefcase.

'Hold that up to the scanner,' his face ordered. 'Now!'

'It's okay. It's just a letter.'

'A letter?'

Murdoch nodded, opening his case. He held out the letter, which was a bit chewed in places and had holes in it, but he had done the best he could to tape it back together. 'This is my confirmation letter.'

The policeman almost looked puzzled. 'You have a letter? Aren't you online?'

'No.'

'What happened to it?'

'My dog got it first.'

'Uh, huh.'

'I've got other stuff. Proof,' Murdoch said eagerly, reaching into his case. 'News clippings, photographs.'

'Alright, I believe you,' the policeman said. 'What are you? SNP? Lib Dems? Twentieth Century Scottish Socialists?'

'Highlands and Islands Coalition Against Road Charges.'

'Never heard of it.'

Murdoch tried not to wince and forced another smile. 'You will.'

'You better hurry, Parliament is opening soon.'

'It is? I mean, it is.' Although he wasn't exactly sure when it was supposed to open. One of Bodger's bites had obliterated that part of the letter and the dog had chewed almost all of the booklet telling him about the workings of the Parliament.

He climbed back into the pod and waved to the sphere. The policeman with his face didn't wave back. Hovering again, he could see the newly built Parliament Building, almost an exact replica of the Welsh Assembly, but larger, and cheaper. Outside stood a statue of Alex Salmond, stoned to death on that very spot as he tried to placate the Local Council Tax Rioters of 2012, before they stormed the Scottish Parliament and razed it to the ground. To Murdoch's surprise, the pod flew over the building and kept going. He pressed a few buttons, but the controls wouldn't come back to him. Auto lockout. Damn. If he was already late, he was going to be even later now.

He set down in a field of pods. He couldn't even see the Parliament over the surrounding buildings. Then he saw a sign. PARLIAMENT TUBE LINK. But there was no stop, no shelter, no escalator downwards, nothing.

'State your destination.'

He looked round. There was an intercom below the sign.

'State your destination.'

'This is Donald Murdoch. I'm a new MSP, I –'

'State your destination.'

'The Parliament Building.'

He screamed as the ground disappeared below him. He was falling down a great metal tube, passing through rings of lights. Then he realised he was floating, almost flying in a strange sort of way. He could feel air currents all around him, holding him up, slowing him down. He shot out of the floor of the Parliament Building and landed on his feet and hands, leaning back, looking like a crab, or a crazy Cossack dancer. Quickly, he stood up, and looked round, expecting to be the centre of attraction and steadied himself for the rush of reporters. No-one took any notice of him. He wasn't sure whether to feel disappointed or relieved. At least his briefcase hadn't burst open. He tucked his shirt in and pushed a hand through his tangled hair.

Someone coughed.

A man stood up from behind a long curved desk with the word RECEPTION wrapped around it in black, bold letters. He held up his hand and motioned Murdoch to approach with a bend of his fingers.

'Mr Murdoch, I presume.'

'Yes.'

'You are late.'

'Am I?' Murdoch held up his arms. 'I couldn't read the start time. Bodger got to the letter first.'

'Bodger?'

'My dog.'

The man shook his head and made a tutting sound. 'Such are the perils of communicating by paper. Still, your circumstances have changed enough for you to become ' "wired up", as they say.'

'Definitely,' agreed Murdoch, although the receptionist wasn't listening to him. Instead, he was reaching down.

On the desk were five small signs: LABOUR, LIB DEM, SNP, CONSERVATIVE and INDEPENDENTS. A badge lay beneath the last sign. Even upside down he recognised his face, and a sort of word.

He frowned.

It couldn't be.

'Donald Murdoch, agent of H.I.C. Has a sort of James Bond ring to it.'

Murdoch took the badge. His face leapt out of the holographic panel, grinning like a madman. Were his teeth really so big, so white? He shook his head. H.I.C. 'I can't wear this.'

'It's merely a temporary badge. Moira will sort everything out for you.'

'Moira?'

'Your personal assistant. Moira Indi 4 to be exact.'

'Where do I find her?'

The receptionist pointed. 'She's over there. Waiting.'

Murdoch nodded. 'Thanks.'

He turned round and headed for the other end of the foyer, past the metallic statues forged in strange ballet-like poses. There were three women in front of him, all dressed identically. He was so busy wondering which one was Moira that he didn't notice one of the statues jump down beside him until he was tapped on the shoulder.

'Mr Murdoch, or may I call you Donald?'

'Jesus!'

For some reason he was held his case up to his chest and backed away slightly.

'It's alright, Mr Murdoch. I'm Moira.'

'M-m-my personal assistant?' He moved to the side slightly. The metal statue had a woman's face, but if he moved quickly enough he could see that the side of her head was metallic. It was almost as if the face had been projected on to the metal.

'All MSPs have a Moira or a Malcolm as their personal assistant. It saves expenditure on human assistance and valuable office space.' She held out her hand. 'I am Moira Indi 4. Welcome.'

'Thanks,' said Murdoch, shaking hands slowly, expecting an ice-cold grip, an ice-cold, vice-cold grip, but the handshake was warm and perfectly normal.

'We must hurry. Parliament is almost open. We will talk on the way. There are important matters to deal with.'

'Sure, go ahead.'

'First, your salary. As an independent, opposition MSP

your annual salary is £300,000 per year. Would you like that in one lump sum or twelve monthly instalments?'

Murdoch stopped, words seemed to stick in his throat. 'I get £300,000?'

'I know it is disappointing, but you have to realise that had you been a member of a mainstream opposition party you would have been entitled to £400,000, or £450,000 if you were a Liberal Democrat coalition member. Labour MSPs get £500,000, of course.'

'Of course.' He couldn't stop grinning. 'Uh, £300,000 in one lump sum is fine.'

'I will arrange payment.'

'Great, my bank account is —'

Moira held up a silvery hand. 'I know, Mr Murdoch. I know almost everything about you.'

'Everything?'

'It only takes a fraction of my memory. 1000 bytes to be exact.'

'Is that a lot?'

'I am sure I will have to allocate more memory now that we are working together.'

Murdoch looked back towards the reception. 'I had expected some reporters.'

'I am afraid we are not major news. We must hurry, Mr. Dewar will be speaking soon. Once he is finished there will be a vote on some Government legislation. Did you access the stick you were sent?'

'Ah, the stick. I'm afraid Bodger got that as well.'

'Your dog.'

Murdoch brightened. 'Hey, you do know some things about me.'

Moira ignored his remark. 'I cannot enter the chamber with you. My energy matrix conflicts with the virtual array.'

'The what?'

'You will be sitting next to Jarek Nowinski of the Scottish Nationalist Party. I am sure he will act as your mentor for today.' Moira stopped. 'I cannot continue, Mr Murdoch. You must go on alone. Good luck.'

Alone? Great. There was an archway with a phrase above it that meant nothing to him. Was it Latin? Gaelic? Inside was different. He had to stop and take in the rows of people who were floating in the air. Someone waved to him. A man with thick dark hair and high cheekbones.

Murdoch touched his chest. Me? The man nodded, waving him over. A million times more friendly than the receptionist had been earlier. The handshake was strong and vigourous.

'Hey, Donald Murdoch. H.I.C., eh? You don't look like a boozer. I'm Jarek Nowinski.'

'Pleased to meet you.'

'Sit down.'

Where, thought Murdoch, then he noticed a floating blue halo about waist-high. He put his hand out and felt the edges of a transparent seat.

'Not very comfortable,' confided Nowinski. 'Makes you want to head for one of the bars at the earliest opportunity.'

Murdoch nodded, gingerly slid on to his seat and reached out, guided by the neon blue outline of a lectern in front of him. A panel winked into existence in its centre. He looked up and couldn't stop gawping. All of the government MSPs sitting opposite looked the same. He closed his mouth. Not exactly the same, he realised. Half were men, half were women, but they were identical to each other, even down to the same grey clothing.

'Clones,' confirmed Nowinski. 'Scottish Parliamentary parties have the right to allocate candidates after an election. The Labour Party uses clones. They all wear a control cap and vote in unison, and I don't mean the old trade union.'

Murdoch looked to the rows of seats that stretched between the Labour MSPs to the opposition benches where he sat. Here, the MSPs wore the same clothes but they were clearly different people.

'Lib Dems,' snarled Nowinski. 'They get to wear the Labour suits but not the control caps. Not that it matters.'

Murdoch leaned forward to take in the MSPs sitting beside him who represented the Scottish Nationalist Party and four independents, including himself from H.I.C. He grimaced. What a name, the sooner he saw Moira about a badge change the better.

The lights began to dim. 'Chin up,' whispered Nowinski. 'Here comes Donald.'

'I've never seen a virtual presentation before,' Murdoch admitted.

'Yeah, well it won't be long before they get old Donald's corpse out of the cryo fridge. Once we've got death licked we can bring all the politicians back to life. Of course, we want Sir Sean back first.'

Suddenly Donald Dewar was there in front of them. Walking. Talking. Even though he had died years ago. It was too much for Murdoch, who wasn't listening to what the First Minister was saying.

Nowinski tapped him on the shoulder. The SNP MSP was grinning from ear to ear.

'What?' mouthed Murdoch. Then he tilted his head, aware of a trilling, a high-pitched tune.

Nowinski flipped out his mobile phone. Immediately, Donald Dewar started to disappear. There. Gone. There. Gone. He folded over. He stretched. His legs separated from his body. Black streaks passed across his image, and all the while, Nowinski laughed.

The screen on his lectern began to pulse. Murdoch leaned over to read it.

MOBILE PHONE VIOLATION
SWITCH OFF NOW OR LEAVE THE CHAMBER

The Lib Dems tutted. The opposition cheered and applauded, but the Labour clones sat impassive, oblivious to the sabotage of their virtual leader's speech.

'Don't we swear allegiance to King Harry?' Murdoch asked.

'Not this year,' Nowinski told him. 'Not with Cornwall occupied by an army trying to put down an independence uprising.'

'Right, I forgot.'

'Yeah, Englishman killing Englishman. Kind of puts a damper on old Miliband's tenth anniversary as PM, eh?'

Murdoch nodded, aware that a message was on his own screen.

GOVERNMENT LEGISLATION
AGENDA ITEM 001
NO AMENDMENTS
VOTE YES
VOTE NO

Murdoch chewed his lower lip. Agenda Item 001. What was that? He'd have to get his mail rerouted from now on, or have Bodger locked in the living room.

'How do I vote?' he asked Nowinski.

'Just touch the screen.'

Well, he would touch no, obviously. He was in opposition. He touched the word and sat back. Instantly his lectern glowed red. All of the government lecterns opposite glowed green, as expected, as did the Lib Dem lecterns. Even Nowinski's was that colour, and every other lectern he could see. Only his was red.

'What are you doing?' hissed Nowinski.

'Voting no.'

'Don't you know what this Bill is about?'

'Er, uh, no.'

'It's the increase in remuneration to MSPs. A twenty per cent pay rise.'

'But I'm earning £300,000.'

'So what? You're a representative of the people. You deserve that £60,000 pay rise. Listen, I gave up being a Super Councillor to become an MSP. I'm out of pocket.'

'I didn't know what item 001 was about.'

'Well, get your act together, kid. Everyone voted for this Bill, except you. Even the Gordon Brown Memorial Party voted yes.'

'Sorry.'

'Okay, okay. C'mon, let's go.'

'Where?'

'Outside, to meet some sponsors.'

'But what about the rest of the business?'

'That's it. The important stuff is over until this after-noon. Here, take a look at this.'

Nowinski opened his jacket. On his tee-shirt was a picture of a group of saltire-faced people riding a rollercoas-ter. Below was the legend *BRAVEHEARTLAND: A Gibson Corporation/SNP Co-production.*

'America, that's where the big money is. Who do you want to meet first? Disney or Pepsi?'

'I'm not sure.'

'Nowinski shrugged. 'It doesn't matter. We'll have a bidding war. H.I.C., eh? Maybe we'll get some drink companies interested, a Japanese whisky firm.'

Murdoch smiled, allowing Nowinski to steer him out of the chamber. Everyone was on their feet, getting ready to leave, except for the government clones. They sat, waiting, as someone went round, removing their control caps. Outside, he looked for Moira. There were several metallic bodies walking about, wearing human faces whenever they looked his way.

'Over here, kid!'

Nowinski was standing at a section of wall that was covered in names. Company names. Ellese, Pepsi, Ford, Kodak, Microsoft. The names went on and on.

'This is the sponsors' board,' Nowinski told him. 'You only give interviews in front of that board. Try and mention one of the products behind you. That guarantees a little extra in your bank account.'

'I thought I was earning enough.'

'Hey, champions of democracy can never earn enough. Here's your Moira.'

How can you tell? Murdoch wondered.

'Greetings, Donald. I trust your first morning as an MSP went well?'

First morning? He glanced at his watch. It wasn't even eleven yet. 'I didn't know what item 001 was about.'

'That is unfortunate, but there is only one other item of business today.'

'Let me guess,' said Murdoch. 'Item 002, MSP holidays.'

'Correct.'

'Hey, Donald!' Nowinski was sipping an Irn Bru tube in front of the sponsors' board. Two reporters were next to him; one held up a finger camera.

'Let me introduce you guys to the fourth independent MSP. He flew all the way here in a giant whisky bottle. This is Donald Murdoch from H.I.C.'

The reporters looked at him. He looked at the reporters, and could tell by their faces that they didn't know what to ask him. He took the Irn Bru tube Nowinski offered and smiled as broadly as his holographic miniature on his name badge.

'Cheers, gentlemen,' he said, as he was shuffled to the correct point in front of the board, eager for the chance to earn some more money. He could put it to good use back home, help the villages stand up against the Free Kirk, and break free of their anti-technology shackles. Any second now he would think of something quoteworthy, displaying his grasp of the democratic process that had led him here, and how it linked to the drinking of Irn Bru.

Any second now.

'Cheers,' he said, raising the drink again, waiting for that second to arrive.

David Hutchison

THE ACHILTIBUIE STONE

It was hot in the back of the car and the seats were sticky. Nine-year-old Douglas had his favourite shorts on. The ones with Nessie sown onto the right pocket. He enjoyed the suction feel as he pressed his legs against the warm plastic then peeled them off.

Vrrrhhmmmmm. Douglas recognized the noise. They'd just gone over the cattle grid. They must be nearly there. He stuck his head out of the window.

Uncle John glanced in the mirror and commanded, 'Douglas. Stop that!'

'I'm looking for the mill.'

As the car went over the stone bridge, Douglas peeked down and saw that the old mill looked just the same as when he'd seen it; a whole year ago. The windows were boarded up with red shutters. It seemed a shame that no one lived in such a brilliant house. He would buy it when he grew up and live in it with Kate MacLeod; Kate with fiery hair and freckles. He thought all these things in a flash and then he was over the bridge and the mill house was gone.

Coming up on the left was Achiltibuie Stores and the petrol pumps. Kate and him had explored the ruin on the hill at the back and had found a black marble fireplace. They had been chased away by Cruachan, the store's mangy collie dog. On cue, as if the hound had sensed his thoughts, Cruachan came rushing towards the car, slobbering and barking madly, trying to bite at the tyres. Satisfied that it had scared the car off, Cruachan swaggered back to patrol the pumps.

Uncle John muttered, 'Annie should have that brute tethered up.'

The car ambled through the scenic village, past stone cottages with rusty corrugated iron roofs, crofts partitioned by dry stone dykes. Douglas looked seaward and saw the piping school where Kate's father worked. Douglas remembered trying to learn the chanter there last summer; only because it looked like a snake charmer's pipe; it didn't work on slow-worms. He'd had slavered over the wooden mouthpiece and overstretched his fingers for a few weeks then had given up. He liked the guitar Auntie Jean had given him though. Uncle John had supplied a songbook with all the chords written down. He could play 'The Banks of the Ohio'. That was only three chords, D, G and A. The words were really vivid too. All about putting knives into people's breasts and everyone being sad.

Vrrroooommmm. They went over another cattle grid with a different higher tone. They turned right down the steep road towards his Auntie and Uncle's house situated at the top of a croft that sloped down to the sea. Neat and whitewashed, with a diamond-patterned tiled roof. He looked to his left and saw Kate's house. Almost the same but with an extension and a satellite dish. Kate's mother used the extension as an artist's studio. At the bottom of Kate's croft he could see hairy blobs of orange and black; the Coigach herd; Highland cows, the subjects of her mother's paintings. Uncle John parked the car. Auntie Jean scurried out of the house and hugged Douglas.

'My how you've grown!'

'Hi Auntie Jean.'

'How's your mother after her operation?'

'She can walk without the metal corset but the doctor said she's to have plenty of rest.'

'Good.'

Douglas took his bag into the house of glossy wood-panelled walls. Auntie Jean's garish handmade rugs were scattered upon the floors like fantastical jellyfish beached on a sea of lino.

Auntie Jean said, 'I've put you in the end room upstairs.'

Douglas ran up the stairs and opened the door to the end room to the smell of fresh paint. On his left there was the single bed complete with a candlewick bedspread. On the right a dormer window looked out across the Summer Isles. The cast iron fireplace was still artistically filled with cones and pebbles, a scary painting of a clown hanging above it. Uncle John's brass telescope was lying on top of the mantelpiece.

Douglas arranged his books on a table and put his clothes away. He opened the window and looked across to the neighbouring croft. The Highland cattle were rushing up the hill to a figure with long red hair. It was Kate. She looked taller than last year. Douglas grabbed a small tube from his bag, flew downstairs and ran to the creaking gate in the dyke at the top of the croft.

'Kate!'

Kate ran up to the gate and smiled shyly.

'Hi Dougie. Mam said you were coming today.'

'Yes, I've just arrived.'

'Come on.'

Douglas went through the gate. Kate ran down the path that followed the dyke down to the shore. Douglas tried to keep up with her.

'Wait for me!'

Kate slowed down and giggled, 'Hurry up, slowcoach!'

Douglas caught up with Kate. They slowed to a walking pace. He held his hands up to shade his eyes from the sun and peered at the islands in the distance. The Summer Isles. Such a magical name. He knew the names of the nearest two islands. They were Goat Island and Horse Island. Last year he had borrowed Uncle John's telescope but hadn't been able to see any goats or horses. Maybe they lived on the other side? He held out a tube of condensed milk to Kate. His face was red from running.

'I've brought the milk. Tell me about the Celts again!'

Kate took the tube of milk.

'They were fierce warriors ruled by the Blue Queen.'

'I remember. She was called the Blue Queen as she rubbed blue berries on her before she went into battle.'

'Yes, and she would offer the gods a sacrifice. You know, like a pet animal.'

'A hamster?'

'Sometimes a person.'

'Cool. But we can use milk instead.'

'Yes, milk's fine.'

They arrived at the bottom of the croft. In front of them was the bullaun, a large boulder with cupmarks.

Kate skipped around it.

'The Blue Queen had a special sacrifice stone with holes in it. Just like this one.'

Douglas climbed on top of it.

'And the sacrificed pet's blood would fill up the holes.'

Kate held the tube over a cupmark and started to squeeze a white worm of condensed milk into it.

'And the Queen would ask the gods to help her in battle.'

Douglas said, 'Make the wish now!'

'Tomorrow at the match, Janice Wilkie will fall and cut her knee.'

'Don't forget the goal.'

'Oh, and Douglas will score a goal.'

*

The football match was at the school playing fields. Kate watched from the sidelines as Douglas ran forward with the ball. Janice Wilkie unsuccessfully tackled him. She fell and Douglas scored a goal.

Janice held her knee and screamed, 'Foul, foul!'

*

That evening Douglas and Kate put some more milk in the stone.

The voice of Auntie Jean echoed down the croft, 'Coooeeee. Douglas. Dinner's ready.'

Douglas jumped off the boulder and started to run up the path along the edge of the croft. Half way up he took a short cut and clambered over the dyke. Some of the stones tumbled down and Douglas went sprawling into a clump of bracken. Auntie Jean had seen Douglas fall and ran down the croft. Kate arrived first.

'You okay, Douglas?'

Douglas sat up and looked at the stone at his feet. It was the size of his head.

'What's that?'

Moss had fallen off the stone to reveal strange carved markings. Kate sat down beside Douglas and ran her finger along a V shape.

She said, 'Rune markings. This must be ancient.'

Douglas said, 'Do you think it's the Blue Queen's?'

Kate said, 'Could be. Probably Viking though.'

Auntie Jean arrived. She saw that nothing was broken and sat down beside Douglas. She untied the corner of her blouse, popped it into her mouth then rubbed some dirt off his forehead. Douglas squirmed.

'Auntie Jean, don't!'

'You okay?'

'I'm fine. See what we found.'

Douglas and Kate held up the rune stone between them.

'Well I never. Where did you find that?'

Douglas said, 'It fell out of the wall.'

A voice echoed over the wall. Kate's mother Sandra leaned over the large gap in the dyke.

Sandra said, 'Kate MacLeod, what are you up to?'

Auntie Jean said, 'The kids are fine. Look what my Douglas found.'

Douglas said, 'It fell out of the wall.'

Kate said, 'It's a rune stone.'

Douglas said, 'Belonging to the Blue Queen.'

Kate looked at Douglas.

Douglas said, 'Or Vikings.'

*

Uncle John was looking though a book on archaeology.

'It must be worth a fair bit, Jean.'

Auntie Jean was leafing through holiday brochures.

'Enough for a holiday abroad, no doubt.'

Douglas was scrubbing the rune stone with an old toothbrush.

Douglas said, 'Abroad. Wha', like Skye?'

Uncle John and Auntie Jean laughed. Uncle John got up, went over to the phonebook and looked through the pages.

'I'm going to phone the museum. Perhaps they'll buy it?'

Auntie Jean went to the bathroom and came back with a can.

'Here Douglas. Use some of your uncle's false teeth cleanser.'

She sprayed the rune stone with foam as Douglas scrubbed away. Uncle John picked up the phone and dialled.

'Yes, I'd like you to put me through to the curator. Yes, I'll hold.'

*

It was early evening and Kate was playing the computer game 'Build an Iron Age fort'.

Her father, Hugh MacLeod, stroked his brown beard as he peered over an old map.

'Come here a minute, Kate!'

Kate carried on playing her computer game. Sandra was sitting in a comfy chair playing Sudoku.

'Kate MacLeod. Your father is talking to you. Put that computer off right this second, my young lady!'

'Yes, Mam.' She sighed, saved her game, got up and walked over to her father.

'Kate. See this map here? See this line running down here?'

'Hmmm.'

'Where did you find the rune stone? Was it on this line?'

'I didn't find it. It was Douglas.'

'Okay. Where did Douglas find it? Look, there's the path down to the sea. And there, where the old ruin is.'

Kate chewed her finger then pointed on the map.

'There.'

'Are you sure?'

'Yes. It was just up from the big rock wi' holes in it.'

'Thanks. You can go back to your game now.'

Sandra looked up expectantly from her game of Sudoku.

Hugh smiled and said, 'It's ours. The rune stone was found on the old boundary wall. Our croft extends several metres past it.'

'Isn't it treasure trove or something then?'

'We'll be due a percentage of its value. I'll see the lawyer tomorrow.'

Sandra put down the Sudoku.

'Shouldn't Douglas be rewarded for finding it then?'

'That boy shouldn't be climbing over my wall anyway.'

Kate turned from her computer.

'Dougie could have been killed!'

'Right. Young lady. It's bed for you with no supper. And another thing, I don't want you playing around with that Douglas Sutherland.'

Kate ran upstairs to her bedroom. Her walls were covered with posters of historical warriors and heroes. She stifled back the tears. A warrior princess would not cry! She heard shouting from downstairs and the sound of a door slamming. A few minutes later there was a knock at the door of her bedroom. Her mother came in with a tray of food and sat down.

'Kate. You okay?'

'Yes Mam. Where's Dad gone?'

'Off out to the pub I expect.'

'I wish Dougie had never found that stupid stone!'

Sandra stroked Kate's hair and gently placed the food tray into her lap.

'There, there, petans. Sit up and eat.'

*

After school Douglas and Kate were walking home along the road. Kate was talking about the rune stone and the Vikings.

'And the Goddess Freya was the most powerful of them all.'

'What special powers did she have then?'

'I'll tell you at school tomorrow.'

'Not in tomorrow. The people from the museum are coming to pick up the stone in the morning.'

'That won't take all day!'

'We're going to get our photos taken at the museum too.'

'Oh!'

'Do you want to come and see the rune stone cleaned up?'

'Cleaned up?'

'I gave it a good scrub and got all the dirt off. It's a kind of red colour.'

'You've not damaged it? They usually clean these things with tiny brushes.'

'I used an old toothbrush.'

'That should be okay then.'

'So are you coming to see it?'

'Dad's banned me from going round to your house.'

'Why?'

'Don't know. He's gone funny. Anyway I've got a photo.'

Kate took out her mobile phone and displayed a close-up photo of the markings on the stone.

'I'm going to look up the markings on the web.'

Douglas said, 'Wish I had broadband.'

Kate said, 'The museum also has some ancient skulls.'

Douglas said, 'From Viking warriors?'

Kate said, 'Yes, and the Celts. Skull goblets encrusted with gold, necklaces made from shark's teeth.'

'Cool.'

*

Professor Jörgestone was an old man with a long grey beard
and tweed suit, like a wizard done up for a grouse shoot.
Kate watched from the other side of the dyke as Douglas
showed him the hole.

'And I fell down here.'

Professor Jörgestone said, 'Hmmm. The other stones
are fairly typical of the area. Lewisian gneiss.'

Kate looked through the hole in the wall at the
professor.

'What's nice about it! I've got to go to school.'

'Lewisian gneiss is a type of ...'

'It was a joke!'

Kate waved and ran up the hill.

*

Uncle John and Auntie Jean were standing on either side of
a posh glass display cabinet. The rune stone sat importantly
on a white plinth within it. Douglas was sitting below the
cabinet facing a group of photographers.

One photographer said, 'Come on Douglas. Smile for
the birdy!'

Douglas managed a grimace. Uncle John ruffled his
nephew's hair. Auntie Jean adjusted her new dress and
beamed for the cameras.

*

That evening at Kate's house everyone was sitting in the
kitchen. Hugh was staring at the photograph in the *Press &
Journal*. Sandra was peeling vegetables at the sink. Kate was
at the table painting a model of a broch, made from pebbles
glued together on a base of plywood.

Hugh read from the newspaper, 'Professor Jörgestone
of the blah, blah Institute, can't pronounce that, said that it
was the most significant find of the century, blah, blah,
Viking rune marking from the 8th century.'

Kate came over to look at the photograph in the
newspaper.

'What a face Douglas has on him!'

Hugh scanned further down the page and read out, 'However there is a dispute of ownership of the boundary wall where the stone was discovered.'

Sandra said, 'Kate, dinner's almost ready. Can you clear the table please.'

Kate cleaned her brushes and removed her model from the table.

'Mam, can I go round to Douglas's for a while? I'll be back in time for dinner.'

Hugh looked up from his paper.

'No, you can't go.'

*

That evening Kate was in her bedroom painting her broch. She heard a tapping at the window. She went over to the window, drew the curtains and peered out into the moonlight. A small stone struck her cheek.

'Ouch!'

She looked down and saw Douglas.

'Come down!'

Kate said, 'Shhh! Dad will hear you.'

Kate crawled out of the window and down over the porch like an orang-utan. She dropped onto the back of the dilapidated garden seat and landed on the ground.

'Dad wouldn't let me out.'

'My uncle wouldn't either. But I've an idea.'

'What?'

Douglas shone his torch at a tube of condensed milk in his hand.

'Let's ask the Blue Queen's stone to help. After all, Janice Wilkie did fall and cut her knees today.'

'Only because you tripped her up. Mind, you did score a goal.'

'Well let's try it anyway.'

'Okay.'

Douglas passed the tube to Kate and pointed the torch beam down the path. Half way down the field they saw ghostly white figures coming towards them.

Kate said, 'Ghosts?'

Douglas shone the torch and a few sheep ran away.

Douglas said, 'More like ghost sheep!'

When they got to the boulder Douglas shone the torch

over a cupmark. Kate filled the hole with white worms of condensed milk.

'I wish things could be like before we found the stone.'

'Yes, I wish our families would get back to normal.'

They walked back up the croft. Kate scrambled quietly up the garden seat, over the porch and up the drainpipe. Douglas waved with the torch then headed home.

*

Shiori Isimaru, a young Japanese woman, looked out of the window of the train. She watched the landscape pass by. She looked back to her laptop and scrolled through her RSS feeds. Suddenly she peered closely at the screen. She clicked on a link to a news article. She scanned the article and dialled her mobile.

'Can I speak to Professor Jörgestone? What? Shiori Isimaru. No, with a U. My father. No, I can't hold. Five-thirty, okay. Bye.'

Shiori clicked through her phone to a photograph of an elderly man. She got up and started packing her laptop. The guard went past.

Shiori called to the guard, 'Where's the next stop?'

The guard said, 'Kingussie, in five minutes, miss.'

Shiori said, 'Thanks.'

Shiori moved down the carriage and started to gather her belongings together. The train stopped and Shiori got off at Kingussie station. She sat down and cradled a styrofoam cup of tea while she waited for a train heading back to Inverness.

*

Shiori entered Inverness Museum and Art Gallery. She climbed the stairs and went through the glass doors. In the foyer she saw the large glass case holding the rune stone. She looked closely at it and the neatly printed card below it. '8th C Rune stone. Found at Achiltibuie, Ross-shire.' She went up to the reception desk where a young girl was sitting reading a book on the Brahan Seer.

'Hi, I'm Shiori Isimaru. I've got an appointment to see Professor Jörgestone.'

The receptionist put the book down and said, 'I'll just call him now.'

A few minutes later the professor arrived. He looked like a wizard with his long pointed grey beard and twinkling eyes.

*

It was another sunny day on the croft. Douglas and Kate were standing in the background as a Grampian TV crew was filming the scene. Uncle John and Hugh had just finished building up the dry stone dyke together. They both smiled and stood back. Shiori fitted the rune stone back into the wall.

Shiori said, 'Rest in peace, father.'

Everyone clapped.

Phyllis McFudgeon, the famous TV reporter, said, 'And now Japanese artist Shiori Isimaru replaces the stone. Let's talk to her. Hello Shiori.'

'Hello.'

'So why did you place your sculpture here?'

'My father was an archaeologist and travelled all over the world, but this was his favourite place. I carved this stone as a memorial to him.'

'Why the rune markings?'

'Vikings were his speciality. The inscription says, "rest in the great hall of Valhalla".'

'And when did you put it here?'

'Last summer. I'm doing an artist residency in Cromarty.'

Phyllis said, 'You must have been surprised when you saw it in the paper?'

Shiori said, 'I saw it on a news website. I couldn't believe it.'

'I believe that the timing was fortunate?'

'Yes. My residency had just finished. I was on the train going to London to catch my flight back to Tokyo when I got the news.'

'Thankyou Shiori. Now let's talk to the young people that found the stone.'

Phyllis looked around for Douglas and Kate but she couldn't see them.

'Let's have a closeup of the stone.'

The camera crew started to move the equipment as Auntie Jean passed around scones and Sandra handed out cups of scalding tea. Douglas went up to Sandra.

'Mrs MacLeod, can I borrow that jug of milk?'

'Certainly Douglas.'

Douglas and Kate carried the jug down the croft to the bullaun. They poured some milk into the hole. They started laughing and running around the boulder. Auntie Jean looked down and was about to shout when Uncle John touched her arm.

'Oh, let them be.'

Linda Jackson

EARLY GULLS OVER MORAR

Mallaig was finished. The boats hung about the harbour with the fishermen sat pished in the pubs nearby. We've nothing to pass on to our youngsters up here; and the island kids come off the boats and just run rabid with our weans instead of going to the school. We used to teach them the tricks of the catch, they would tell us stories of eagles up on the Sgurr. It was a productive time of exchanges – netting and romance, work and storytelling.

The arse is out of the fishing now but I never took to the drink. I carried my hip flask from Mary, always a dram and a prayer before taking the boat out but God, these men in the bay now. Christ – they're done.

Mary's been solid through it all and now works in a fancy tourist café where they sell fish suppers for a tenner, fish brought up from other places.

'Are you awright there Jack?'

Jack doesn't answer, he just staggers off to the Seaman's Mission. His wife ran away with a young loon from Ullapool, but aye well he was always a crabbit bastard of a man.

It was Mary that took me to the new medical centre. She found me one night down by the pier, sitting there on the street in the rain.

'The fishing's finished here Mary, it's done.'

'C'mon now Andrew, c'mon.'

She swept her hand then over my brow and bent into my eyes.

'C'mon that'll be you, up you get.'

The doctor was a youngster from Alness, he was too embarrassed to talk and I was humiliated – by myself, by the weakness.

I hoped that the anger would come and stop me greeting there in front of the boy.

'There you go now Mr Robertson, take these, you'll be alright.'

In the waiting room, Mary checked the labels and tried to hide a look of worry. Outside the place, I pulled on a roll-up and I looked at Mary emptying the rubbish from her bag into the bin. I loved this woman but didn't know what

to do anymore, the strength in my wanting seemed to have
drifted off with the boats.

'Everything will come up good,' I said to her with a
comforting hug. The truth couldn't work now. Her wee
shoulders were starting to fall forward, worry.

The rain drizzled gently about us.

'Here ye go.' I laid my coat over her shoulders.

Clutching around her, we hurried home to the house.
With the rain wet between us, I kissed her tenderly, I began
to kiss her hard but she stopped, kind and knowing that ...
well, just knowing.

'Come on now, enough of your carry-on, let's get
something on to eat.'

Later we drank tea. 'That wee job that John Carmichael
has got is not bad, Andrew, and they'll need some new
drivers soon.'

I fingered the card that the doctor gave me. It was a card
about stopping smoking.

It burned in the grate.

'I'll look into it in the morning then.'

'The receptionist gave me a card for you about smoking, it's
in your coat pocket but well I think this is not the time eh?
God knows what we'll be left to decide for ourselves eh?'

She upped and offed into the kitchen. I lay back in the
chair, a wee doze.

He loved this woman and he used to know how to hold
her. He was strong, tall with good muscles still but he used
to know how to hold her, he used to feel the bit between his
teeth with the wanting of her.

For near a year now, he couldn't, what with the fish
and the multi-coloured tarpaulins over new knick knack
shops. Aye.

Andrew slipped out of their bed near two in the
morning, he took the boat from its moorings. He loved
the smell of the harbour at night, he loved the early gulls
swooping. Light splayed across the wooden beams of the pier
as he pushed off for Morar. That had been their place. Mary
and him all those years back. He pulled his coat round him
and felt for the old shell in the inside pocket; it still had sand
in it. That had been a great day.

With a heart feeling newly light and determined, there'd
be no more waiting – he had a purpose.

Paula Jennings

THE GIFT

The present is a gift
say the smug punners

but when you unwrap it
it's already gone.

I'm training myself
to unwrap it fast.

This is the slow discipline of meditation.

Vivien Jones

THE MILL
Acorn Bank, Cumbria

This oat mill was working then,
not just something to peer at
on a day out, but noise and dust,
men shouting, water falling
from lades, in and out, the wheels
grating, husks ankle deep.
The miller's boar roaring his lust,
dizzy hens weaving underfoot.
Small boys, massing like September wasps,
dropping pebbles, earning thick ears.

Their sticks defeated dragons in their path,
their knees were meshed with scratches, their
arses were streaked with grass-stain, they
scratched the pigs' backs with their sticks
through the infinity of summer holidays.

This Easter Day's child carries a worksheet
and a pencil, chewed, that must be returned.
The silent mill walls are studded with boards,
drawings of mechanisms, a pictured history.
The stream, unemployed, flows by, the lades
creak, the great paddled wheel unconnected.
The child ticks his boxes, his parents beam,
they head to the shop for a postcard.

Alex Laird

STRAWBERRY YIELD

We went that sunny day, us grandchildren
With collecting jars.
Bees droned from flower to flower,
Moths flushed from disturbed grasses.
Rail tracks glistened as the smell of
Tar-oil oozed from driven key blocks.

A war-torn world boomed its weariness
While we filled jar after jar
With plump wild strawberries.
We never knew of danger
Though the world floundered in it.

Look, we cried, showing our gathered treasure
Having picked the fruit all along the cutting
Fanning out over the soft wide grass banks
Where, looking back, saw her there waiting
Knowing we would return to her with bounty.

Grandfather claimed miracle,
That such sweetness prevailed
From cinder and crushed slag.
Under his feet timber sleepers
In the heat, sweated their creosote.

We stood by as wagon loads of coal
Clicked their way along the straining tracks
Shepherded by the common shunting pug.
The great mouth of an iron works waited.

Helen Lamb

1962

My small world is bound
by beech and privet,
a singing river.
Hiroshima could still be
the shiver
of breeze through birch trees.

In the old stone school,
belly after belly
swells the rumble.
We gnaw on rubber
suck on lead till
the hot, hungry gallop home.

But the kitchen is empty.
The broth pot stands
cold on the stove.
Simmering silence
summons me
through the shadowed hall.

Up close to the Bush TV,
my mother,
on her knees,
wrings a yellow duster.
The newsreader cannot
promise us tomorrow.

And now my world grows vast
and dark.
Nagasaki could be
the crack in her voice,
correcting me –
Cuba is not in Africa.

William Letford

THE LAST MINER

My memories from the strike are vivid but it's difficult for me to put them in order. Memories don't work like that. They don't start from yesterday as bright as summer then fade to a grey morning in autumn. It's more like I've got a basket full of them. Little bits of life all jumbled up in different shapes and sizes.

Like when my dad would come home on a Saturday evening with bin bags full of cakes and bread. I didn't understand it at the time, I thought we were rich on a Saturday. The bakers would leave everything they hadn't used for the two nights previous out the back for the miners to collect. That was my father's job. Collect the cakes and the bread and share them out amongst the families, but not before he let me open one and peer inside. Every time I pass a bakery the smell engulfs me and I see the inside of that bag. Dark and full of treasure.

I chose the same thing every week. A yum-yum. A twisted length of pastry coated in icing sugar. Sweet, sticky and delicious. I remember phone calls and my father being far away in England. I remember my mother looking out the window and turning off the TV and holding me on her knee as someone chapped the door and we would just sit there, quiet, until they went away. I remember my grandfather standing in the kitchen stamping his walking stick and shouting. He had been a miner too. And I remember a Christmas when everything I got was wooden. There was a wooden drawing board with a ream of paper attached to it and a handwritten note from Santa Claus. He told me that most years the elves had so much work to do they had to buy a lot of their gifts from the shops in town, but since I had been a particularly good boy this year they'd made all of my gifts themselves. There was a P.S. at the end of the note. 'Don't forget to look behind the couch.'

A silver BMX was waiting there for me as I clambered over the sofa. Both my parents took me out into the street to teach me how to ride it. I was talking about that memory with my mother on the day of my dad's funeral. She told me that my aunt had sent them money from Manchester so they could buy it.

*

My grandfather died sometime during the strike and on the day he died my dad had sat me down to tell me a story. My dad had been about the same age as I was then. He was walking home from school when he got in a fight with Craig Macelvoy. It was a young boy's fight. They could've gone all day without doing a whole lot of damage, until an older boy stepped in. The older boy was called Clem. There's a Clem in every generation and when my dad began to describe him I recognized him, except to me his name was John. Clem was the boy that would spend an afternoon trying to catch a pigeon so he could wring its neck. He would keep a ferret as a pet and look after it so he could send it down rabbit holes. When Clem stepped into the fight he had decided – in his own unique way – that my dad was the rabbit and Craig was the ferret. So the rabbit was to be held down and the ferret was to eat it. Clem pushed my father's face into the ground and lifted his jacket so his back was bared. Craig didn't set to his task with much gusto. Clem shoved him to the side and bit my father so hard he broke the skin in four places.

*

My grandfather was working night shift so he wasn't long out of his bed when my dad walked into the house. He was at the kitchen table settling down to his first coffee and cigarette of the day when my dad sloped in and presented himself, snottery-nosed and teary-eyed. My grandfather didn't look up.

'What happened?'

'I got in a fight, da.'

'Well, did ye win?'

'There wiz two eh thum.'

'So there wiz two eh thum. Did ye win?'

My dad turned and lifted the back of his jacket as far as he could. He said he heard a long stream of air coming out of my grandfather's nose. He told my dad to sit down until he'd finished his smoke. Once he'd finished, he closed the lid on his tobacco tin and walked to the corner of the

kitchen to put on his working boots. He asked my dad the
names of the two boys as they walked out the front door.

*

My grandfather was a young man then and kept a good pace
all the way to Craig Macelvoy's house. He rattled the
letterbox. Craig's dad answered and stood for a moment, but
when my grandfather said nothing he asked,
    'What can I do for you, Bill?'
    Bill was my grandfather's name.
    'Your son wiz fightin wae ma laddie, Jim.'
    Jim shrugged. 'Boys fight Bill, ye know that yersel.'
    My grandfather turned my dad around and lifted up his
jacket.
    'There wiz two that set about him and done this, Jim.
Noo get yer laddie oan tae the front grass here so they can
settle it one tae one.'
    'Bill, am no gettin ma son oot here so he can fight in
the street.'
    My grandfather didn't miss a beat.
    'That's fair enough Jim. If yer no gettin yer laddie oot
ye can bring yersel oot. Noo go inside and get yer boots oan
so we can settle it oan the grass here.'
    Jim turned his head to shout for his own son.
    None of the two boys had much heart for the fight.
The spectacle only lasted a few seconds before Craig let his
legs go out from under him. My dad and my grandfather
walked away without a word.

*

On the way to Clem's house my father said he was terrified.
He knew he couldn't beat Clem in a straight fight but the
presence of his own father held him in place. Clem's dad had
also been on night shift and when he answered the door his
eyes were already angry. He was a big man and decided to
ignore the niceties.
    'Whit's this aboot then?'
    Clem and his dad shared the same name.
    'Yer laddie wiz fightin wae ma laddie, Clem.'
    'And?'
    My grandfather repeated the process of turning my
father around and lifting his jacket.

'There were two that done this, Clem.'

'I still don't see whit yer doin at ma door, Bill.'

'Ye can bring yer laddie oot here so they can settle it one tae one.'

'No gonnae happen, Bill.'

'Well bring yersel oot then. Right now.'

Older Clem took a moment to consider this.

'If there's a lesson tae be given tae ma laddie a'll be the one that's givin it, and it'll be a harder lesson than you or your laddie could manage. Leave it wae me Bill, he's ma son.'

My grandfather nodded agreement. Before they left the front path they could hear young Clem screaming in the living room. As they walked along the street my grandfather put his arm around my dad's shoulder.

'The reason that laddie is the way he is, son, is cause that man beats him so hard.'

My dad never lifted a hand to me his whole life.

*

My grandfather was six years dead. Santa and the elves had long been put to bed and my nights were now filled with street corners and cheap cider. I think I was singing. Maybe I was just shouting. Whatever my vocal chords were doing I was marching down Broad Street after gulping down a litre bottle of Electric White and watching one of my friends vomit all over the local graveyard. Something landed on the pavement about a metre away from me. Something wet. A water balloon or a sponge, it came from above anyway. I looked up through the streetlights and saw the silhouette of a head poking out from one of the windows. A guy called 'Toasty' had recently moved into that flat and we'd been watching the comings and goings of a new group of young delinquents with the wary eyes of a pack of mangy dogs. I was alarmed that he had thrown something at me so I let him know,

'Whit the fuck eh you dane?'

'Who the fuck eh you talking tae?' he shouted down at me.

There was obviously a problem so we discussed the situation further.

'Who the fuck de ye hink you're talking tae?' I shouted back at him.

'Talkin tae you, fanny baws, want me tae come doon there and boot yer heed in?'

'C'mon then.'

'Jist you wait there, I'll be doon the noo.'

'Nae bother.'

As soon as his head disappeared another head, with long hair, appeared at the window.

'You better run away,' the girl shouted, 'his big cousins are here and one's twenty-one and the other yin's twenty-three.'

I looked across the street to where one of my friends stood. He was holding his stomach and retching beside the Tollbooth steps. I turned around and caught a glimpse of my other friend's heels as he melted round the corner. I didn't care. I was fourteen. The Electric White had worked its magic. My fists were four times their normal size. I had a chest like a weightlifter — which was puffed out accordingly — and my head was the size of a large cannonball. I had planned to use all three alcohol-acquired attributes to beat down my foes. A guy appeared at the entrance to the close door and just stood there. So I stormed right up to him. Before I had taken five strides, the other two — the twenty-one and twenty-three-year-old — leapt out of the close. I'd been ambushed. The oldest and biggest of the three planted his Nike Air trainer into my stomach. One blow sent me sprawling. I remember tasting blood as I was given six or seven kicks to compound my lesson.

*

One of the kicks had caught me square in the face as I was trying to get up. It broke my nose. So I was quite a sight when I walked into the house but it wasn't my face that was bothering me. I was more concerned about getting to my bedroom without my parents finding out I had been drinking. Sure enough, as I passed the living room my father was there, watching TV. I hadn't cried, I think the cider had fixed that, but when I saw my father jump from the couch toward me I broke down into a bloody, blubbering mess. I related the story to him, tweaking it where necessary. Now that I think back, by the time I had finished I was an angel, set upon by demons. Men demons. He got a cloth and cleared the blood from my nose, telling me it was broken.

He took the cloth back to the kitchen and reappeared with his working boots dangling from his right hand. My heart fell right out of my body and landed on the floor in front of me.

'No, dad.'

'Take me to where it happened.'

'No, dad.' I was pleading with him.

He grabbed me by the collar of my jacket and hauled me off the sofa and out the front door.

My body was numb as we walked up the hill toward Broad Street. I remember the sound of the air rushing in and out of my lungs. When we reached the scene of the crime I piped up.

'I don't even know whit door's their's, dad.'

'Just point at the windae, son.'

We entered the close. He took the stairs two at a time and rattled the letterbox. No answer. He rattled the letterbox again. No answer. He lifted the letterbox and shouted inside.

'Ye cannae hide forever.'

We heard movement inside the flat. Someone was coming to the door. When the door opened my dad just stood there. Words began to tumble from the guy wearing the Nike Air trainers and as the words were tumbling from his mouth my dad looked at me and said,

'Did this guy hit ye, son?'

I nodded. He leant forward and yanked him from the doorway onto the steps that led further up the close. As the guy landed on the stairs the words were still tumbling from his mouth. He tried to get up. I saw my dad's elbow rise and fall as he planted him and declared, 'Shut up, this is a time fur listenin. If you ever,' I winced at the dull slap of knuckle against skin, 'touch ma son again a'll be goin tae the jail but at least a'll still be fuckin alive.'

I heard the guy's jumper rip as he was dragged up and thrown back into the flat. There was a moment of silence. Then the click of the Yale lock as my dad closed the door gently behind him.

As we were walking home the man walking beside me – a man that seemed different to my father for the duration of that walk – put his arm around my shoulders and said,

'You hivnae been drinkin the night, hiv ye son?'

*

So now my dad's three years dead. I'm sitting in my living room and my own son's lying in front me, not even six months old. His eyes are as bright as ice as they roam around the room. Was my father dreading that moment or waiting for it? Maybe it was a bit of both, but I think he needed that night. And now, of course, I'm wondering. There's one thing I know for sure. I might not work miles underground, I might not work inside the veins and heat of the earth, I might be half man, half desk – but the last miner hasn't died in this family.

Rowena M. Love

STRIKE A LIGHT

You wouldn't think that a love of words could come from coal, would you? Yet for me, the events of the winter of 1973–74, culminating in the miners' strike, struck a chord that still resonates.

Coal means different things to different people. For coal-miners in hard hats, white circles round their eyes standing out from the dirty faces like pandas in negative, it's a way of life. For the environmentalist, it is fossil fuels and rape of the land. To Joe Public, it might be the romance of an open fire, or the drudgery of hauling heavy buckets of coal and cleaning out the grate. But for me, coal is inextricably linked with language and imagination.

I was far too young to appreciate the finer aspects of the Government's 'Three Stage Programme' or the stand taken by the National Union of Miners. Adult talk made no sense to this youngster. Surely a State of Emergency had to be a place? Did stagflation have horns? I'd heard of people being two-faced, but what was Face Three?

All that winter, I'd hear the name of Mick McGahey be invoked; all the syllables running together in my ears until it was a word to conjure with. 'Mickmcgahey' and hey presto, weeks could suddenly have three days instead of the usual seven.

For me, when the NUM declared their all-out strike on the 10th of February 1974 in support of their pay claim of 30–40 per cent, it was the start of a magical period that would cast a spell over my entire life. I'd spend the day dreaming about dark-time, when I could curl up in a room lit only by firelight and flickering candles.

I remember it all so clearly: the crack as a piece of coal split; the whistle and wheeze of escaping gas; the sound of running water into a metal pail as Mum dampened the dross, and then the reek of it pinging my nostrils. Shadows fought battles worthy of Wallace on the wall or cooried in corners like cowards.

My mother was from mining stock, and would build the fire accordingly: this was no sad cluster of coals where you could count the individual embers, but rather a steep bank of heat with flames that seemed to go half way up the chimney. Like Janus with a foot in either world, your front would be burning while your back was cold. As the night wore on, faces would flush, knees would brighten with their mantle of tinker's tartan and our chairs would get pushed further and further back until we were almost out the door, but still our focus would be that fire.

Mum would tell stories of her Ayrshire childhood with tale upon tale of her miner grandfather and uncles to fire the imagination. In that warm darkness, their world was brought to life: Davy lamps; the cage; the harsh reality of the coal face; the wives washing their moleskins; towels warming by the fire while they shaved, scraping away any ingrained dirt with their cutthroat razor; their travels to the mines of Canada and South Africa.

There were more than just stories of the past, as the flames breathed life into ghost stories and fantasies. We'd stare into the glowing coals and look for monsters or fantastic creatures, taking our turn to recount where they had come from or what they would do.

'Look, do you see that one? Up in the corner.'

'The dragon?'

'No, no, to the side of that. See the face, and that blue flame's like her hair. Well, she's a princess and ...'

Those nights by the fire didn't simply fuel the imagination, though. As well as the stories, there was a whole range of word games that gave me the very building blocks of language. Every night there would be bings of words, their sounds echoing as their meaning was hacked from the darkness. An elderly aunt lived with us then, and I can still hear her 'Definition, please!'

It never struck me as ironic that in a time of a miners' strike, a coal fire should be so central to our activities of word games and storytelling, but so it was. As spring approached, so did the lighter nights, but the real end of those enchanted days came when British industry returned to the five-day working week on the 9th of March 1974, the state of emergency ending two days later when the miners' union accepted a £103 million pay deal. The close family gatherings round the fire were over; soon they were only a rich seam of memories, but one that would forever fuel a love of words and of storytelling.

DUFTON PIKE PICNIC

Dufton Pike wasn't a big hill:
but mirth slowed us down –
it's hard to laugh and still climb.
We got to the cairn in perfect time for lunch.
Flat rock, sun-warmed, and we were set.
You dug in the khaki knapsack,
surely a casualty of at least one World War,
and came up with the goods. Dry goods.

You didn't do posh picnics.
Sandwiches are for sissies, you said.
Your idea of lunch just a trip to the butcher, the baker
(plenty of candlepower in the sun already).
No butter, no spread, mayonnaise a word
you'd struggle to spell, if you knew it at all.
You slapped the roll into my hand. Slapped the meat
into the roll. While I slapped a smile onto my face.
Or tried. What I wouldn't have given
for something just a little more moist.

Be careful what you ask for: your old refrain.
Moments later, clouds were mopping up sunshine
like bread with gravy, letting it ooze out as rain.
You took back the roll, held it high: sacrifice
to a rain god. Then, kidding on you were a waiter,
in a uniform as black as the sky,
and a phoney French accent,
you presented it to me with a flourish.
Marinated in laughter,
what should have been a soggy mess
became a banquet worthy of kings.

Since then, when it comes to picnics,
while most people are praying hard
for cloudless skies, I can't help wishing
for a little rain.

Peter Maclaren

REGISTERING A DEATH

Ushered politely through a panelled door
(a sombre job to settle up a friend's affairs)
certificates are read, and folded up,
returned safely to their envelope,
he writes in longhand with a gleaming nib.
Three weeks from his retiral, so he says,
seeming quite chatty for a man of death,
while the dim room inspects us both.

At length, led on by his civility
I offer up the detail drawn from far
that though I never knew the man
my father's father, too, was registrar.

He checks my name, while his mind sieves
the patient traffic of so many lives
shared out across the solid polished desk.
'I think I've met him,' he replies,
'he visited my office once
when as a junior I began this job.
A crippled foot? Strong nationalist?
But human, for despite his post
He'd talk to you. So, you're the grandson?'

A few brief phrases pulled from one man's past.
I see him off to keep a luncheon date
(a group of them met weekly in the town)
walking frock-coated, kid gloves in his hand,
a bright gardenia winks from his lapel.

Reacting now to one man's death
I sense the extra loss compete
across three generations' span
of never knowing the other man.
Sharp like a slate a sudden panic flares
for after *my* going what's the chance of talk,
of grandson's memory for details?
It fades, there's none,
that track ends here with me.
The room lights flicker, we complete our task,
shake hands, this business ended,
yet strangely always going on, going on,
this daily structuring of human lives,
not bitter, not forgetful.

VESTED INTEREST

Following the track back
to the Lodge
we found doors bolted, curtains pulled
against intruders,
the loch's brilliant light,
the azaleas
and the rock thimble of Suilven

Through a gap the furniture
stood sheeted still,
yet by the house door
four seats shone in the afternoon sun,
a business gift from some shipbreaker friend.
Only a silver square marked its origin,
teak from an admiralty yacht long foundered.

Behind the house the vegetable garden
the servants' quarters where you must have stayed,
a practice stag's head on the nearby wall.
'Did your friend not work here?' asked my wife
pushing out the keel
into widening ripples of memory.

In the space of the night, while the hotel slept,
I dreamed of you
walking apart
in some strange city,
wearing clothes I didn't know,
unaware of my gaze.

With the morning
thirty years from that love's shipwreck
I gaze out at the mountain's wise forehead
and watch it breach the clouds of a new day.

SEVILLA

Up the Giralda's sloping ramps
urging his sweating horse
the muezzin five times daily
dismounts, tethers the beast,
regards the rooftops
and calls the faithful to prayer.

Across the square
in the cool gardens of his Alcázar
strolls Pedro the Cruel
shaded by palms in the aromatic air,
plash of fountains
over glistening pebbles.

Six centuries on
I can build you no palaces
nor set a city at your command
but walking together
in the warm October air
I offer you a simple hand.

Lois McEwan

LICHEN

Lichens can colonise almost any undisturbed surface. Most lichens grow very, very slowly, often less than a millimetre per year, and some are thought to be among the oldest living things on Earth.

— Stephen Sharnoff, *Lichens of North America*

Nana was making the funny noise again, sucking and slurping in her throat like the sea caught in a blow-hole. The sea hated being stuck; it was getting rough, the waves pushing higher and higher. She didn't want to stay in the room with Nana in case the sea rushed out of her mouth and drowned them both. She sat up in bed, riding the mattress like a raft on the waves.

Mummy, Nana is ...

She went to the front room while Mummy saw to Nana. She didn't need a nap anyway. Nana was bellowing but the clock was ticking, slow as a strathspey. She slid her foot along the floorboards to the beat of the clock; bump and glide, bump and glide, Scottish country dancing tomorrow night. She needed her ghillie shoes but they were in the bedroom and Nana was yelling:

Zoo house, zoo house.

But Lockerbie didn't have a zoo. She had never been to one. Maybe Nana thought she was in a zoo, lying night and day in the bedroom with its sickroom smell, like an animal's cage.

Zoo eyes, zoo eyes.

Nana sounded wild and inhuman. Daddy came hurrying down the hall. He was cross, she could tell by the speed of his step. But then he was cross a lot.

Can ye no keep her quiet?

Zoo eyes.

Mother, stop it, Mother ... Lichen.

She had forgotten Nana had a proper name, just like a real person. Nobody else in Lockerbie was called Lichen. She had never heard of anybody called Lichen anywhere, apart from Nana. She didn't like her own name, Agnes. It was dogsbody drab but at least it was normal, a name people had. Better than being called Fungus or Mould.

Lichen grew over Nana's face and body, outcrops of white and orange, yellow and turquoise, spreading rough, blotchy and broken like a disease. Lichen closed over Nana's eyes and mouth and sealed them shut, until she was a stone slab lying on the hillside in the wet grass with the lichen growing over her forever like corals on a reef. Now Agnes knew the name of the beast in the room but she was afraid to think it. She picked up a lace doily from the back of the armchair and put it over her face, like lichen.

Whit are ye playing at Aggie? Come and get a sweetie.

Agnes followed Mummy down the hall, past the door to the back bedroom, not looking at the dark lump under the bedclothes. She kept her eyes on her feet; bump and glide, bump and glide into the kitchen.

Dinnae dae that the now. Here ye are.

Mummy held out both fists.

Neery neery nick nack, which hand will ye tak? The left or the right, the right or the wrang?

Agnes tapped the right; a Murray mint, striped black and white like a zebra. She tapped the left; a barley sugar twist. There was always a sweetie in both hands.

Daddy came in.

Come oan Aggie, the watch is already started.

Nana moaned again but quieter. Mummy clicked her dentures with her tongue.

We've goat tae gang, woman.

Daddy slipped on the stairs, almost running to open the street door. There was a man on the doorstep.

I thocht ye were deid Mr Stevenson, or gone away like. I've been knockin an knockin an the wind, it's like a stepmother's breath oot here the ...

We're closed.

... way it cams funnellin doon the street at ye. I fell awf my bike comin doon the Lamb Hill an the wheel's aw bent.

Mr McIntyre's breath, visible steaming clouds of it, reeked of fresh Scotch on top of stale Scotch. It was not nice to see Mr McIntrye's smelly breath billowing towards her.

Ma mother's nae weel, Mr McIntyre, nae guid at aw.

Nana could still be heard from the door but she was

fainter, like a wireless just off a station, the words all crackled out of shape.

But I've goat tae get tae Fechan the nicht.

Are your legs broke man?

Mr McIntyre pushed his cap back, speechless, shaking his head. She thought for a horrible moment he was crying but it was a dewdrop flying off the end of his nose. His red flaky neb was greeting for him.

Ah canny ...

He stopped to sniff, a snail's trail of snot leaking out of his nose.

A've goat tae gang oan watch, fur the Observers, Mr McIntyre. We're late.

Ah canny walk aw yon way man.

There's a war oan. Come on Aggie.

Ah did war work masel, ken, fur the last war, in the munitions at Gretna. Ruined ma hauns makin the deil's porridge.

He held up his hands, his knobbly witches' fingers shaking in her face.

An now ah canny haud oan tae ma bike sae ah fall awf. The ruddy Huns, ah'd stick eve-ry last yin o thum up agin the wall, ah'd gie thum ta-ra.

He aimed an imaginary tommy gun.

Ra-ta-ta-ta-tat.

His coat had no buttons, just a bit of rope tied round the waist. It had slipped down at one side. His cap fell off into the gutter. Agnes picked it up. There was only a little bit of mud on it.

Bluddy German bastards.

Jim, the wean.

Och sorry hen, ah didnae mean onythin.

Right ye are, Mr McIntrye. The wife will help ye.

Mr McIntyre stuck his head up the stairs.

Hullo Missis Stevenson!

Daddy took her arm, dragging her away up the High Street, the sooty sandstone terrace burnt orange in the horizontal sun, shop windows flashing with molten light.

What's the devil's porridge? said Agnes.

Oh, the armaments. Nitro-glycerine mixed wi, ah, nitro-cotton in big tubs, white, lumpy stuff. It was Conan Doyle cawed it the devil's porridge, that wrote Sherlock Holmes.

LICHEN   127

He should have written a horror story about that McIntyre; The Man with the Shaky Hands or The Claw mibbae heh heh heh.

A huge devil with Mr McIntyre's red neb was mixing porridge in the Devil's Beeftub, the big green hole in the hills. The beast had a Nazi leather coat tied on with rope. He stirred the porridge with his pointy tail, then took it out and licked it. The devil rolled his eyes, porridge sticking to his Hitler moustache, shovelling handfuls into his mouth with his bony claws. Lumps exploded in his belly, snap crackle pop. His eyes went round in circles and streams of burning sulphur belched out of his nose and mouth. He laughed, heh heh heh, rumbling like thunder round the Moffat hills.

He could keep it in the Devil's Beeftub.

Whit?

The devil. His porridge.

Ye daft besom. Come oan now, we're late.

He took her arm to cross the road, past the noise and warm beer smell at the Blue Bell, across the road, into the lane where it was cool and damp, even in the summer. Her feet slipped over the cobblestones; bump and glide, bump and glide. She brushed her hand along the wall, the sandstone leaving red dust on her fingers, soft cushions of moss and rough blisters of lichen scraping off under her nails. Lichen.

Daddy, why is Nana called Lichen?

Whit now? Because it's her name, why else?

Nobody else is called it.

She was French mind, it's a French name.

Bump and glide, bump and glide.

But French girls are called things like Marguerite and Antoinette. Lichen doesn't sound French. It sounds ...

She's French, it sounds French. It's just naw posh like Antoinette. Run on and tell Dougie we're here. He'll think we're no coming.

She shot out of the lane like a cork out of a bottleneck, up the steep green side of the hill. Dougie wouldn't mind them being late because he played dominoes in the library with Daddy, but it was good running.

The sheep scattered across the grass like clouds over a green sky. Daddy was miles behind. He needed his motorbike to get up the hill but there was no petrol. She wasn't allowed on it anyway, not since Mummy fell off halfway up the Lamb Hill. Daddy didn't notice till he got to the top and Mummy was left sitting with the sheep. Now he was left halfway up. She sat down to wait for him.

She could smell burning. A plume of smoke was curling out of the shelter and down the hill. You'd think the observation post had been hit, but it was Dougie's pipe, even though the baccy was terrible because of the war, might as well smoke carpet, Daddy said, or hay. But they needed the hay for the animals.

When Daddy got to the top he was puffing as if he was smoking already, but then he lit his pipe too, before it got dark which meant No Smoking. Sometimes he did anyway and she had to Look Out in the Blackout for people coming because of his eyes. Daddy sooked furiously. The pipe smouldered and foul-smelling smoke curled out of the bowl.

Does it taste like the bedroom carpet or the rug in the living room? she asked.

Daddy did not answer. Dougie was muttering in his ear, mibbae something secret she wasn't meant to hear. He was in the Masons like Daddy, with an embroidered satin pinny like the one she wasn't meant to know was in the black leather case under Mummy and Daddy's bed. She had opened the case to look and touched the shiny material. She wanted to try it on but was too scared. They would look funny, Daddy and Dougie, sitting side by side in the shelter blethering in their satin pinnies like housewives but with their hairy legs in tackety boots and sooking on their pipes like weans' dummies.

She put a twig in her mouth and sooked it. It might have been dirty but they weren't looking. They could not hear her or see her. She was the invisible girl. She went round the shelter and rolled down the Lamb Hill over and over until she minded about grass stains. Nothing to play on here, not like Kintail Park that had three swings. Victoria Park just had flower beds, but not now because everybody had to Dig for Victory. There were already plenty of vegetables and everything else but they must grow more tatties and neeps to send to the people in the cities, in Glesga, London and Liverpool, then maybe they will stay there and not be evacuated to Lockerbie with their nits and impetigo. And they were so ungrateful they didn't want to give their banana rations to poor little Peter Stronach like everybody else, even though he could eat nothing except bananas or he would swell up like a barrage balloon and maybe burst.

They sometimes came out to the Lamb Hill, the evacuees. It was too dark to see now in the shadows. She ran back up the hill and round to the front of the shelter. Daddy was unfolding a piece of paper from his wallet and hooking his glasses round his little red ears.

Listen tae this yin. A wee preview, afore I send it tae the Annandale Herald. 'Come, see Raleigh's man o' steel, tempered well fae hub tae wheel.'

Daddy always wrote his adverts as pomes, but he never read them to her or Mummy, only to Dougie.

'It will serve a hundred years, sound in frame from brakes tae gears. Up hill, down dale, the man o' steel will never fail.'

That's good, Bert. The man o' steel. I like that. Jist like MacDiarmid. Jist ride o'er tae Langholm on yon man o' steel an show it tae him.

That's its name. I didnae mak that up, it wis Raleigh.

Oh right. Ah'd rather huv a motorbike like yous onyway.

And Murray Grieve, or MacDiarmid or whitever he calls himself the now, disnae live in Langholm ony mair.

Weel, ah'm nae poet, I dinnae ken aboot it. Ah'd better be gettin back.

Ah've nae finished.

Ma dinner will be burnt black.

Daddy relit his pipe. He kept his hand over the bowl, the smoke seeping out through his fingers like the steam off the devil's porridge. It would make his hand smell orange like a monkey paw. She heard the air crackle in the baccy like bracken on fire and the whoosh as Daddy sooked, then the wheeze as the smoke seeped into his chest. He coughed, let his lungs sigh and whistle.

Good for ma asthma, he said, banging on his chest like the door of a broken cupboard that wouldn't open or shut any more.

There was nobody to see the tiny orange fire in his hand, nobody up in the sky. She lay down on her back to have a look, just to make sure. A buttercup tickled her ear. She put

it under her chin but of course it was too dark for Daddy
to see if she liked butter. She did, they had butter, war or no
war.

Unless the man in the moon could see the pipe, his face
white and lumpy like tripe with the plough, the big dipper,
full of the devil's porridge. He could spill it on their heads,
the milky whey pouring down like the Snowflake rocket.

Will they ever bomb Lockerbie, Daddy?

Mibbae. If a bomber on his way back fae the shipyards
in Glesca or Belfast had yin left they might drap it if they
saw a licht. They'd need damn good eyes tae see ma wee pipe
fae up there, a lot better than mine onyway. Da da da dada,
da da da dada.

Daddy was humming A Scottish Soldier again, which
meant he was thinking about Billy over in France who might
not come back. She tried to remember her big brother's face
and couldn't, because now he was a soldier he was
different.

Da da da dada.

Daddy only ever hummed the first few bars then
stopped. A few minutes later he'd start over again.

Da da da dada.

Last time Billy came back on leave he brought bookends;
two little carved fireplaces and two tiny metal cooking pots,
a little old woman on one and a little old man on the other,
like Mummy and Daddy. They were little old people because
she was a late baby, everybody said, and she wanted Billy
to come back from France to Lockerbie where it was safe
and there weren't any guns or bombs or fighting, at least not
since that Hogmanay Mr McIntyre gave Sandy Callander a
belt at the Blue Bell. Nothing ever happened here.

There was something flying out of clouds over Lockerbie,
like a big black bird but higher in the sky.

Ye'll catch yer death lyin oan yon wet grass. Pit yer
cardie oan.

She stared, listening for the engine noise.

Are ye no listenin? Pit yer cardie oan.

It's a plane.

She pointed up.

It's no, is it? Canny see onythin. Is it behind a cloud?

Ssh.

Can ye tell whit it is Aggie?

It's a bomber but no a Hurricane.

Is it a Heinkel? Mind yin crashed oan Cairnsmore.

No, it's a Yank, a Mitchell. It's coming the wrang way fur a German jist now onyway, it's coming fae Luce Bay.

Are ye sure Aggie? The enemy can come fae anywhere, jist oot o nuthin. You nivver ken when it's comin.

I'm sure.

We'll check the book when we get hame.

Daddy?

Uh hmm.

Whit if it was an enemy plane?

We'd fire the rocket and sound the siren.

Could the rocket hit the plane?

Naw, a Snowflake canny bring doon a plane, it's jist a flare. Yin time it hit the fuse pocket oan the bomb an it went awf. Gave them a fright.

Mr Stevenson, Bert.

Dougie was standing halfway up the hill. He was bent over, panting like a dog.

Your mither's taken bad.

Daddy was right, neither of them had seen it coming.

She couldn't sleep. She stuffed the corners of the quilt into her ears but she could still hear Nana, and feet going up and down the hall. They hadn't even checked the cards. Daddy had forgotten about the plane and sent her to bed and she hadn't even been naughty. Her skirt was muddy from lying on the grass, but Mummy hadn't seen it.

The quilt was soft, the feathers prickling her ears like grass growing underneath her head. The stars were moving around the sky, but they couldn't be. A plane was moving through the constellations, covering and uncovering the stars. She couldn't see what it was because the shape kept changing; a Lancaster, a Heinkel, then a Stuka, wings flapping like a raven with a swastika on its beak. The pilot turned round and he was Nana in Nazi uniform, flying the plane and shouting:

Ich möchte nach Hause gehen.

Daddy was trying to fire the Snowflake rocket and she pulled at his arm trying to stop him because it was Nana, only she was talking German like on the newsreels, but the rocket shot up and Nana exploded like a clay pigeon.

Ich sterbe, shouted Nana.

There was a blinding flash and a fireball fell out of the sky in a huge arc before hitting the ground, sending up two prongs of flame in a big orange V. There was fire all around. Fire was falling down from the sky and it landed on the ground. She was stepping backwards to avoid the fire and she stepped back and back until she was against the wall and couldn't go any further. The ground was burning; the path, the hillside, the hedges, the rooftops, the trees. Everything was burning until it was burnt black. Then it lay on the ground and rotted away into holes of lace and lichen grew over it like a veil.

She was suffocating, hot wool in her mouth. Mummy was in the room.

Why did you gang right under the quilt? Ye'll boil.

Mummy, Mummy, it was a plane.

Sssh, the doctor's here.

Is Nana better?

Nana's gone.

Gone where?

Where we all go in the end.

James McGonigal

UNDERSTUDY

When sunrise warmed the hills' shoulders
they rippled with pleasure – such
a treat of heat after darkness.

I was studying for the role of my father
and found hesitations – a glance of unease –
worked like a breeze

stippling shade under a lime tree.
Soon I wore the part like horse skin
visible only when bleeding or pestered by flies.

David McVey

THE D ROW

Mrs Stroud always hid behind the *Glasgow Herald*. She was cold and thin and bony and it hid her well.

Until Mrs Stroud's Primary Five class I'd never seen a *Glasgow Herald*. We got the *Daily Record* in our house. It was small and handy and had lots of pictures and football. In the mornings, when Mrs Stroud gave us sums to do or questions to answer, our heads went down over our work and she pulled out her *Glasgow Herald* and hid behind it. Everything was still and quiet except for the scratching of pencils, watery sniffs and the crackling when Mrs Stroud fought to turn over one of the huge pages.

We sat in four rows, each two desks wide, running away from the teacher. As Mrs Stroud faced us, the row furthest left was the A Row, then there was the B Row, the C Row and, out to her right, the D Row. We changed desks every Friday afternoon. On Friday mornings, Mrs Stroud gave us an English composition to do, and read her *Glasgow Herald* as we wrote. When we were finished, we turned to a new page in our jotters and wrote at the top *This is My Best Writing*. Mrs Stroud dictated a story to us and we had to copy it down as neatly as we could. I was always rubbish at this and my writing was wild and untidy. 'Ye're jist like me,' my aunt said when she saw something I'd written, 'Ye're too brainy. Yer brain goes too fast for yer haun.'

By early afternoon, Mrs Stroud had marked our work. Those with the highest English composition marks got to sit in the A Row, the next best in the B Row, and so on down to everybody with the worst marks in the D Row. Some people never left the D Row and Jim Barrie was one of them. He was bigger and older than the rest of us because he had been kept back a year, but he wasn't slow or stupid or anything. He just didn't want to be in school, didn't like school work and couldn't be bothered. He was tough. He was the only Celtic supporter in the school but nobody would pick on him for it.

One Friday, Mrs Stroud read out our English composition marks and I had to move from the A Row to the C Row. It had been my first time in the A Row and I had got to sit next to Audrey Campbell, the most beautiful girl in the class. I had been too scared to say much to her and had just enjoyed sitting and working with her next to me. She smelt nice, of soap and some kind of scent. Now I was back in the C Row. Usually I was there or in the B Row.

When I got home that Friday, there had been more arguing, but it seemed worse than usual. My mum had actually thrown a cup at Donnie (my aunt called him my mum's 'fancy man') and it had smashed off the mantelpiece. I was sent out to the Minimarket and told to buy toilet rolls.

'But there's loads of toilet rolls in the lavvie!'

'Look, jist bloody *go*!' said my mum.

When I got back things were quiet but nobody was happy. Mum said she was going out to Barrowland which was what she always did at weekends when she wanted to annoy Donnie. Donnie said *he* was going out for a drink with the boys from work. I went to bed early so that I'd be asleep when they got back. My bed was in the same room as theirs.

Next week at school I settled into the C Row. One day, Mrs Stroud set us sums to do, and for a few minutes I watched as she peeled back each page of the *Glasgow Herald* and, when she got to the crossword, folded the whole paper back on itself and then in half again. I looked around the class: Audrey Campbell, her long, dark hair pulled into a ponytail, was at the front of the A Row and Gordon Waddell was the lucky dog sitting next to her. Across the gap from me, in the D Row, Jim Barrie sprawled back in his seat. He hadn't bothered even starting his sums.

There wasn't much talk at home that night. There had been more shouting. I half-wakened during the night and heard noises and angry voices from the double bed, but nothing made much sense until my mum roughly shook me awake. The light was on, my mum was dressed, and there was no sign of Donnie.

'Get up and get dressed.'

'Eh? Whit for? Whit's the time?'

'Never you mind. Bloody dae whit I tell ye for a change.'

I put on my school clothes, looked at the alarm clock – it was just past two – and walked dreamily out into the lobby. My mum handed me shoes and a jacket and told me to put them on. Donnie came out of the living room, wearing a dressing gown, and asked my mum, 'Whit are ye daein?'

'I'm going,' she said.

'*Going*? Where are ye going?'

'Away. Fae *you*.'

'Wi the *boy*?'

'Well, I'm no gonnae leave him wi you, am I?'

'Don't be bloody daft. Don't leave. Where are ye gonnae go at this time o night, eh, hen?'

Another argument was coming. By now we were out on the stairhead and they realised they couldn't bawl and shout at each other without waking up the whole close. We went back into the lobby and shut the front door. My mum told me to wait in the bedroom.

I sat on my bed and tried to think about things far away and better. I thought about Audrey Campbell, how beautiful she was, how she smiled, her scent and how it felt good just to see her. I thought about being in the A Row and about the composition that had got me there. Mrs Stroud had given us the title 'What I Love About My Family'. Mine had been mostly made up but she didn't know that.

I even thought about Jim Barrie. He didn't bother, he didn't care, he never worried about anything and I really wished I could be like that.

My mum came in. She'd been crying and just said, 'Go back tae yer bed, son.'

I lay awake for the rest of the night. Neither Mum nor Donnie came back in. When I finally got out of bed, the house was empty, as usual; they both started work early. I lit the gas, put the kettle on and filled a big bowl with Rice Krispies. It was just a normal school day. Friday.

In the C Row. Billy Gunn was supposed to sit next to me, but he was off sick again. He was really brilliant at sums and science but hopeless at English so he always struggled to get higher than the C Row. Now he had started to do badly in arithmetic as well, and be off sick a lot.

This week's composition title was 'Leaving Home'. I wrote a really sad story about a poor boy in Glasgow whose mum wanted to escape from her house and her job and her life. She woke the boy up in the middle of the night and they left. They really did escape in the story, but the boy broke away from his mother and went off himself. After playtime we got ready for *This is My Best Writing*. This week's reading was about somebody English called Sir Thomas More and his family and how they lived. I was glad to get it finished and hand in my jotter.

In the afternoon, we got our jotters back. 'A little far-fetched,' Mrs Stroud had written in red about my composition, 'but very well told. Excellent use of English.' She gave me 16/20, which might be enough to get me into the A Row. I looked at my *This is My Best Writing*: 'As usual, correctly taken down,' Mrs Stroud had written, 'but careless, untidy, messy and sometimes barely legible.' My mark was 8/20, which was better than last week.

'Now,' Mrs Stroud boomed from the front, 'for a change, we will arrange you in rows according to your *This is My Best Writing* mark ...'

I watched the rows fill up but was still standing waiting as the last two C Row seats were taken. For the first time ever I would be in the D Row. Mrs Stroud pointed me to the desk next to Jim Barrie. Like most of the D Row, he hadn't bothered to empty his desk or move out.

I tried to act friendly and said something really stupid like 'I've no been here before.' He just looked at me and said, 'Shut it ya fud.' A voice from behind me said, 'We don't like swotty poofs in this row.' I looked over at Audrey sitting, as usual, in the A Row. She looked far away.

That night, Mum went to Barrowland again and Donnie went spying on her. He said he was just making sure she was okay in case Bible John was still on the go, but he really just wanted to see who she was dancing with. I stayed up to watch a scary film on STV but I was sleeping by the time they got back.

I went for the messages with Mum on Saturday morning, and in the afternoon Donnie took me to watch our local junior team. Neither of them said much, and they got annoyed if I tried to talk to them. On Sunday I had BB Church parade, and then played outside for the rest of the day. I didn't tell Mum about the D Row. She wouldn't have been interested, anyway.

On Monday I thought about how there were people sitting in front of me and behind me who *never left* the D Row. What must that be like? Then Miss MacKenzie burst

in suddenly. She was the Assistant Head, took a Primary
Six class and was really old and strict. She had pulled me up
in the corridor a few weeks before when she heard me saying
'fitba' instead of 'football'. Mrs Stroud lowered her *Glasgow
Herald* and then slowly put it away. Miss MacKenzie had
hauled in a miserable looking boy. I recognised him, one of
her Primary Six class. He was supposed to be brainy and he
was also in the school football team.

Miss MacKenzie closed the door and asked Mrs Stroud
if she could speak to us. She turned to face us, pushed the
boy towards us, and screamed, 'Here is a boy – *here is a boy!*
– who does *not* know the date of Christmas Day!'

Silence.

'Isn't that *shocking*?'

I looked at the boy and felt sorry for him. I couldn't even
laugh at him. I was in the D Row, I didn't know what I'd
find when I got home, but at least I didn't have Miss
MacKenzie after me.

'I am taking this boy round *every* class in the school so
that we all know – so that *he* knows – how shameful it is to
be so ignorant!' She opened the door, thanked Mrs Stroud,
and pushed the stricken boy out. Still no one said anything.
Mrs Stroud seemed to have lost interest in her *Glasgow
Herald*. Audrey Campbell, Gordon Waddell, everybody was
back at their sums, except Jim Barrie. 'That boy,' he said to
me, 'he's a diddy, jist like you ur.'

As I did my sums, I practised being as neat as I could.
Even if Mrs Stroud pulled the same trick on us on Friday, I
wanted to be out of the D Row.

Michael Malone

ART IN THE PARK
(for Ronnie Rae)

They wur in among the trees, ahint the big hoose et
      Rozelle.
Richt there oan the grass, like they'd drapped frae a plane.
Huge they wur. Huge wae effort. Huge like a god's thochts.
– Whiddye mak o' them? ah asks ma wee boay.
Hud tae drag him away frae the black boax,
afore his een went widescreen.
He pints, finger oot like a dirk
– Dad, that one has a big butt.
– Furgoadsake, you watch way too much telly, son.
N' the word is arse.
He jist luks up et me n' says
– Whatever.

The Yoke this wan's ca'ed. He's hunched ower.
Heid awa tae the side, like Gourock.
Ah move closer fur a guid look.
– Dad, let's find some branches, so we can play at sword
      fighting.
Ah run ma hauns ower the granite. See, ye think it's gray,
but up close it huz a' these speckles o' black n' flashes o'
      green.
– Dad, I'll be Darth Vader,
the wean skips ower wae twa sticks. – Who are you?
– In a meenit, son. Am huvin' a moment tae masel'.
Noo, he's juist starin' et me n says
– Whatever.

See, son. It's aboot Jesus n' his pain. Bit it's become mair
      than that.
Nature's ge'in a haun' here. The stone's gray like a sufferin'
      sky,
n' the trees are stretchin' their airms oot tae share a touch.
Tae soothe. The earth is aroon the base reachin' up
tae pull the granite back in. N' see here, moss and lichen
... n' wid ye luk et that? That lichen is like a rid stripe
doon the statue's ribs. Whaur a wound micht huv been.

Ma boay stoaps wavin' his sticks aboot,
– Dad, I cannae believe you are actually my dad.
Ah jist luks doon et him n' says
– Whitivur.

WOUNDED KNEE

My black trousers stumbled to a point half way
to the skull-grey cap of my knee
while I steered my way through the corrals
of school playtime, avoiding the gunslinger
glare of bullies, who'd queue
to lasso with threats.

Pencil point stabbed between my shoulders,
beef-jerky breath in my face
and a low growl in my ear ...
          ... as soon as the bell rings, you're dead.

I was faster than any of them.
Knees and fists pumping the air,
I was the best rider
the Pony Express never had.
A half-breed scout, I wore
a Colt pistol under my belt
and an eagle's tail feather in my hair.
A combination that won
neither friend or foe
from reservation or ranch.

A fall ... and the bony plate of my knee
became a wound with hard baked gravel
ground under the torn and grieving skin.

I grew my thumbnail especially
for that moment when the scab was ripe,
when the blood had hardened
to a brown as deep as the colour of Apache skin.

I would tease off the scab ...
... until baby pink skin winked in the sunlight,
fresh for the next gallop across the prairie
and the race into the unreachable horizon.

Greg Michaelson

BEFORE THE FLOOD

1.

Late afternoon, high on the north-west flank of Ben Nevis, the cloud rolled in from across Loch Linnhe. Visibility quickly dropped away.

'I can't see the others,' said Bill, anxiously. 'Maybe we should call them.'

'They're still ahead,' said Jes, switching her sunglasses to heat vision. 'Let's keep going.'

Soon they could barely make out the path, but the sound of the burn, and the reassuring beep from Henry's wrist-tracker, told them they were still on course. Twenty minutes later they emerged from the cloud. In front of them, the peak pierced a sea of rippling whiteness.

They crossed the burn and followed the track round the hairpin, gently climbing widdershins, then zigzagging more steeply up to the summit.

In the twilight, Jo and Chris came down to meet them.

'You took your time!' said Jo, helping Bill off with his backpack.

'We took it steady!' said Jes. 'Let's set things up before it gets too dark.'

'There's a while yet,' said Henry. 'And we've got to get it right. We'll not do this again.'

'They are going ahead, aren't they?' said Bill.

'Don't worry!' said Chris. 'They've spent all the money and the whole world's watching so they can't afford not to.'

'And they really haven't tested it?' said Bill.

'They're not telling anyone if they have,' said Chris. 'They must be so confident it'll work first time.'

'What happens if it doesn't?' asked Bill.

'They'll wind up with eight very expensive orbiting dustbins,' said Jo.

'Don't be so sceptical!' said Henry. 'This is a historic day. A turning point. Limitless free energy.'

'Yeah, yeah,' said Jo. 'They said that about nuclear power. And five hundred billion dollars is hardly free.'

'Come on!' said Jes, plugging together the sensor array. 'It's not long now 'til sunset.'

Henry stabilised the tripod and helped Jes mount the glistening dish of hexagonal detectors onto the pan-and-tilt head. Meanwhile, Chris, Bill and Jo cleared a patch of ground behind the ruins of the observatory, unfolded the dome and inflated its panels. Then they anchored the dome's nylon guy ropes to the rusting iron stanchions that once tethered a radio mast.

'That's it!' said Jes to Henry. 'You check the picture and I'll go inside and call Glasgow. There's too much noise out here.'

She disappeared into the dome.

'That was unnaturally easy,' said Bill, standing back and inspecting the squat, green hemisphere. 'I'll turn on the systems. It's going to be a cold night.'

He set off round to the back of the dome.

'I'm whacked!' said Chris, sitting down heavily next to the telescope,

'Are you alright?' said Jo, anxiously.

'Don't fuss!' said Chris, taking the pen-sized monitor from his inside pocket and swiping it across his left cheek. 'It says my blood sugar's fine.'

'So why's the red light blinking?' asked Jo.

'The battery's low,' said Chris. 'I'll recharge it when we get home.'

Jes stuck her head out of the dome's red door flap.

'How's it looking?' she called to Henry.

'Looking good!' said Henry. 'It's locked onto EuroSat-1's reference signal and bringing up the image. Everything's still a bit fuzzy but the focus should be fine by the time we're on.'

'Great!' said Jes, 'I'll tell them.' And disappeared back into the dome.

As the great sea of cloud beneath them lit orange, red and purple in the setting sun, the dome began to glow.

'Firing on all cylinders!' said Bill. 'Should be nice and warm by the time we're finished.'

'Glasgow says they can see our pictures,' said Jes, rejoining the others. 'We're live in ten minutes.'

'Let's get on with it then!' said Jo.

Jo stood beside the telescope. Chris and Bill stood opposite her adjusting their holo-cams. Jes was to one side, shielding her RedFang headset from the mounting wind. Henry squatted beside the 3D display.

'The picture's great!' he said. 'Have a look.'

Above the display hovered a golden ball, rimmed with twinkling red lights.

'Get away!' said Chris. 'That's one you prepared earlier!'

'I wish!' said Henry. 'No, that's EuroSat-1 all right!'

'Come on people!' said Jes, 'They're almost ready for us.'

'Yes, yes,' said Jo impatiently. 'We've rehearsed this over and over again.'

'Quiet!' said Jes. 'I'll count us in. Five, four, three, two and one. We're live!'

Jo straightened up and looked directly at Chris's holo-cam.

'This is Jo McFadden for SBC 7,' she said. 'The weather's grand and we're all set to bring you the great switch-on live from the top of Ben Nevis.'

Jes gesticulated at Bill. Bill panned his camera across the horizon and into the blackening sky.

'Our very own EuroSat-1's right over head,' said Jo, 'but we can't see it with the naked eye: it's much too small and too far away. But we've got the next best thing.'

Jes waved at Henry.

'It's a clear night,' said Jo, 'and our ultrawave telescope's giving us a crystal clear view.'

Henry gave Jes and Jo the thumbs up.

Jes, intent on her ear-piece, gestured at the sky.

'And we've just heard that they're ready to switch on the system,' said Jo, excitedly. 'AsiaSat-1's in the sunlight over the Urals, so first we'll see its energy reaching EuroSat-1.'

Suddenly, a jet of vibrant light leapt from nowhere to join the east side of the ball hovering over the display.

'Then we'll see EuroSat-1 linking up with AmSat-1 over the Rockies, and AfSat-1 over the Drakensbergs.'

Pencils of light left the ball from the west and north.

'Finally, EuroSat-1 should start beaming energy back to the Great Cumbrae ground station.'

A third shaft of light sprang from the base of the ball down into the display.

'That's just so amazing!' said Jo. 'I'm almost speechless!'

Jes made vomiting motions.

'So many people said it was impossible. So many said it was tampering with the very fabric of nature. But after nearly ten years of extraordinary challenges, we've finally harnessed the sun's energy itself!'

Jes made a chopping motion with her right hand.

'Thank you all so much for joining us,' said Jo. 'This is Jo McFadden for SBC 7. Now back to the studio.'

'That was grand!' said Jes. 'Well done everyone!'

'And here's one I did prepare earlier!' said Henry, extracting a bottle of champagne from his backpack.

'They're so right about great minds!' said Bill, producing another.

'One track minds, more like,' said Jo. 'I'll find the mugs.'

'Better pack the 'scope up,' said Jes, moving towards the tripod.

'No,' said Henry. 'Leave it. Let's celebrate!'

They huddled round the 3D display, the golden ball still hovering in the centre, transfixed by the eldritch lights. Henry opened his bottle, filled the mugs and handed them out.

'None for me, thanks,' said Chris.

'Spoil yourself!' said Henry.

'Go ahead,' said Chris, 'but I'm not sure how much life's left in my monitor so I need to pace things.'

'Well,' said Jes, raising her mug. 'Here's to us! Slàinte!'

'Slàinte!' they all chorused.

Suddenly the display began to flicker. Henry squatted down and fiddled with the touch screen.

'Bloody hell!' said Henry, clearly rattled. 'It's certainly not our equipment playing up.'

The team stopped drinking and stared intently at the projection. As the links from EuroSat-1 to AmSat-1 and AfSat-1 faded away, the energy beam down to Great Cumbrae grew brighter and brighter.

'But it shouldn't do that!' said Henry, alarmed. 'It should have shut itself down!'

'So is that bad ...?' asked Bill, laconically.

'Bad?' echoed Henry. 'It's catastrophic! Instead of sending most of the power from Asia on to the other satellites, EuroSat's channelling it all straight down to our receiver station ...'

With a cataclysmic roar, the world lurched sideways.

2.

Jes picked herself up and felt herself all over.

'Bloody hell, that's sore,' she mused, gingerly fingering the bruises down her left side. 'And it's really cold. Wonder how long I was out for?'

She checked her watch. It had stopped.

'Anyone there?' she shouted. 'Bill? Chris? Henry? Jo?'

'Jes?' cried Bill. 'I'm over here by the cairn. My leg's all smashed up.'

'Hang on,' said Jes, stumbling over Chris.

She quickly bent and checked his pulse.

'Chris?' called Jo. 'Are you alright?'

'He's with me,' replied Jes. 'He's still alive but out for the count.'

Jo staggered across and knelt beside Chris.

'I think he's gone into shock,' said Jo, her voice shaking. 'We need to warm him up and give him some insulin.'

The two women slowly dragged the unconscious Chris into the dome.

'Stay with him,' said Jes. 'I'll check Bill and look for Henry.'

'No need,' said Henry shakily, joining them. 'And I'm more or less okay before you ask.'

'Any idea what happened?' said Jes.

'Felt like an earthquake,' said Henry.

'We've really got to get help for Chris,' said Jo. 'His monitor's conked out. And I've no idea how much to give him without a reading for the jab-pack.'

'Contact Glasgow,' said Jes to Henry. 'Tell them to send the helicopter to get us all out of here.'

Jes left the dome and made her way across the summit to Bill, silhouetted against the moon-lit cairn.

'How are you doing?' she asked him.

'It hurts like buggery,' said Bill, 'and I feel like I'm burning up.'

'Do you think you could stand if I helped you?' asked Jes.

'Of course I can't bloody stand!' said Bill caustically. 'But that doesn't matter.'

'Why doesn't it matter?' asked Jes, watching him quizically.

'Look!' said Bill, pointing up at the sky. 'Look at the Great Bear!'

'What's wrong,' asked Jes.

'The Pole Star should be overhead!' said Bill wildly, 'but if you follow the pointers it's almost halfway to the horizon!'

'What are you saying?' said Jes.

'It's the Earth!' shouted Bill. 'It's been knocked off its axis!'

'Come on,' said Jes, far too calm. 'It was just an earthquake. Did you bang your head? Maybe you still can't see straight.'

'You stupid bloody woman!' screamed Bill. 'My head's fine! Just look at the bloody stars!'

Henry joined them.

'Bill's totally lost it,' said Jes, moving away from the cairn. 'How soon are they sending the chopper?'

'I can't get through,' said Henry, following her. 'There's no service, not even for emergencies.'

'Is your mobile broken?' said Jes.

'I don't think so,' said Henry. 'Anyway, I can't get through with Jo's either.'

'What about the ultrawave link back to the studio?' said Jes.

'That's down as well,' said Henry.

'Could our unit be broken?' asked Jes, without conviction.

'It's fine,' said Henry. 'I ran the diagnostics. There's just nothing at the other end for it to connect to.'

'Bloody hell!' said Jes. 'There's no way we can move Chris. Or Bill, by the look of him. Do you think one of us could get back to the van?'

Henry fiddled with his wrist tracker.

'This is deeply weird,' he said. 'It's seems to be working normally but the moving map says we're somewhere beyond Dover. That's over a thousand kilometres away.'

'Can you re-calibrate it?' asked Jes.

'Fraid not,' said Henry. 'It's automatic. Supposed to use GPS. But it's showing almost no signal strength.'

Jes stood silently, nervously picking at her cuticles with her finger nails. Henry watched her expectantly.

'I think it's too risky trying to make it down unguided,' she said finally. 'The wind's growing stronger and it's getting even colder.'

'Blows like rain,' said Henry. 'We better get Bill into the dome.'

They rejoined Bill.

'Did you tell him?' asked Bill, feverishly,

'Tell me what?' said Henry.

'You didn't, did you!' said Bill.

'What didn't you tell me?' asked Henry,

'Not now,' said Jes.

'Not so bloody fast!' screamed Bill, as Henry and Jes gently helped him up. 'Jesus wept! I can't stand it!'

'Take it steady,' said Henry. 'It's not too far now.'

Inside the dome, Jo was crouched next to Chris.

'How's Chris?' asked Jes, easing Bill down besides them.

'I tried to give him a shot,' said Jo, 'but he still won't respond to anything and his breathing's getting shallower. I'm really frightened I gave him too much.'

'Keep trying,' said Henry. 'But we need to help Bill right now.'

Bill's left trouser leg was dripping with blood. Henry cut up the seams with his Scots Navy knife and gingerly inspected the damage. The femur was snapped clean through: one ragged end protruding through the livid wound.

'How does it look?' moaned Bill, the knuckles of his clenched fists white in the soft glow of the dome's LEDs.

'Not so good, I'm afraid,' said Henry. 'We need to get you to a hospital. There's nothing we can do here.'

'We're not going anywhere before it gets light,' said Jes. 'Let's try and make ourselves comfortable.'

As they lay huddled together, the rain fell more and more heavily, and the wind pounded the dome, each buffet straining the moorings.

'I don't really like this,' Jes whispered to Henry

'There's a big storm coming,' said Henry quietly. 'The dome's not meant for this sort of weather. I hope it holds.'

At dawn, Jo was stirred from her fitful sleep by crazed scrabblings and screechings. Sitting up, she saw the shadows of myriad beasts darting across the dome's translucent walls.

'Jes! Henry! Wake up!' shouted Jo.

'What's happening?' called Jes, getting up quickly.

'I don't know! I don't know!' cried Jo. 'I'm so scared!'

Stepping awkwardly over her colleagues, Jes opened the window flap and peered out. In the half-light, terrified animals fled through the driving rain: deer, foxes, rabbits, wild-cats and sheep, amidst a seething carpet of mice and voles.

'You can't be as scared as they are,' said Henry, joining Jes at the window. 'It's as if they know something dreadful's about to happen.'

'How's Chris?' asked Jes.

'He's really cold,' said Jo. 'Could you have a look at him? I can't bear to.'

Suddenly, the rain stopped and everything went quiet.

'The storm's about to hit,' said Jes, thinking quickly. 'We need to keep really close together.'

But as they tried to manoeuvre Bill and Chris across the jumbled floor, a huge gust caught the front of the dome, ripping the guy ropes from the panels. The dome flipped on its back, tumbling its occupants on top of each other. With the next gust the dome broke up, the panels whipping away into the whirling vortex. Frantically, Jes disentangled herself, grabbed hold of Henry and Jo, and pulled them away from the stricken encampment. Sheltering behind the crumbling observatory wall, they hunkered down and clung to each other.

3.

The storm had passed and the sun had risen. Chris was dead: Jo sat beside his zipped-up sleeping bag, silently rocking backwards and forwards. Bill, his wound suppurating, was now running a high fever. Henry wandered the debris, fiddling fruitlessly with a mobile phone.

Jes paced up and down, arguing furiously with herself.

'Why aren't they looking for us? Maybe they don't expect us back yet. But we'd have stayed in touch. They must know something's up. One of us needs to go for help. Someone's got to stay with Bill. Henry and Jo could stay. But Henry knows the way down and I don't. Jo's badly in shock. We can't leave her on her own with Bill. Jo and I could stay. Or she could go with Henry and I could stay. But there's nothing any of us can do for Bill. We could all leave him but he'll probably be dead by the time we got back for him. He'll probably die anyway. Why aren't they looking for us? Maybe they can't? Why can't they? Jesus fucking Christ! What a total nightmare! I can't bear it here any longer ...'

'Henry, Jo,' said Jes, sounding as decisive as she could, 'I'm going for help. Come or stay. I don't mind. But I'm going.'

'Don't you think we should wait?' said Henry. 'They'll be looking for us.'

'I think they'd be here by now if they were coming,' said Jes, firmly.

'Maybe they don't realise we're stranded,' said Henry. 'Anyway, I think we should stick together.'

'I'm going for help,' repeated Jes. 'Bill's in a really bad way. We've no medical supplies. We've practically nothing to eat or drink. One of us has got to go.'

'Why don't we all go?' said Henry. 'Jo?'

'No!' said Jo, emphatically. 'I'm staying with Chris! He's sure to wake up soon. Please don't leave us!'

Jes looked hopelessly at Henry.

'All right,' said Henry. 'I'll stay as well. Maybe I can bodge the link's fuel cells to boost one of the mobiles.'

'Fine!' said Jes. 'You both stay. Which way do I go?'

'The path starts at the back of the ruins,' said Henry. 'It's quite steep going for the first stretch. When you reach the Y junction, turn left and follow the burn. You can't go far wrong.'

'Thanks!' said Jes, without conviction. 'I'll be back as soon as I can.'

'Happy trails!' said Henry abstractedly, returning to his mobile.

Jes set off down the mountain track. Below her, the vast layer of cloud still stretched away to the horizon. On the heather clad flanks of the summit, a throng of sheep and deer stood watching her accusingly.

'Stupid bloody animals,' muttered Jes to herself. 'Why don't they go further down?'

Eyes to the ground, she carefully picked her way along the boulder strewn path. But as she neared the fork, she stumbled, landing heavily on her bruised side. Tired and tearful, she lay back in the heather.

'Come on girl!' she said to herself. 'Keep it together! No one else is going to. You'll soon be safe ...'

The sound of waves breaking on rocks shattered her reverie. Jes got up and looked around. The clouds beneath were dispersing. Terrified, Jes stood and stared at the white flecked foam of the unknown sea.

Jason Monios

EZRA POUND AT PISA

In 1945, the sixty-year-old Ezra Pound was arrested in Italy and taken to an American military prison camp at Pisa where he spent six months awaiting transportation to the USA to be charged with treason. For the first twenty-five days he was kept in an open air cage, with a spotlight trained on him at night.

Thoughts of when he was young,
a mind grown old in imitation,
romance, song: the mind of a troubadour.
Now older, still a sprightly sixty,
a danger to his country, a danger to freedom,
a danger to himself, they say.

Caged, the sun hostile
like the territory, not the only edifice
in Pisa, nor the least solidly constructed.

Reinforced with airstrip steel.
Guarded, watched, displayed
to the camp. A traitor, a critic, a poet.

Old-fashioned torture, the daytime sun,
spotlights strove through the night, tin can
for company. Mind cracks in the arid glare,
lets in the spirits of the Italian plain,
lets out the voices of the past.
No white noise, no air con, no tactical deprivation.
No Gitmo torture, no Abu Ghraib.
Just an old man, steel, sun,
a platoon of broken men.

Richard Mosses

NELSON'S BLOOD

'You got a copy of *Die Last*?' The guy in the white shell suit looks at Stu warily. Like he doesn't trust him, like Stu's going to sell him dodgy goods. What does he expect? All Stu's goods are dodgy by definition.

'Sorry, mate.' Stu shrugs and eyes him warily back. Like he doesn't trust him, like he's speaking a little too well for a guy wearing a shell suit in the Barras on a Saturday afternoon. The windswept pavement is littered with chip wrappers, large-breasted women spilling from the dispersed pages of a *Sunday Sport*, crisp packets and a crowd hungry for a cheap bargain. Whether it's an antique hidden under grime and salvaged from an auld yin's home after she popped her clogs, or a cracked copy of Windows, you can find it here. Not so much a flea market as a slice of street-level survival.

Stu looks up the street, catching the eye of another vendor, a regular, with a proper stall, not happy with a lad and a suitcase setting up camp next door, but they're all in this together. The stallholder shrugs. Stu looks shell suit over once more. 'I might have it next week. If you're keen?'

'I just thought you might have got a copy already, from the States, you know?' The guy in the shell suit twitches his head slightly, as if wanting to see who Stu had been looking at. He seems ill at ease – many of the punters are though. They smell the illegality of it all – deep down they get off on it.

'We dunna do that.' Stu's sure this guy's a ringer, he feels it in his bones.

'You know, download 'em, like MP3s.'

'If you wanna give that a go, I'm no stopping ye.' Stu is almost certain now. Slowly he changes position. It'll be a shame to lose his stock, hazard of the job, but he can get more. His sister Suzy's suitcase on the other hand ... 'Listen, I've got *Escape From Hell*. If you're interested?'

'I dunno. I don't mind all that God stuff, but my partner's a Catholic ... Hey where are you going?' Shell suit's last minute slip seals Stu's certainty as he's already sliding away.

Stu sees dark suits appearing out of the crowd to left and to the right, like Agents of the System in that film. How right they were. But Stu has his secret weapon. Kali Panthers are the best running shoes a thief could have. In-built state-of-the-art predictive shock absorption in the soles, combined with terrain dampeners and near perfect traction even on wet or slippy surfaces like metal or marble. Stu isn't a thief, but the Panthers come in handy all the same. And in Stealth Black they look fuckin' cool too.

Stu skips through the crowd like a knife through butter, pleased by the sounds of anger, outrage and commotion erupting in his wake. He dodges past a couple of dark suits covering this exit. He hears pounding on the pavement behind him and thinks he feels the rip of air as an arm reaches out to grab him. Stu dances past a Barrowlands ironwork sign, sprints effortlessly over the road, skipping round the cars just in time, and spins off into Calton. Zig-zagging through the maze of white roughcast houses, stained with black and green patches of damp beneath sills, he escapes the long arm of the law and nips into the back garden of the grey-walled three-story tenement where his Nan lives.

Stu warms the pot, throws in three bags and tops up with boiling water. While the tea is standing he takes the milk carton out of the fridge and takes the tray through to the front room. 'I got the best milk jug out for you.' Stu puts the tray down onto the coffee table, smiling from the old familiar joke. 'I also got something for the housekeeping.' He slips forty quid into the jar on the mantelpiece. Constructed from tiles and bearing a gas fire on full, he braves scorching his legs and knocking over one of the porcelain ladies dressed like shepherdesses.

'You don't need to, son. I can manage.' Stu's Nan is proud of her grandson – he's already got a job as well as his college course.

'I know, Nan. But Grandda's navy pension will only stretch so far and I like to make sure you've enough for your teacakes.' Stu smiles. 'Shit, that reminds me ... Sorry, Nan!' Stu dashes back into the kitchen before his Nan can tell him not to bother. He takes out several foil-covered domes and lays them on a plate. Stu feels guilty letting his Nan think he's got a proper job, that's why he spoils her. It's not like he's doing anyone any harm – he's just using his natural talents, like his Grandda taught him to.

'Listen, son.' Stu's Nan graciously accepts one of the teacakes offered to her – she insists to herself she'll only have the one. 'I found something amongst your grandfather's things.' Stu's Nan rummages around on the floor beside his Grandda's chair. She thrusts a fat bottle at him. The black liquid inside sloshes about thickly.

'What is it?' Stu pauses pouring the tea to take the bottle. The glass is brown and thick. The bottle is about the size of a quarter of voddy, shaped with a stubby neck and a wide rounded contour to the body – like a hip flask. It is stopped by a short fat cork and sealed with black wax. He turns the bottle over to look at the label. A shield of browned paper bears a faded coat of arms, of which Stu can only make out a lion on the right, a man with a funny hat on the left and a crown on top of a shield. Beneath this is printed *NELSON'S BLOOD* in thick curly capitals and below that is a date, *1805*. 'What is it?' Stu repeats. Having once been his Grandda's, it's almost like a holy relic to Stu.

'Alcohol.' Stu's Nan finishes pouring the tea. 'I'd never touch the stuff myself, but I was sure you'd find some use for it.'

The theatre is full to the seams. This is both a good thing and a bad; anonymity, in contrast with too many pairs of eyes that might see something, even in the dark. Stu, Jim and Davy wait for their moment, sat in the back row. It is almost too easy. But it is hard enough to make it worth the effort.

The adverts for perfumes and phones fade away and like a mouth-watering menu the trailers begin. Stu makes a mental list of future projects. Halfway through he gets up and apologises under muttered breath as he pushes past half of the back row as he makes his way out to the main concourse. He nips into the toilets and has a quick slash while reading a script excerpt from *Dr No* the cinema chain have hung above each urinal. He feels like Bond, the gadgets, the spying, the danger. Classy girls with nice skin, silk dresses and loose knicker elastic are in short supply in the East End though, more's the pity.

Stu prepares the most important device he carries and walks out confident, if a little nervous as the kick of adrenaline raises his heart rate. He takes a deep breath of hot butter and hotdog and strides up to the discreet door beside Screen Six. A short stab and the key goes in, a quick flick and the lock turns. He opens the door and walks up the short flight of stairs. An ex-girlfriend had once worked here and unknown to her, like the films he distributed, Stu had acquired a copy of the key she had been entrusted with.

The room smells of dust and hot plastic. The projectionist has left and there's about an hour before they come back to check the disk has changed over. He brazenly puts his hand in front of the shining lens, a huge thumbs up is briefly seen on screen to the consternation of the crowd. The second last trailer is showing. Davy and Jim can't miss the bat-signal. The back row are displaced and displeased once more.

Two knocks and Stu opens the door. Jim is already whipping out the tripod from under his long leather coat like it's a backup shotgun in a bank robbery. Davy takes a ridiculously small box that is mostly screen and partly phone out of his pocket. Perched on the tripod the camera tapes the first reel of *Die Last* – not that there are any real reels used anymore in the multiplex – from the best seat in the house. Stu checks his stopwatch.

Sure they could swipe the disks and make off with them, but they're a small outfit and the encoding is still beyond their ability to break – as soon as someone does the film companies bring in their latest algorithms anyway. So it's old fashioned filming from the back of the theatre for them – but this way no bugger gets up and crosses the camera. The tricky bit is changeover.

Davy goes back down to his seat, ready for the few minutes of buttonhole camera work. In many ways the perfect picture, with a moment or two of movie from a different angle, is a signature of theirs. They'll have to figure out something better. Perhaps Davy can fashion a machine that they can leave hidden in the booth in future?

A few moments before change over, Stu and Jim leave the booth with the camera and the tripod. They wait while a stringy lanky looking youth goes into the box to make sure the disks change over without a hitch. Then they jump back in as soon as he's gone.

Mission accomplished, the lads congregate on a bench in the shopping mall outside.

'I got us something to celebrate with.' Stu takes out the bottle of Nelson's Blood and waves it around. He strips off the wax with his thumbnail and teases out the cork, which comes free with a satisfying ›pop‹. The others look on wondering what he's got. Tentatively, Stu sniffs the bottle. A confused range of rich scents mingle together; jam, black, burnt sugar and a metallic note.

'What is it?' Jim reaches out for the bottle.

'Alcohol.' Stu grins, but moves out of Jim's reach. 'My Nan gave it to me. Said it was once my Grandda's.'

'Go on then, give it a swallow.' Davy urges Stu, clenching both fists and raising them slightly.

Stu tips it back and feels the thick liquor slide slowly into his mouth. It tastes of berries and burnt toffee, a bit like red wine and a bit like rum, but there is an odd coppery aftertaste. Then Stu thinks he can smell the sea, like a day out to Largs he had with his Grandda when he was a kid. He thinks he can hear the snap of canvas as the wind catches a sail and somewhere there is shouting and metal clashing and a deep booming and wood splintering. He starts and realises he had closed his eyes, when he opens them to see the lads looking at him. The buzz fades slowly like the smoke from a strong spliff.

'So, what's it like?' Jim reaches for the bottle again.

'Bloody weird, but nice.' Stu passes him the bottle and waits to see what happens when Jim drinks. He thinks he can see the same moment as, briefly, after swallowing, Jim pauses and blinks too long. A satisfying sulphury burn rises up Stu's gullet.

'Hey! Pass it on.' Davy snatches the bottle from Jim's hand.

'Careful, Davy. You're driving,' warns Stu.

'I'll only have a wee swallow.' Davy tips it back and soon the three of them can see it in each other's eyes — the shared experience, a memory none of them could have.

'Hey, youze! What you doin' here?' The shout of indignation and challenge comes from a group of youths coming up the escalator from the shops below the cinema. Stu quickly recognises them as the leaders of the East Kilbride Young Team. They have every right to be annoyed.

This is their turf. Stu grabs the bottle from Davy, stoppers it and stashes it. The lads leap to their feet and run for the nearby doors to the roof of the car park.

The doors swing shut into the faces of the EKYT in hot pursuit. Stu glances back and sees them barrelling out of the entrance, Davy and Jim hot on his heels. Ahead of him is a shopping trolley some guy is loading his messages from into his car. On impulse Stu jumps on the back, waits a moment for Davy and Jim to climb on the sides, and begins to push off. The guy notices them and shouts, no doubt wanting his quid back. Stu takes one from his pocket and flicks it at him with his thumb like it's a gold doubloon. He laughs a hearty laugh and the trolley gains momentum.

Behind them the EKYT seem to have gotten the same idea and commandeered their own vessel. The two trolleys glide across the open car park. Two inside the basket and one pushing. The moon comes out from behind a cloud – the moonlight turns the wet tarmac to silvered sea.

'Cap'n, we've got cannons.' Deadeye Jim gestures at the box in the belly of the trolley. Six magnums of Moët Et Chandon.

'Open all ports and prepare for battle.' Cap'n Stu adds another push and jumps onto the back of the boat.

'Cap'n, we've a dip ahead.' Black Davy turns and Cap'n Stu sees the short ramp down to the next level nearing.

'All lean starboard,' Cap'n Stu commands. The trolley turns to the right and they head back towards the EKYT.

'Cannons ready, Cap'n!' Deadeye Jim finishes stripping the foil and shaking the last bottle. He has placed three magnums on each side, the necks sticking through the wire bars.

'Prepare to fire.' Cap'n Stu pauses, waiting while the EKYT come into range. 'Fire!'

Deadeye Jim bangs the base of each bottle. A spume of foam erupts from each of them sending a gas-propelled cork soaring into each of the EKYT members in the other ship. The lads all hear the heavy impact on wood, the yells from sailors struck by debris and the snapping of loose sails. A roar of protest erupts from the enemy trolley, soaked and bruised, they in turn come about.

The trolley has lost some of its momentum and Stu jumps down and pushes again. The guy whose trolley they stole is heading towards them yelling incoherently. 'Lean to port,' commands Cap'n Stu. The trolley turns to the left and skims a puddle leaving the man soaking in their wake.

The EKYT are nearing once again. 'Prepare to repel boarders! Get ready to fire!' 'Aye, Aye,' comes the reply. Once more Deadeye Jim strikes the champagne and the corks pound the opposition. The short blonde guy looking to leap is caught in the face, but with a snarl he looks set to jump anyway, then Black Davy swings a fist at him. He reels back and the EKYT are overbalanced, their trolley tips over.

The lads hear the terrible tearing of sail and stern, the guns go eerily silent and the enemy ship capsizes, taking down all hands. The lads cheer their victory and slide down two ramps gaining momentum as the Pirates of the Odeon speed across the high sea.

'You got a copy of *Die Last*?' The guy in the blue denims looks at Stu warily. Like he doesn't trust him, like Stu's going to sell him dodgy goods.

'Fresh from the screen.' Cap'n Stu grins his most charming grin. 'I've a few other things you might like, too.'

What does he expect? All Stu's goods are dodgy by definition.

Anne B. Murray

WAVES

When and why do we wave?

In a room full of strangers, when we see someone we know.
Or in greeting, or goodbye.

But sometimes the waves seem purposeless.
I wave back to children waving at a passing train.
Neither will I see them nor they see me again.
Or, standing on an island pier,
My wave returns those from the departing ferry
even though I know no one on the boat.
Perhaps that's it.
It's not I nor they who wave.
It is my wave that waves to theirs.
It is just, somehow, the right thing to do.

This thought gives me comfort;
for it gives me to believe that one day
when my mind has gone, and done with giving instructions,
my hand will continue to do the right thing, unbid.

Like my mother now.
Gestures, even words, are often the right ones
even though she neither recognises nor remembers either
     them nor me.
'Safe home,' she mouths as I leave;
then waves, waves from her small windowed world
for I don't know how long after I've gone.
I drive off, eyes on the road ahead, one hand on the wheel,
the other held out the open window, waving, waving,
my wave meeting her wave
in an understanding of their own.

Alison Napier

INVISIBLE MENDING

'Two fish suppers, a bag of onion rings, a single white pudding and a portion of curry sauce. Just salt, no vinegar. Thanks.'

I memorised the order and calculated the cost. Eleven eighty.

I am called Sue and Cathy calls me chip suey.

I waved a chilly haddock through batter and dropped it into the boiling ocean of oil, lobbed nine onion rings from the freezer to the fryer and thought about the hoopla at the shows, took a hundred mil tub of sauce out of the fridge and slammed it into the microwave and set it at thirty seconds, slid back the glass doors and tonged out a yellowing five-inch length of deep-fried oatmeal, lard and seasoning, and started scooping chips from one section of the stained stainless steel unit to the other. The fish floated to the surface, the onion rings bobbed like life-belts nearby.

I netted them, landed them, and then in various combinations served the glistening food onto polystyrene containers and wrapped them in two layers of paper. I put the packages, already seeping, in a thin plastic bag. The microwave went ping and I opened it, pressed a plastic lid on the tub and placed it on the counter. Eleven eighty, I said. He gave me twelve. I gave him two ten pence pieces. He put one of them in the plastic collection box shaped like a gaping trout, in aid of deep sea fishermen, that sat on the counter with a chain round its neck for security.

I did a greasy version of this nineteen more times. This was the best job I had ever had by a long chalk. What's a long chalk, I wondered and decided to look it up on Google when I got home.

The Happy Haddock had a café attached, through a swing door like in a saloon bar. The walls were covered in tiles with dolphins and seashells on them. I knew I would be serving there after my break, working with Cathy who couldn't cope with the lunchtime rush. Poor Cathy. Just out of hospital. Poor Cathy. Fixed smile and dead eyes, slow careful speech in case anyone finds out. But everybody found out anyway. Salt and vinegar on that? Oh sorry I'll do another one. Silly me! Just salt was it?

I changed out of my white coat, wondering why I dressed
as a doctor to serve up fried food, and tied a large striped
red and white apron round my waist. Tinker tailor doctor
butcher. A plethora of failed careers. I had had many failed
careers but this was not going to be one of them. Let's hear
it for chips. Are the chips down? No sirree they are not.
Chip fryers against the bomb, against the world, against the
bloody wall if you like.

Now now. See her go.

That's me, Sue with her clipped raven-black hair and
her eagle eyes. Waiting with the patience of a penitent.
Darting and diving between tables, dodging customers as
they hover and flap by the till, tall orders scratched on a
notepad, flitting backwards and forwards, backwards and
forwards. Sue is a very good waitress.

Sue can see the writing arced like a rainbow on the
window, kcoddah yppah eht, and she imagines she is a
customer in a busy seafront taverna on a Greek island,
gazing out onto ocean and heat, breathing the joyful clean
scent of Mediterranean blossoms. A waiter brings a carafe of
wine and one glass to her table. She pours, sips, sips again.
She stares at the sea, at the olive-brown men and women
who live here in the impossibly white scatters of houses.
People chatter and she relaxes in the unintelligible
exchanges. Nothing is required. She has never been to
Greece but that is what it is like in the postcards. All
shimmering white and blue and bloody flowers. No sign of
the Jobcentre though, is there, no sign of the dole queue, or
the clap clinic, or the old folk's home. Just out of the picture
were they?

This morning I got one letter. Dear Ms Summers. That's
what they call me. Ms Summers' madness more like. The
letter was quite friendly up to that point. Dear Ms Summers.
Okay. Ha ha. Think I'm going to ruin my breakfast with
that, the only peace of the day, no sirree, toast just popped
and kettle boiled, teabag sinking murkily in the mug, the one
that says Free Tibet, bleeding out tannin and caffeine,
dripping off the teaspoon no matter how fast I rush it to the
sink, brown stains to wipe later, butter melting in high
cholesterol lakes, no way do you interrupt this.

This morning I got one letter and it was from Kay. Dear
Ms Summers. This is what she calls her little sister. We are

not close as can be gleaned from the salutation. Kay and
Sue Summers. What a pair. Two abandoned espadrilles.

Dear Ms Summers. Please find enclosed quarterly cheque
as arranged. No acknowledgement is required. Sincerely, K
Summers. I tore both bits of paper neatly into four and
dropped them in the bin where they landed on top of the tea
bag. That would be the envelope and the letter. Not the
cheque. It got propped up against the still-warm toaster.
Nice. Enough for a week on Crete or an electric bill or a
new exhaust. Enough.

Kay is seven years and four months older than I. She is
very attractive and has blonde hair. She is very attractive and
has blue eyes and is slim. People say she should be a model.
She wears short black skirts and jackets and white shirts
and looks like a lawyer. She is a lawyer. Black and white. She
is the executor of our mother's will.

I sat in the kitchen for ages after that. My tea went cold
so I gave it thirty seconds in the microwave, ping, and my
toast went cold but I ate it anyway. I'm glad this kitchen is
big enough for a table and chair, its got a cracked bottle-
green sofa in it too, and a parallelogram bookcase and a
double bed and a bicycle. You'd have to call it a bed-sit
really. Toilet, shared, one floor down, bath, shared, in the
basement. A shared bath is nothing like in *The English
Patient*. It is spinal tap and icy drips and nowhere to put
your knees to keep them warm. I'll just wait my turn
thanks.

I can hear my mother tut-tutting in the corner. Did you
wash behind your ears? You'll never amount to anything if
you don't apply yourself. Look at you. I just don't know.
How could you do this to me. Full of yourself, aren't you.
Well if that's the worst that ever happens to you. And other
useful pieces of advice. Mother mother mother. Dead and
buried. Lucky sod. Sorry. My mother ship is a fish and chip
shop so off I sail, tucking the folded cheque into the back
pocket of my jeans.

'What's the soup, do you know?' asks Cathy.

'You can travel the world in a plate of soup, Cathy.
Spanish onions weeping from the Civil War, peeled and
finely chopped and dragged in orange net sacks across the
Pyrenees and up through France, collecting garlic from
Gascony and warding off lechery and evil spirits as you go.

Sauté, that's fry, Cathy, fry in a little olive oil, rich and dark
and Mediterranean, the way you like them, and you're away.
Lentils, because that's what soup it is seeing as you asked,
slipping in in the pockets of refugees on barges from the
mysterious East under cover of darkness. Only mysterious
because I've not been, you understand, apart from the all-
inclusive in Tunisia, and no I did not see any lentil
plantations in case you're wondering, but there was a lot of
fried stuff and chips in the hotel, just like here, only tougher.
Everything was tougher.

    'And in the markets they always try to get you to buy
things even after you say no, so I wore dark glasses and even
though I looked at them and the stuff they were selling I
knew nobody could see my eyes. And that's what I learned
on holiday even though I did buy you that olivewood camel.
But mostly lentils are from Egypt and Ethiopia, the starving
places. Deserts. Someone puts them in the plastic bags, and
onto a boat, through the Straits, the pillars of Hercules, up
the storm-lashed Bay, unloaded on the coast, driven to up
here and here they are, orange mushy and soupy. Jeez.
Wound-ready salt and peppercorn bullets all the way from
the South Seas. Stock cubes from Norrrrway of course. What
did I tell you? Fancy a coffee? Or tea? You sit, I'll get it.'

    'Mad, you are, mad. Just a quick coffee then seeing's it's
quiet.'

    Cathy has written her life story on her arm. Contours
and lifelines far apart and close together mapping a journey
she never planned, criss-crossing like nomads in the endless
deserts, her ancestral songlines, her invisible mending. Some
people look and look again and look away and wonder if she
is a junkie, heroin tracks skidding across her skin, up up
and away under the sleeve of her shirt. But I know that she
takes a brand new blade out of her disposable razor, six in
an economy pack, and holds it up to the light and moves it
slowly in the late evening sun-dazzle and watches the
rainbow pattern lurch across the wall. Backwards and
forwards. Don't ask me how I know, I just do. Sometimes
you can tell things about people. It's the eyes. Sometimes the
eyes are too full of themselves. This is not the worst thing
that has happened to her. Once it slipped and an arterial
route was taken in error, these things happen, and one
hospital led to another and the pills they gave her are barely

legal but there you are. And that's not the worst either, cause and effect, cause and effect.

I visited her in the second hospital, and she hid at first, then a nurse led me to her room and knocked and went straight in and there she was, sitting on the bed reading *TV Times*. Bloody hell Cath it's got an ensuite. Any vacancies? Then we talked. She is not the only one to have made her mark in this world. Sharp as a tack.

We manage to get our coffee, sitting outside the back door smoking on upside-down beer crates with newspaper cushions and take turns to jump up when the door bell rings, nee naw, electric donkey, and serve lunches in between times. A quiet day. Cathy did not need me after all.

Cathy sleeps with men if she sleeps with anyone but once she slept with me. We don't talk about this because she says she was drunk and didn't know what she was doing. Which wasn't how it seemed to me but if she doesn't want to remember it then who am I. Forced recollections are rarely the best. We were camping, in Argyll, and the midges got into her tent so she came into mine. Because of the midges. We smoked to keep them away and we drank because that's what we do. We tried to zip two sleeping bags together and couldn't and laughed and laughed and fell against the sides of the tent and each other and she was my whole world for hours and hours. And that's okay. That's when I saw her arm first and I kissed it all the way up from the wrist to the shoulder, following the nomads across the desert.

'You clear up, Cathy, I'll get the till.'

The desert sands are more treacherous than you would think, they creep and cover and make it all look nice like the beach on a postcard. And other times there you are playing in the sweeping swooping dunes and a gust of grit blows right into your face and pebble-dashes and sandblasts you from all sides and you spit and shake your head and it's not the dunes at all and you and Kay are not Lawrence of Arabia and his big sister with towels and sunglasses riding across the marram grass because everything's been blown away like Skara Brae, and people are shouting across the desert and waving their arms and running in that heavy thick way adults do in deep sand. And then ages after men in yellow jackets came, they must have been roasting, pulling a dinghy, and then ages after ages after that and then. Tragic mother of two missing at sea. The search was called off last night after a blue and white inflatable lilo was found washed up on rocks near the. Holiday makers raised the alarm when they heard the transistor radio still playing by her beach towel an hour after she had gone into the. It is understood that her children will be taken in to the care of the local authorities until such time as the.

Cathy knows this story is as full of rubbish as a deep-fried pizza supper but we all have our lies to tell so she lets me do my own embroidering and mending. Cause and effect. Sometimes Kay kills my mother and sells me to bandits, who then lose me in the medina after I dodge into a carpet shop and I am found by the Ambassador's wife who raises me as her own until they are posted to Malaria (are you sure that's a country Sue?) and I can't bear the mosquitoes so I run away and end up in a bedsit here. Sometimes I tunnel so deep into the sand that I reach the arterial route noisy with traffic and I step onto the open top deck of a shiny red city tour bus and am whisked away, wind in my hair and a commentary in three languages round all the sights in the capital until I end up in the terminal and the driver takes me home to his family in a two up two down in Bethnal Green. More usually it's the boring version, that would be the real version Sue would it be, says Cathy? Mother walks away from two children leaving stunned teenager in charge? Then dies from an infected insect bite on an island in the north Aegean sea? Oh Kay. It was only nineteen years ago.

Nee naw. 'Sorry we're just closing. Open again at six.'

Come home with me Cathy, come home to my kitchen sofa bedroom and we will stuff tee shirts into our rucksacks and head for the hills. Set up camp on the magic midgeless mountainside that looks out forever across the sparkling Aegean sea, dine with me in the seaside tavernas with the bloody begonias and heady hibiscus and I will weave jasmine stems into your hair and lick wine stains from your mouth, I will part your lips with morsels of cheese and olives and apricots and kiss your war wounds from coast to coast. I know, I know.

'See you later Sue. Phone me and we'll go for a drink. Maybe do something at the weekend?'

'Yeah, I'll phone you after I've had my tea.'

There is a message on my answering machine. 'Sue it's Kay. Your sister. Come over at the weekend, let's just la la la not listening. I know what day it is and so do you and it wasn't blah fault or blah blah. Okay? Just come.' Ping. I memorise the order and calculate the cost. Jeez. Not bloody likely, not by a long chalk.

I'll go and have a bath now, make some soup, maybe do some mending.

Helen Parker

HIDE AND SECRET
Extract from a teenage novel

Chris Miller and his girlfriend, Rachel McKay, a newcomer to Edinburgh, are harbouring an illegal immigrant. Yusef, known as Joe, arrived in Edinburgh hidden in a lorry, traumatised and badly injured. To further his chances of achieving refugee status, Chris and Rachel are trying to teach him English and to familiarise him with the city.

Early summer tourists were already out, admiring the sights. Chris led Rachel and Joe into Princes Street Gardens, where they bought cans of cola and stood for a while, watching a busker playing his bagpipes. Joe looked puzzled. 'Man,' he said, and touched the knee of his trousers.

'Trousers,' Chris supplied.

Joe looked around and pointed to a woman wearing a skirt. 'Woman!' Then he indicated the piper. 'No woman!'

Chris and Rachel laughed. 'It's a kilt!' Chris explained. 'Scottish men wear a kilt.' It had never seemed unusual to him.

'Kilt,' Joe repeated slowly. 'Scottish men wear kilt.'

They stood on the bridge and watched trains underneath them slowing down to enter Waverley Station, then they walked up the steep path towards the castle, pausing occasionally to turn and admire the view of the city. At the entrance to the castle, they stopped. 'Have you ever been in?' Rachel asked Chris.

'Yeah. Loads of times. We ought to take Joe.'

'But it's so expensive,' Rachel groaned, looking at the ticket prices.

'I know what! We should take him to the Tattoo! He'd see hundreds of bagpipers, and dancers, and all the traditional Scottish stuff! And the Festival Parade! You get a kind of preview of everything that's going to happen.'

'The Festival? It's not till August, though.'

They looked at each other, then at Joe. They read each other's thoughts. Who knows what might happen to Joe by August?

'We'd better get on with English lessons fast,' Chris concluded.

They left the castle, walked down the Royal Mile, and turned off along George IV Bridge, stopping to look down at the big empty space, where several old buildings had been burned to the ground. 'There's a boy in my class who's chosen this for his project,' Chris told Rachel. 'We have to do *something historical with a local flavour*. A fire started in a nightclub there, and because the buildings are so tightly packed, and so tall, it spread very quickly.'

'Like the Great Fire of London,' Rachel remembered. 'How did this one start?'

'No one seems to know whether it was deliberate, or an accident.' Chris turned to Joe. 'There was a big fire,' he explained. Joe looked blank. 'A fire,' Chris repeated, looking round. There was a billboard advertising an action film. He pointed to the picture of flames, then to the big hole where the buildings had been destroyed. 'A fire.'

Joe gazed at the hole, and the colour seemed to drain from his face.

'Come on,' said Rachel, linking arms with him. They walked on, and stopped beside the life-size statue of Greyfriars Bobby.

Chris patted the little bronze dog. 'Do you know the story?' he asked Rachel. She shook her head. 'The dog's called Bobby. His owner was a shepherd, who brought his sheep to market at Greyfriars somewhere around here. When he died, Bobby refused to leave his grave. He sat faithfully on the grave for fourteen years, and the landlady from a local pub gave him dinner every evening.'

'Fourteen years!' Rachel marvelled, and patted the statue. 'His name's Bobby,' she told Joe. 'He was very faithful.'

'Bobby,' Joe repeated. 'Faceful.'

'Faithful,' Rachel corrected, sticking her tongue out in an effort to emphasise the t-h.

'Faithful,' Joe repeated correctly.

They turned back towards the city centre. Joe stopped outside a butcher's shop. 'Maybe he's hungry,' Rachel suggested. 'Let's buy a burger when we get back to Princes Street. It must be lunchtime.'

But Joe was pointing at something. 'Haggis!' Chris told him. 'Delicious!' He licked his lips and patted his stomach.

Joe laughed and pulled a face. He turned to Rachel. 'I've never tried it,' she admitted.

'Never tried it?' Chris mocked with a grin. 'You can't be a true Scot and not eat haggis.'

'But it *looks* disgusting!'

'Looks aren't everything,' Chris joked. 'It's very tasty. But it reminds me that I'm starving. Come on, let's get some food.'

Returning through the gardens, they crossed Princes Street to the side where the shops were. The pavements were crowded with visitors and weekend shoppers. The warm June sun had brought everyone out in their colourful tee-shirts. The Japanese tourists were taking photographs, the Americans were exclaiming over the tartan souvenirs and local children were begging their parents for ice creams.

Chris glanced at his watch. One o'clock. No wonder he was starving. 'Come on, let's ...' He began over his shoulder to Rachel. The next moment, he found himself sprawled face down beside her in the entrance to a department store, with Joe on top of him, squeezing the breath out of him. Scenes from television flashed through his mind: bombs, earthquakes, and explosions. Terrorist attacks!

He opened his eyes and twisted his head to one side. His glasses were on the floor beside him. He reached for them. Nobody else was on the ground, just the three of them. Shoppers passing by around them had leapt back, scared, puzzled, even amused. A small, curious crowd was gathering.

'What?' he gasped, 'What's the matter? What happened? Joe? Rachel? Are you okay?' He wriggled and pushed Joe off him, managing to sit up. The passers-by began to pass by again, skirting around them warily. The baffled crowd started to melt away.

A middle-aged couple had stopped. The man squatted down beside Chris. 'Are you all right, son? What happened?'

The woman knelt down beside Rachel. Joe sat up and looked around, dazed.

'I don't know,' Chris said, adjusting his glasses.

'It was the one o'clock gun!' said Rachel suddenly. 'Joe didn't realise, er, he thought ...' She struggled to her feet and tugged at Joe's elbow. 'It's okay. We're okay,' she said to the anxious woman. 'Thanks.' She held on to Joe and marched outside.

Chris scrambled up. He turned to the man. 'Thanks, er …' He followed Joe and Rachel. Joe was leaning against a bus shelter, looking like a ghost, his dark, fear-filled eyes gazing past them, unaware.

Rachel was still holding on to Joe's arm, fighting back tears. 'I think it was the one o'clock gun,' she repeated, her voice trembling. 'He's never been in town at one o'clock before. He must've thought …' A tear slid down her cheek.

Chris put a hand on her shoulder. 'It's okay. Come on, let's go.' He was embarrassed. He didn't want to stand there any longer, with people staring at them curiously as they walked past. Chris steered them back to the gardens, where they sat on a bench. 'I'm going to get food. Got to keep our strength up,' he said, longing for normality. He left them sitting in the sun, while people strolled by, ignoring them.

Five minutes later, he returned with burgers and milkshakes. Rachel picked at hers while Joe ate mechanically. Chris was a bit ashamed of his appetite, but he finished his burger and Rachel's, and noticed with relief that Joe's colour was returning.

On the bus home, Chris tried to explain to Joe. 'Every day, Monday, Tuesday, Wednesday … Every day, one o'clock, you can check the time.' He pointed to his watch. 'Boom! One o'clock. Every day.' Joe just stared at him in uncomprehending amazement.

Vix Parker

MY BREATH IN HER BODY

I was driving home on the A9. It was the first accident I've ever seen. I've seen the aftermath of accidents before, I've crawled past the wreckage of cars crumpled at the side of the road, I've seen the broken trees, dented barriers, glass shards. I'd never seen an accident happen.

It had been a glorious day. The sun was going down long and red across the mountains, the sky a high pale blue. I'd been stuck indoors all day, in a meeting, and it was good to be out on the road, fleeing north. I wasn't paying much attention to what was happening up ahead. We were doing about fifty miles per hour and there wasn't another stretch of dual carriageway for ages. It was annoying, yes. There was a car ahead of me, and a jeep towing a caravan ahead of the car. I had the radio on; it was some programme about books I think. I wasn't really paying attention. I was thinking about the conference I'd been at. What I was going to have for tea. What time I'd be home. I was aware that the car had pulled out to pass the caravan, and then I was aware of the caravan braking, hard. My feet responded without even consulting my brain, and my car was already slowing when the caravan started swinging wildly around. I pressed down on the brake with my whole body, my arms stiff against the steering wheel. I could hear the squeal of my tyres on the road and it sounded strange and otherworldly, as though it wasn't really happening. My car stopped and I glanced in the rear-view mirror, thinking it was lucky there was no-one to run into the back of me. There was this noise, a sudden loud BANG! that made me flinch. It all happened in the space of a few seconds, but I was so aware of everything that it seemed slowed-down. The caravan had tipped onto its side on the road, blocking the right carriageway. The jeep had ridden up on something, I couldn't see what. I didn't really think about what to do. I put on my hazard lights, turned off the engine, got out of the car. The driver of the jeep and the passenger had climbed down from their vehicle and were standing stunned beside the wreck of their holiday. They were old, the woman leaning on a stick. The car that overtook them was stopped a little further up the road and the driver was being sick onto the verge. I walked round to the front of the jeep and saw what it was parked on. It was a red car. The front of it was completely crushed and mangled, the bonnet a sharp W sticking up into the air, the engine horribly broken and parts strewn across the road. Both airbags were inflated and I couldn't see who was inside the car.

It was so quiet. There was a waterfall tumbling over rocks not far from us, running into a river which paralleled the road for a little way before running beneath it and away across the sunbathed landscape. I heard a buzzard call, high and lonely above us. A car coming the other way slowed down and stopped, the driver got out.

'Shit,' he said. He took his mobile phone out of his pocket, flipped it open and dialled 999.

Another car had stopped behind mine, and the driver and passenger appeared behind me. The first man called out that he'd phoned for an ambulance. The second one walked past me and looked in at the window of the driver's side of the mangled car. He tried the door but couldn't get it open. He rubbed his right hand over his face and his watch glinted in the sunlight. He looked back at his partner, who had remained beside me. 'There's a kid in the back,' he said.

The woman clacked over to him in her high-heeled shoes. She tapped on the window and smiled. It didn't look like a smile, even from where I was standing. She said something to the man and he went to the back and opened the boot. It was a hatchback; it had no rear doors. The man spoke to the child inside and reached into the car, drawing out a skinny blond-haired boy about seven or eight years old. He set him down on the road and the boy's legs buckled, but he didn't fall. The woman held out her arms to him, and he staggered to her, rubbing his chest where the seatbelt had bruised it. She hugged him against her and I realised that she was crying. I wondered if she had children of her own, if she was thinking how lucky she was that he wasn't hers. The man, her husband or partner, had gone to the passenger side and opened the door there. The first man joined him and they pulled out a man, the father.

'Can anyone do first aid?' the first man called.

'I can,' I said, but I said it so quietly that nobody heard me. I cleared my throat and tried again. I was feeling sick. 'I can,' I said a bit louder. The woman heard me and looked up. She dragged the sleeve of her nice suit across her face.

'She can,' she called to her husband or partner, and she pointed at me.

I felt like I was gliding as I moved toward the car. I hardly seemed to be moving at all. I was taking everything in at some level, but nothing was registering. I had entered a space where time was irrelevant. Everything was happening right now. The sound of the impact was still in my ears.

My work had sent me on a one-day course in emergency first aid a year and three months previously. For a while I'd had a neat packaged face mask in my bag, for doing CPR, but I'd taken it out a few months ago because I'd never used it and it was taking up space. I wasn't sure I could remember anything from the course. I remembered having a baked potato for lunch, with coleslaw. I remember it because the coleslaw had been particularly nice.

I skirted the car which now had both its boot and bonnet raised to the sky, and looked down at the man they'd laid on his back on the verge. He was about my age, with hair styled so that it looked dishevelled and stuck up from his head. He was wearing an open-necked cotton shirt and jeans. He had a cut above his right eye which was leaking blood down the side of his face, but that seemed to be all. I could see that he was breathing even from where I stood; ragged shallow breaths. I crouched next to him and took his wrist. It was heavy and limp; much heavier than I'd expected. I found his pulse easily, it felt the way it feels to hold a butterfly in your cupped hands. I knew I was supposed to move him into the recovery position, but I couldn't quite remember how, or what it looked like. I remembered the instructor at the first aid course, a big, heavy-set man with a paunch, lying prone on the floor and instructing the smallest, slightest girl in the group to roll him into position. She did it easily, and grinned up at us watching her, and blew her hair out of her eyes.

I reached across his body and took the man's left leg, bent it at the knee. It felt strange touching him like this, when he was unconscious. When I didn't know him. I took his left arm and pulled it towards me, across his body, pressing down on his knee so it acted like a lever. He rolled onto his right arm. I gasped at how easy it was. I laid his knee down, still bent, and placed his left hand beside his face. He was still breathing. I brushed a stray piece of hair away from his forehead and wondered who he was.

The others had got the woman out of the driver's seat.

'She's not breathing,' the first man said.

I looked up at him but couldn't see his face because the light was behind him. I swallowed, but my throat had gone dry and made an odd clicking sound. I wished that someone else here could do first aid properly, could take over.

'How long will the ambulance be?' I managed to ask. The man shrugged.

'They said about half an hour.'

I looked at my watch, but I didn't know what time it had been when he called, so I couldn't work anything out. I looked down at the man lying beside me. He looked like he was sleeping. I thought that perhaps we should have left them in the car, in case they were bleeding internally or something. I thought about the woman, not breathing. I wondered if she was dead then, if she wasn't breathing. I knew I was supposed to do something, that they were waiting for me to do something. I crawled over to her. I didn't think I could stand. There was a smell of petrol coming from the car, and I wondered if it was safe. We were right beside it, on the rough dry grass. The sound of the waterfall went through everything. Someone was letting cars through one at a time. I wondered where the old couple were, then I saw them across the road, sitting on a rock, holding each other. Someone was standing beside them.

I forced myself to look down at the woman. She had curly dark hair, such soft hair, and I wondered where the boy got his blondness from. Her face was very white, but she didn't look damaged at all. I wondered what had happened. I wondered if she was already dead, and I felt suddenly very tender towards her. ABC, I thought. Airway, breathing – what? I couldn't remember what C stood for. I touched her face very gently. I had to put my finger in her mouth but I didn't want to. I had to. I took a long deep breath and held it. I put my finger into her mouth, and it opened. I couldn't remember what I was supposed to be looking for. I fingered her tongue, then hooked it over to the side of her mouth, and turned her head towards me. Breathing. I bent over her and put my cheek up close to her mouth. I could smell her perfume, something subtle and sweet. She wasn't breathing. C. Circulation? That would make sense. I lifted her wrist and although it was lighter than the man's, it was still heavy. Her hand flopped limply over mine. I couldn't find a pulse. I pressed my ear to her chest, but there was nothing. I tried to will her to breathe, to cough and sit up. I wanted it to happen so badly I almost believed that it would. I wondered how much time had passed now since she'd stopped breathing, and how much time it was supposed to be between not breathing and brain-damage. I thought about the lifeless dummies we'd practiced on at the course. A torso. A child. A baby. I didn't have a go on the baby or the torso. I did the child wrong – when I blew into its mouth, its disgusting latex rubber-smell mouth, its chest didn't inflate like it was supposed to. The instructor came over, said I hadn't tipped the head back far enough. I felt ridiculous. I tried again. The chest inflated.

I tipped the woman's head back and it was nothing like using the dummy. I couldn't remember whether I was supposed to blow first, or compress. I closed her nostrils with my finger and thumb and opened her mouth by pressing down on her chin with my other hand. I put my mouth to her mouth and thought how it was like kissing, but also not. I closed my eyes and blew. I realised that I wouldn't know if it was working with my eyes closed, and opened them. I blew again. Her chest moved. I thought about my breath going into her lungs. I thought about my spirit, my life-force entering her body and willing her to live. She didn't move. I closed her mouth and measured the space between the dip in her collarbone and the end of her breastbone. She was wearing a pendant on a thin gold chain, like a thread from a spider's web. The pendant was a tiny purple stone. I wondered if the man had given it to her. I found the mid-point of her breastbone and placed the heel of my left hand on it, with my right hand over the top, fingers twined together. I noticed how bony my hands were, how white at the knuckles. I pressed all my weight onto her chest, and released. Her breastbone gave, rose up. It was nothing like using the dummy. I didn't know if I was doing it right. I did it fifteen times, fast but steadily. I picked up her wrist again. Nothing. I put my ear to her mouth.

Nothing.

'Mummy?'

I looked up and the boy was standing there. The woman who had hugged him was trying to pull him away.

'Wait,' I said. 'Let him come.'

I don't know why I said it.

He came and knelt at her head and stroked her hair. He looked at me and his eyes were bright blue with tears.

'Can you help?' he asked.

I wanted to tell him yes, that everything would be fine. I didn't want to lie to him. I didn't know what to say.

'I'll try,' I said. 'But your mum's really –' I wasn't sure what to say. Unconscious? Possibly dead? I fumbled for something, and came up with 'not well.'

He nodded. The woman told him to come with her, but he pretended not to hear, or else he really didn't hear. I looked up at her again and I realised that I was in charge. I'd never been in charge of anything like this.

'Let him stay,' I said. 'How's the man?' and she turned away to check on the man.

'Sit down there,' I said, and pointed to a space halfway down his mother's body. 'Hold her hand,' I said. He took her white limp hand in his small one and began kneading it. His lips were moving but I couldn't hear what he was saying and wasn't sure if he was talking to her or praying.

I tipped her head back again and blew into her mouth twice. Then I did fifteen compressions. Then I checked her pulse. Then I started again. I don't know how many times I did this before we heard the faraway thud thud thud of the helicopter. I was so tired. I didn't even know if I was making a difference. I just kept on going. The helicopter noise got louder, blotted out everything, then slowed to a whir in a field across the road. I could hear sirens as well, once the noise of the helicopter died down. Two paramedics appeared in fluorescent coats, toting their medibags. One of them spoke to the man who'd dialled 999, while the other one thanked me and took over. Suddenly there were police and medics everywhere. One of them took the boy, who started to cry and turned to stare at me desperately as they took him away. I stared helplessly back, hugging my arms across my body because suddenly it was cold, the sun had gone below the hill-line and it was so cold. A policewoman asked me to sit in her car while she asked me about what happened, what

I'd seen. I told her as much as I could remember. She said I'd done the right thing, that I did a good thing, that I may have saved the woman's life. I'd started shaking, but I was trying hard not to let it show, just to hold it inside. When she let me go I walked past the wrecked car and the broken caravan. They were taking the woman on a stretcher over to the helicopter. The man had been put in an ambulance. I'm not sure what happened to the boy. The old couple had gone, too, and the driver of the car that passed them. All the other traffic had been turned around or diverted. Mine was the only one left, its hazard lights still flashing in the dusk. I got into my car and drove the silent, empty road for a couple of miles, then I pulled over into a lay-by and I started to cry.

I thought about my mouth on the woman's mouth and thought I would never be able to kiss anyone again without remembering that. I thought about my breath going into her body. I thought about my spirit entering her while hers floated away on the evening air, while her son pressed her hand in his and her husband lay sleeping on the grass.

Allan Radcliffe

COLD CHICKEN ROLL

Dad pulls up behind Kenny-from-next-door's van. Outside, Mum plants her non-slip boots firmly in the slush and places a plate-filled tray in my arms: homemade steak pie and tatties, sprouts, green beans and carrots and a trifle. Grandad's favourites, suffocating under clingfilm.

'You take those in to your Grandad.' Mum dismisses me with a smile. Not a smile, just upper and lower lips pressed hurriedly together to let me know I have my instructions.

I shoulder the filthy wooden gate and trudge up the three steps to the front door. I'm always first into the danger zone, like the dogs they send in to scout out bombsites. Tray balanced on one knee, I use my elbow to poke down the front door handle. The door springs open. 'Grandad!' I back awkwardly into the hallway. I don't bother to ring the bell anymore. Grandad can't hear it and, even if he could, he wouldn't be able to get up to answer. In the hall, the acrid smell of old man pee mingles with Glade. Mum and Dad are behind me.

'Now, don't let him upset you,' Mum mutters in my ear for the umpteenth time today. 'Grandad says some inconsiderate things, but he doesn't mean it. You know he doesn't mean it.'

I let Mum pretend it's me who gets wound up by Grandad. It makes the grief he gives her easier to take. This morning, he's already been on the phone twice, the first time to tell her 'NO TEE BOATHER COMIN',' the second to bark that he 'JIST WINTS TEE BE LEFT ALANE!' He's 'ENTITLED TEE SIM PEACE AN QUIET AN NO TEE HAE FOWK GOAN OAN AT HIM THE HALE TIME!'

Mum, ever ready with a reasonable response to the unreasonable things Grandad does, says, through fastened teeth, 'He'll be thrilled when he sees you. We'll be in and out in an hour, give him his New Year and go and that'll be that. It'll be a nice wee boost for him.'

'Grandad!' I call, using my knee to bump open the door to the front room.

And there he is. Slumped in his decrepit chair by the

three-bar electric fire. Head back, mouth wide open, snoring so hard his body shakes.

Mum says Grandad's looked the same since she was a kid. If you look at the photos on the mantelpiece – Granny and Grandad grinning widely on Mum and Dad's wedding day and on holiday at Brodick Castle – you can sort of see what she means. The fight's never left his eyes. Or maybe it's the ancient, black-rimmed NHS specs that have stayed the same, blinking in and out of fashion down the years. Or the drinker's complexion, the thinning skin scorched by ruptured blood vessels.

Grandad's tiny now and his clothes hang from his withered frame. His hair is shocking white, plastered down and tinged with yellow at the fringe. His eyes crinkle up at the edges when he's talking, so that no matter how slack his mouth gets you can see his intelligence. Beneath high, blade-sharp cheekbones, his flesh has retreated into tight hollows on either side of his face and the folds of his neck and jowls look like they've been sooked under his jawbone.

The front room looks cramped since he sanctioned us to move his bed downstairs. It's dimly lit, the carpet patchy, the Rice Krispie wallpaper withering. But it's still his room, his territory, his carpet, his wall, his bits and pieces, his stuff that's been around longer than I have. The picture of the blue-faced lady on the wall above the fireplace where it's always been. The ancient record player, the dog-eared Chic Murray albums, the toby jug, rimmed with grey ash, on top of the telly. There's my third-year photograph, the one that makes me shrink in horror every time I see it, acne-ridden and unhappy and in pride of place in the centre of the mantelpiece.

We creep into the room and take up our positions. I perch on the bed, Dad in the armchair next to Grandad. Mum lowers herself into Granny's old chair with the stick still hanging off the back and the black tar stains on the ceiling above where her permed head should be. Mum leans forward and furtively whispers, 'Dad.' Then a wee bit louder, 'Dad!'

He starts awake causing the three of us to flinch.

Grandad takes a moment or two to come round, peers at each of us in turn.

'Oh aye,' he says, almost nonchalantly, not shifting,

slowly working his mouth up and down, loosening his jaw.

'How you doing, Dad?' Mum asks. She hasn't taken her coat off. She sits huddled protectively inside it, her hands stuffed in her pockets.

'Ach, much the same.' He pulls himself into an upright position, gropes for his Superking Blues, lights up, sucks and inhales with breath that whistles like a radio between stations.

'Happy New Year, Dad,' says Mum.

'Eh?'

We three, as one, tilt our heads to examine Grandad's right ear. He hasn't got his hearing aid in.

'Where's your hearing aid, Dad?'

'Eh?'

'Where's your HEARING AID?'

'Ach, I canny mind. Simdy mistae moved it.'

Simdy always gets the blame. Even on Christmas Day, when the three of us spent half-an-hour searching for the remote control for the telly, because Grandad wanted to watch *Titanic*, and Simdy had pinched the remote. Not that it mattered in the end. Grandad eventually forgot what we were looking for, what film he wanted to watch. What day it was.

'Happy New Year, Dad,' says Dad, offering his hand.

'Och aye, Happy New Year, Brian.' They shake. 'Aye, a' the best.'

'Happy New Year, Grandad,' I shout.

'Aye, son. Wha's my first fit then? You?'

'What about Dad? He's tall, dark and handsome,' I offer. Dad laughs graciously. Like me, he's the height of nonsense.

There's a bit of a silence. Smiles all round.

'Weel, son,' says Grandad, half-turning to me.

This is my cue to start telling him my news. I embellish all my tiny recent achievements because I know this is my role in New Year proceedings: to give Grandad a 'wee boost,' by amusing him with (mostly fictional) tales of my wild and feckless youth. Throughout my newscast, Mum sits uneasily on the edge of her seat, her eyes darting between Grandad and me. She's still got her smile clamped fast onto her face, but her eyes are wide and tired, her forehead furrowed. Whenever Grandad doesn't hear something, she jumps in

and translates what I've just said. When she can see that
I'm running out of steam, she whispers a new topic for
discussion. 'Tell him about your flat,' she says. 'Tell him
you've been doing your own cooking. Tell him about your
exam.' I ramble on and sometimes she interrupts me mid-
sentence. This throws me, makes me think I've said
something wrong, something inappropriate.

It doesn't matter what I say to Grandad. These days, he
always responds the same way, nodding and laughing in what
he hopes are the right places, even though he can't hear half
of what we're saying. As I talk, he smiles and shakes his head
and winks and raises his eyebrows. He responds with the
advice he's always given me. 'Weel, you mind and stick in at
the skale, son,' and 'Noo dinna you be wastin' time wi'
lassies. They're nithin' bit boather.' In his mind, I'm still that
robust child bringing dead birds in from the garden to show
him and eating him out of cream cakes and fizzy juice. Some
days he can't remember my name and rattles through his
mental register of male relatives, occasionally alighting on
the right one: 'Charlie, Norrie, Jackie, Don, Brian, eh ...'

'Who's wanting a cuppy?' Mum's asking, getting out of
her seat.

'I'll do it,' I say, too quickly. 'Who's wanting what?'

Grandad screws up his face and says 'Ach no, I'm no
buthert,' but I'll make him one anyway because he'll have
changed his mind in five minutes. Mum throws me the
urgent look which means, 'Put the food on. I want to see
him eat something.' I pick up the tray of food from the coffee
table, and glance back at Mum to show that I've understood.
I can't help it: I'm still so bloody eager to please. But her
attention has already flipped back to Grandad, who's half
out of his chair and feeling around for his ashtray. I hear his
vibrating voice as I make my way down the hall to the
kitchen: 'WHIT, AHM AH NO EVEN ALLOWED A
WEE SMOKE TEE MASEL' NOO. YE WINT ME TEE
DEE MISERABLE AS WEEL AS DEEF AN' BLIN' ...'

As expected, Grandad accepts his tea, and even manages
to force down some steak pie and a helping of trifle. Mum's
eyes anxiously follow every fork and spoonful that finds its
way falteringly into his mouth.

Dad's the first up. 'We'd better get going. Miss the
traffic,' he tells Grandad. We're going out tonight, the three

of us, for a few New Year drinks and, hopefully, a laugh. Mum smiles apologetically at Grandad, her expression changing to one of alarm when she sees him trying to get up out of his chair. 'No, don't get up, Grandad,' we all shout in chorus.

Mum says: 'There's a tick ae trifle left in the fridge for later, if you want it, Dad. I'll be down to see you on Friday.'

My turn. 'Well, bye Grandad. I'll come up and see you soon, eh?'

'Maybe I'll get down to see this flat of yours eh?'

I blurt out a laugh, genuinely surprised and pleased that he's remembered. 'Aye, you're welcome to kip on the floor anytime you want.'

He laughs appreciatively.

'Well, bye.'

I hesitate, then place my hand on his bony shoulder and give him a kiss. His cheek feels like cold chicken roll. I kick up the third button on the fire. 'Keep yourself warm,' I say, then head for the door. Behind me, Grandad's voice, like rusty pipes, creaks into life: 'It's aye guid tae see ye, son.'

Now he's got this big grin on his face that won't go away and he keeps shaking his head and having a wee laugh to himself. I think maybe I ought to stay longer but I don't have time. Dad's already got the motor running.

Next New Year, Grandad will be sitting at the end of a row of hospital beds in a mixed ward. He'll have lost so much weight he'll be a shrunken doll version of his former self. He'll only half-recognise his visitors and he'll be placid and polite in their company. Left alone, he'll sit bolt upright in an unfamiliar chair, staring into the middle distance, trying to ignore the gyp his insides are giving him. His eyes will be open and unblinking but there'll be nothing left in his face, no fight in his eyes.

In the car on the way home, Dad listens to that programme where they play all the number ones of the past year. He keeps shaking his head and grimacing and complaining to me that young folk have no taste in music. 'These records are more like number twos,' he says, more than once. I don't argue with him: I think it's rubbish too. Of course, he's trying to be witty, to make light of the situation, to cheer Mum up. I know I should be helping out

by doing the same. Mum's in front of me. I watch her in
the wing mirror. Slumped right down in her seat, still buried
inside her coat, eyes searching the floor. She's doing that
thing of brushing her upper lip with her bottom row of teeth,
which means she's going over and over in her head
everything that happened during our visit, and wondering if
there's anything she could have done to make Grandad more
comfortable. I wish I could find the guts to say something,
or even just take her hand and give it a squeeze, but I won't
because, well, what if that's not what she wants? So I
try to ignore her sitting there, unhappy, and do my best to
concentrate on Dad's jokes and the year's number twos.

Alan Riach

TWO PAINTINGS BY JACK YEATS

1. A Shop in Sailor Town

            and old copper
      DEALER IN
        OLD IRON
under the sign above the door, under the two yellow
    oilskins and caps, hanging
there, a wee boy jangles pennies in his pocket, looking in
the open doorway, one foot on the threshold. What can
    there be
        in the shop's dark shadowy
interior? His wee pal's standing outside on the pavement, a
    scarf
around his neck, his head tilted up, he's looking at all he
    can see
in the window. Their inquisitive backs are facing us. What
    can we see?
Bottles of hair-oil, model ships in bottles, books,
             a pistol hanging on a string, a set of knives
hanging on strings, sailors' boots, a painting of a ship in
    harbour,
two necklaces in a frame, a painting of a beautiful young
    woman (but you
cannot see her face), a big conch shell, a captain's hat,
    another book (a 'Life of ...'),
a flower jar, a box, two watches and beyond these things,
    the shadowy
dark of the shop's interior. The two wee boys are standing
    on the edge of it,
a world of shapes and structures, colours, textures, tastes:
    all things new
and full of prospect, appetising plenitude, of many things,
    and shadows.

2. Sailor Boy

The sailor boy steps up upon the quay
beside the man with the sickly stare and sickle.
The hour-glass sand is pouring down beside him.
The monkey on the boy's sack over his shoulder's looking
     at you.
The parrot in the cage he carries cackles. The rigging
     creaks. The sounds
of men and women and traffic from the town across the
     harbour chime
and tinkle in the continuous filaments of water gurgles,
     lapping
the quay and the tide. The big white clouds blow by.
Some day, even the blue-bright red-striped sailor boy will
     die.
But for today, the sunlight, stepping ashore, and above, the
     high old sky!

MEXICO POEM: TIJUANA BRASS
Bienvenidos a Tijuana
(Auntie Anna's Famous Brothel for US Marines
from San Diego)

Tijuana waxworks. Quiet in the lobby. The woman at the
    counter has no change
for a $20 bill. Back to the street. First, off Revolución, the
    Sierra all around,
now pink and hazed bronze; you can pick up a trace of the
    silence from
the snow up there. The beat, though, is all along here:
    dance, silver, leather
whips? / you like whips? and hand-cuffs? sombreros all a-
    glitter in the evening sun,
the storefronts and the balconies all selling, and you've seen
    it all before, it's all
been done before, oh, so many times! how many times? The
    faces aged into
acceptance, weathered into humour and ways to get through,
the big mustachios, the shiny silver buckles, the cigars, the
    cars as big as helicopters,
the buses from before the Revolution, the filth and sell, the
    poor, and you walk
across the bridge across the Tijuana river, a thin band
    running straight
from the Sierra, one long silver line in its concrete channel,
    and all along the bridge
and the stairs up to it, and the stairs down from it, the
    children are there,
one every few yards, old women too, battering it out on
    crazy drums
in tune with something somewhere, like Gaelic singers
    singing psalms
in Lewis, an old man plays a lively tune on a harmonica
    with his one
right hand, he has no other one, or legs, his flinty flushing
    eyes
are speaking, looking up, the kids cry out with Abba's pace
    and emphasis,

'Man-ay, Man-ay, Man-ay – da daa – na na na na naah!'
El Mariachi songs, the brass of it all, like the waxworks I
    will
not get into now, having too much money to afford the
    entrance fee.
The Mexican flag hangs and runs out like water rippling in
    a huge diagonal,
an oblique oblong in the long slanting light of December,
    4:25PM, that
Pacific border light, no cloud, the dust and snow from the
    distance,
the feel of trafficking, now all around you, the sweet sugary
    smell
from the deepfried pastry, the meat frying for tortillas and
    the sour smell
of burning sweetcorn leaves by the vendors by the
    Cathedral in whose darkness
the grotto is a shrine to which a crowd of people raise their
    eyes
from scattered places in the pews, and a man on the corner
    of Revolooshyoan
is shouting into a microphone: 'No pasarán! No pasarán!'
And down in the empty concrete valley by the river,
    another man is walking
absolutely alone, under the footbridge, on towards the
    impossible mountains,
as if not one thing in the world could yet prevent him.
    Solitude in sandals,
grey suit, the jacket flapping open in the breeze. He does
    not look around.
Not even for a moment. What gives him such authority,
    direction? Hope?

R. J. Ritchie

STREET THEATRE, EDINBURGH, AUGUST

Up by coach for a festive break
a twenty-one-stone Cornishman,
freshly weighed on alfresco scales,
perches precariously on a board of nails
pressed into the nipple-ringed chest
of a burly baldie be-kilted Scotsman
swallowing a flaming torch
as he lies supine on a plastic battered suitcase
on the rain-slicked High Street setts.

Up atop a twelve-foot metal pole
Arizona Jones stands
at the mercy of strangers,
who hold the stay-ropes in unaccustomed hands.
He looks down on the henna tattooists
and the monkey-puppet woman, and over the punters
queuing to fork out eight quid to gawp
at Andy Warhol's Brillo Boxes,
and pulls a paraffin-soaked whip
from a canvas bum-bag.
And the borrowed-lighter-lit whip
being well alight along its snake-long length,
Arizona Jones cracks the whip
and cracks out the flames.

Brave and free, from the Monterey pines
they have crossed a continent and the wide Atlantic ocean,
a thirty-something touchy-kissie couple:
they say they are Daredevil Chicken Club.
The hen-chicken scrambles onto the shoulders
of a pair of stooges plucked from the crowd:
split-legged, she lays an egg.
Into the Hunter Square air the cock-chicken
launches rubbery baby fowl
from a rubbery-baby-fowl launcher
as a wee girl runs about with a big net.
Half-way along a makeshift tightrope,
his full cock-chicken-height high,

one half of Daredevil Chicken Club crouches,
and clucks, and stands and juggles
a few knives and a chicken club
over his yellow-capped, scarlet-feather-crested,
gold-shorted, red-legginged wife.

Nancy Somerville

BUCKET OF FROGS

You and me
heading for the pub
in the full heat
of the mid-summer sun, then

a bucket of frogs
waiting for a bus,
that's what it looked like.
No-one else about,
just you and me
heading for the pub
and a bucket of frogs

squatting on the pavement
in the full blaze
of the mid-summer sun
– more rare in Scotland
than a bucket of frogs
taking turns to try
the high jump to freedom.

Do we leave them
to croak it
boiled in a bucket
or splattered under rubber
in Dalry Road?

Heading for the pub
with a bit of a detour
to the summer-cool canal
with a pail of hot frogs,

talking about gum trees,
other frogs we've known,
books we've read
and the things
that come to you
when you're trying to find the words
with a bucket of frogs in your hand.

Heading for the pub
with a story on our lips
– the day we saved the frogs,

and later
you saved me.

Kenneth Steven

LEMON ICE CREAM

If I close my eyes now, very tightly, I can smell everything. The ice cream that my father is scooping into bowls in green-white curves, the little kitchen with its open dishes of herbs and its baskets of vegetables. The windows are open and all of us — my mother, my brother, my father and me — we are all looking out onto the umber sea of the fields, and the scent that is coming in is from the lemon grove.

I used to get up early in the summer to walk there, just to be there. To lie on my back and listen to the shingling of the leaves and let that scent, the scent of the lemons, fill me completely. And at night when I couldn't sleep in my tiny room under the attic, I would open the latch of the windows and let in the lemon breath of the dark.

I was four years old. Born in Sicily under the shadows of the mountains. My father called Mount Etna *the blue ghost*. And when I was five we left, all of it was taken away as suddenly and completely as a teacher wiping a blackboard. There were little finches my father fed; they came to one of the windows at the very top of the farmhouse and he fed them. Most of the other boys had grown to love hunting such birds; netting them and caging them. But my father had a soft heart; he could not bear to see such beautiful things hurt, and he fed the finches. It was the last thing we did before we left, him and me; we stood there with our palmfuls of seeds, me stretching on tiptoe, the tears on my face. His voice was so soft; those words of kindness he whispered both to the finches and to me. They were for both the finches and me.

We were leaving for America, for New York. It was a time of new hope, new dreams, and no dreams came bigger than America. And the last thing my father took from that farmhouse, that place that had been home to six generations of our family, was the recipe for lemon ice cream. I don't know where it had been hidden all that time; it was as though like a magician he snapped his fingers and brought it out from behind his ear. But there it was, in an old square envelope, with flowing writing on the front. And his dark brown eyes shone as he showed me.

We sailed to America. Everything we could carry was stowed beneath us in this great ship ploughing towards the New World. Marco and I ran everywhere – he was nine and I was five. This was our Ark; we had set out across the sea for a new world and everything we needed was onboard. We went down as deep into the ship as we could, to beside the great engines that roared and shook like angry dinosaurs. We went up to the highest deck and watched the grey swaying of the sea, and the brown smoke fluttering from the funnel.

And we smelled New York before we saw it. We smelled it and we heard it, Marco and I. Very early one morning when the sea had become a pale piece of glass, we scurried up from our cabin, went on deck and leaned out, and we smelled and we heard New York. It was such a mixture of scents, such a tumbling of things, as though an old bin full of rubbish had rolled down the side of a hill. You tried to catch things at random and always it went on rolling. The bin never stopped tumbling out of control, for ever. Hot smells and sour smells and burnt smells and fresh smells and dead smells and new smells. They made us excited, they set us on fire, but my father hushed us as he leaned out too, for he was listening to New York – he was hearing the city.

'Those are the biggest sounds in the world,' he whispered to us, and somehow we believed him that they must be, that they were. He quietened us with those words, he made us listen, and the smells and the sounds gave us pictures in our heads – pictures in ochre and bright green and orange. But when we came to New York a fine rain was falling, a mist like a mesh of flies that seemed to dampen the scents and the sounds and leave only the great looming greyness of the skyscrapers.

We came to our new home, four flights above the street. On the other side of the hall were the Pedinskis, and above us there was nothing but the roof space and the sky. The only place we had to play was the stairs, and we made it our train station, the launch-pad for our rockets, our cave system, our battlefield. On four flights of stairs were Jewish children, Polish children, Italian children and German children. We had nothing but our imaginations and the days were not long enough. We ate each other's food and we never went hungry.

One Saturday in the hot summer we had been outside,

all of us children. We came back panting, full of stories, and sat on different stairs, leaning against the wall. My father came out with bowls of lemon ice cream, his ice cream, and as soon as I bent my head to that bowl I smelled home. I was back in the kitchen, I was up feeding the finches, and I was down in the lemon grove. The tears flowed from my eyes and he comforted me. He rocked me in his arms that evening until I fell asleep.

He kept the recipe behind the old carriage clock in the living room. That brown, crinkled envelope. Sometimes if there was a high wind in the autumn, the fall, and the draught crept under the front door and through the top of the high windows, I would hear it rattling behind the clock, dry like an ancient seed pod. It was there behind the clock, the clock that never lost a second's time, that flickered its passing segments of time like hurrying feet. The clock and the paper.

Then, one spring, my mother fell ill. Everything was beginning again, coming alive, after the long winter, and it was as though she went the wrong way and couldn't come back. It was as if we kept moving and had to watch her getting further and further away, disappearing into the snow. I remember her waving to me as I set off for school in the morning. The pale oval of her face behind the glass, trying so hard to smile. That is how I saw her, that was the last memory of her every day, that painting of the pain of her smile. I remember going with Marco and my father to pray for her in a little chapel at the heart of the city. I tried so hard to pray but my head was full of the evening traffic, the shouting and laughter outside. I wanted so desperately to guard her and keep her safe from harm in that place, but not even there was there sanctuary.

My father seemed to grow old in front of us after she died. I remember thinking that one night when we sat together in the living room: *the clock and my father were set at different speeds*. One night I had a dream, a particularly vivid dream. It was of a field, a great wide field. I could see nothing beyond it, it was the only thing there was.

And I came on my father in that field and he was planted in the ground. Mad as that sounds now, he was planted in the ground. And I began digging out his hands and feet, his wrinkled fingers and toes, and all the time I was thinking to myself – *this soil is wrong*.

I was twelve years old. Marco had left school and couldn't find a job. My father, who had worked on scaffolding high above the city, who had sat and laughed with friends on beams the width of a leg half a mile over the streets, he had grown afraid. He had lost the courage to put one foot in front of the other.

That winter the snow fell and fell and fell. The skies were quieter than silence itself and the flakes spun like ballerinas from the sky and buried the world in white. The noise of the city diminished bit by bit; like a great, old animal New York lurched into its own cave and went to sleep.

The wind fluttered the curtains in the living room. It was six o'clock in the morning and I stood there alone, twelve years old and hungry. My father and Marco were asleep. There was nothing left in the house to eat. The wind came again and I shivered; there was a rattling and it was the old envelope behind the clock, the recipe for lemon ice cream. I felt sadder than ever before in my whole life; it was as though there was only one colour in the world now, the colour grey. And I made up my mind. I felt behind the clock and I found the piece of paper. I put on my shoes and I went out into the grey, sleeping morning with that crumpled paper held tight in my left hand.

And I sold it, I say no more than that I sold it. I do not even want to think of the people to whom I went, nor the place where that was. All of it still hurts too much; it is like some red sore where new skin will never grow again. It is enough to say that I was paid a bundle of dirty notes. I caught the smell of them as I took them and I felt sick. It was the smell of the subway, the smell of the basement where no light ever reached. All the way home my hands smelled of it too, and I wanted to wash them clean, I wanted to scour them until it was no more.

Even as I came inside I felt sick, but not only with that terrible smell. I felt sick with something else and I sat by the window; I hunched there and cried and cried and cried.

Outside, the new day was just beginning, there were voices and sounds and scents. The first light came red and beautiful through the streets; beams that crept and changed all the time.

And when I stopped crying at last I looked down on all of this and I thought: *the snow and the light are bigger, they are bigger than all of us together.* For there were men toiling in the snow, digging out cars and pushing them and swearing at one another and at their wives. Taxi drivers in their yellow cabs were shaking their fists and yelling. They were blinded by the red light that came low through the city; they tried to shield their eyes and they had to stop. All they could do was shout and swear, and I looked down on them from where I was four flights above, and they seemed so small and what they struggled against so huge.

I looked up and listened; I listened to the one room and I listened to myself. I felt utterly empty. I had cried myself dry; my eyes were empty caves. The dirty banknotes lay strewn over my lap and some were scattered over the floor at my feet. They were like leaves that had blown in the window – old, dead leaves.

My father and brother would be up soon, my father to sit there in the living room and look at pictures and wait, just wait; and my brother to drag on his coat and go out into a city that did not want him.

Except that everything had changed now. I looked up and I listened and I realised I could hear nothing at all. The clock had stopped ticking.

THE FERRYMAN

The blue ribbon of a river, too deep to ford,
a great chattering of water a hundred feet across,
and on the far bank a cottage fluttering smoke.

No-one crosses here without the ferryman's consent:
king or commoner, all are in the same boat —
thirty years he's criss-crossed the river for the one coin

a coin for a crossing but for silence also:
the man who travels under cover of owls always
to meet the girl who is not his;

the boy who's running away,
whose eyes are full of ships and storms;
the priest who carries more than he came for.

That coin is worth its weight in gold,
to seal the slip of a tongue,
the spread scent of a secret.

So he has learned to say nothing,
the man with the bracken hair and the big hands —
to let out no more than where the best trout lie.

Jim Taylor

AFTER THE WAR

Dr Reuter was keen to destroy all trace of my father. 'I know it's difficult,' she assured me, gently prising another crippled chair from my arms and tossing it onto the fire. 'After clearing my parents' place last year, I know exactly. But I'm not sentimental. It's much better this way.' She didn't really know, though, I didn't think, as I followed her into the sacred Nissen hut, packed with hobbled furniture, coils of frayed rope and plastic drums from the beach, drawers full of rusty nails, homeless keys and dust-caked radio valves, shelves and shelves of paint pots and jars of odd screws. In a corner she found the welder's helmet and hung it respectfully above a bench covered in tractor parts.

'The Iron Man,' I said. 'That's what they called him after he put this place up. He got it when they bulldozed the aerodrome.' I lifted a warped pile of encyclopaedias off the top of the old telly, the original black and white one. Friends had come from all over to watch David Coleman read the teleprinter. 'The first on the island. Not only did we have a state-of-the-art shed, we also had the first fridge on the isle and the first TV.'

'Ahead of his time,' she observed.

'Trying to compensate Mam,' I said, clunking in the ITV1 button, 'for giving up so much to live here.' I shook my head as the doctor dragged away a mouldy roll of carpet. 'He didn't mind having all the latest things, just wasn't so keen to get rid of the old ones.' I remembered Dad saying that carpet would make for good insulation material. 'Nesting materials for mice, more like,' Mam had replied.

I wrestled a wardrobe out from the mountain of hellary and there behind it, stacked on a dressing table, was a yellowed pile of sheet music. ' "Mozart's Duets",' the doctor read over my shoulder, as the pamphlets disintegrated in my hands. 'Chamber music.'

'Aye. Torture chamber. I couldn't play a note, but Dad made me practice.'

'And look at this,' she said, unearthing my Sony mono player and a couple of scratched records. Mam's – the Joe Loss Orchestra.

'Christmas 1967. They bought me a Beatles record to play on it. Well, Mam did,' I added. 'Dad hated it. "*Yeah, yeah, yeah.* Why can't they just say yes?" He thought it was too American.'

Detecting a sudden build-up of sentiment on my part, Dr Reuter prescribed the immediate destruction of the entire collection. I had to let her do the record player – so much harder to watch a peace offering go up in flames than the punishment exercises.

'I think it's time for a cuppa,' she announced, as flames shot from her volcano kettle. It was a childhood camping relic she'd salvaged from the house in Hamburg.

The other thing she'd brought back was the Volkswagen van now sitting along at North House, just the latest left-hand drive to be parked next door since the craze for German GPs got started. The Health Board rented it for them.

'Dad would have liked your kettle,' I told her. 'A "fiendish contraption", he'd have said.'

'He wouldn't have minded his place being invaded by Germans?'

'No, he liked you guys.'

'Even though we torpedoed him?'

'That's right, because you gave us Mozart. Whereas the Americans who saved his life were a bunch of layabouts.'

'It must have been such a strange, terrible time, the war,' she said, looking across the voe at the ruined gun emplacements.

'Not entirely.' I nodded at the old byre. 'That was like the local dance hall when Dad and Uncle Frank were home on leave. Dad on his fiddle and Frank on the accordion. Mam and her pals came from the airbase.'

'And he enchanted her with his playing.'

'Yeah, she came back after the war.'

'A smart move if you ask me,' she said, standing closer. We were sharing the first sunset of autumn with a few seals and a passing flock of geese. 'Why would anyone want to leave this place?'

'Some folk don't,' I replied, as one of Brahms' finest tunes kindled a broken jersey frame, charred notes flying up on a current of tracer bullets. It had been good, all the same, to see the place through her eyes. I'd come back for Mam's funeral in the spring and stuck around trying to make amends, the old guy on his last legs. Not that he knew who I was, half the time.

'The mind plays funny tricks in your father's condition,' Dr Reuter told me on one of her early visits. 'Sometimes he will know who you are, but perhaps not how old you are.'

'It's better to be a complete stranger, in a way,' I confided, 'than his fuck-up of a son.'

'The black sheep of the family?' she asked, pleased with her command of colloquial English.

I shrugged. 'I think he just wanted me to be like him. Good at fixing things and playing the fiddle. I was only interested in football.'

We dug on to the back of the shed until all that remained was my nemesis, the church organ, or harmonium, to be precise. Dad stepped in when the minister gave up on his 'old squeezebox', carting it back to the shed to use as an instrument of terror against me. First of all he repaired it using an assortment of twine, canvas and pieces of leather. Then he made me run up and down the scales, the notes hooting like drunken owls in the gloom of the shed. I think he had visions of me giving Bach recitals, but Larry Stout and Derek Ratter found me sitting at the coffin-like box and shouted 'Count Dracula!'

That was the last straw. I refused even to play the fiddle again. Me and Dad never talked about music or much else thereafter. His revenge was not to honour the things that were important to me, even with a mention. That included the final of the Northern Isles Cup, in which I scored the winner, witnessed by Mam and half of Lerwick. Dad was fixing somebody's Rayburn that afternoon and never asked me about it, or about anything else to do with football, until one afternoon near the very end.

The belt had gone on the old hoover and I was hocking in the kitchen for a screwdriver. 'What kind of repairman are you, coming with nae tools?' he shouted after me. By the time I went back in the room he had remembered who I was, but not which phase of our lives we were in. 'So, have you a game this weekend, son?' he asked the 14-year-old me. 'No Dad,' I said, hiding my face behind the hoover bag.

Dr Reuter and I heaved the wrecked harmonium out of the shed and played a wheezy version of chopsticks together, before tipping it onto the fire. 'I don't suppose the museum ...' she started at the last minute, but I shook my head.

'It's a goner.' It was the last item to go up in smoke, packed with a few more wads of Dad's German composers.

*

We've been finding wee notes for days now, a singed quaver trembling in a cobweb, scorched semibreves waving from blades of glass. There's music coming at us from every corner. I'm supposed to phone the estate agent to get the advert up and start sending people, but I'm thinking I better just wait till the racket dies down.

Douglas Thompson

TWENTY TWENTY

Darkness was falling and what was all the fuss about, Jakey wondered. One day was much like any other to him. You never could tell when the good breaks or bad were coming your way. Just keep your head down and push through the crowds, keeping one eye out for coppers, both kinds. He laughed at his own joke. These were the twin poles of his life: spare change and the police. For some mysterious reason the streets were particularly packed tonight and everyone he brushed up against seemed excited or angry about something.

Jakey skirted the outside of a throng of people gathered around some firebrand preacher. *The End of Days will be a fitting punishment for the wickedness of our times. Materialism, cynicism, nihilism. Beware the Beast in your midst. You bow and pray every night to your DJs and talk-show hosts and pouting popstars, but I say to you that these impostors of the latter-day world shall all go on one path, into the grasp of the Devil, by God's will, into dark bitter torments ...* Putting on his most pious and repentant face, Jakey squeezed his way through the bodies until he was closely packed like a sardine then began to gradually and quietly relieve everyone of their pocketbooks and bank cards.

Next he found his way to a political rally that was filling out the darkest corner of a large cobbled square below a Gothic church covered in scaffolding. Activists with megaphones were whipping up the crowd towards a frenzy. Jakey pushed in earnestly, his brow furrowed with grave concern for the well-being of the nation, he felt hungry for democracy. *For decades our country has been polluted with radiation and accidents have killed thousands while governments have covered it up, now the final insult: the democratic will of the people has been neatly sidestepped and we see that we have been hoodwinked by this political pantomime ...* When the cheers went up and the bodies shifted Jakey helped himself to some particularly meaty wallets, yes he really felt the extent of their civic concern and generosity.

For days, there had been all this shouting and rallying going on and droves of polis has been trying to herd Jakey and his ilk off the streets and off to the cells or the suburbs. He felt like the last scallywag in town, an institution by Christ, and was just admiring himself in the reflection of a shop window when as if from nowhere two policemen, old 'friends' of his, Muirhead and McWilliams, suddenly materialised and put their heavy hands on his shoulder. It was panda time again.

In the back of the car they laughed and shoved him about as they passed around the exotic credit cards they had found on his possession, even some dollars and euros. *Coming up in the world eh, Jakey? International fucking venture capitalist are we now? Some tourist's holiday ruined by you, ya clatty shite.* As they drove, Jakey sat in the back, rattling his handcuffs and hating the annoying little hairs on the back of PC Muirhead's skull. As if feeling his gaze, Muirhead turned and sneered: *Are we sitting comfortably there then, your majesty?* Jakey was about to mutter in reply: *Then I'll begin*, when the streetlights and traffic lights flickered and went out and a second later they were all thrown sideways by a crushing impact.

*

Stella Ettrick, a sales rep who lived in her car, had found herself locked into a two-mile-an-hour traffic jam all afternoon, trying to get through the city centre. She even had a biker deliver a phone-in pizza to her window.

Now the computer game she had downloaded from the web came to an abrupt halt as her laptop crashed, its hard drive winding down into a series of grating clicks. The streetlights went out. Her digital notepad read gobbledegook instead of her customer database. Using the only number she could remember by heart she dialled her parents on her mobile but found the network was down.

Somebody was tooting their horn behind, trying to turn around. Ahead of her, a few drivers were finally getting out of their vehicles and talking.

A firework suddenly boomed overhead, and she jumped in her seat, biting her tongue. The angry blossom of light spread out, turned from cool blue to green to yellow to fiery red and all the time falling down and down towards her, closer and closer, filling the sky and blotting out the stars completely.

*

Jakey regained consciousness being dragged clear of the police car and laid out in a shop doorway. His head swam and he suddenly threw up onto the pavement beside him. Some passers-by were pulling PC McWilliams, unconscious, from the front of the upside down wreck. Somebody was prodding into the other side and saying: *his partner's had it, he's crushed ...*

Jakey felt like he'd been out for hours, but evidently only minutes had gone by: this was confusing. With his wrists still handcuffed he sat up and wiped a little blood off his head onto his hands, moved his fingers and found his right foot twisted but not seriously. The small crowd of passers-by were moving over now, concentrating on the vehicle they had collided with; where a whole family, apparently unscathed, were being helped out in various stages of tears and trauma from the Chinese lantern that had been their car.

Jesus! Jakey found himself calling out hoarsely, *Don't just leave me here! Can someboady help me or get the key to these cuffs ... ah mean man ah cannie fend fur masel like this ...*

A number of cold disapproving stares turned towards him and he shrugged his shoulders and lay back on the pavement looking up at the stars which suddenly seemed to be blue and falling down then turning green and yellow. He closed his eyes, feeling nauseous again, wondering if he was dreaming.

He was next woken by the sound of a departing siren, and he sat up again: surprised to see that the good Samaritans had all moved on and left McWilliams behind lying on his back on the pavement. A raincoat had been draped over him covering his face: one of those curious human conventions that defy logical analysis. Jakey was shocked for a moment by the comparative silence, the suddenness, the finality of it all. He had been spared, grudgingly perhaps by this mysterious accident: and left here still sitting in chains. The streetlights were still out.

He tried to stand and stumbled slightly on his sprained foot and shuffled, hopped a bit and then on his knees made his way up to the body. His cuffed hands still shaking from the shock, he lifted the raincoat and searched for the keys to his chains. He heard voices, people approaching in the darkness. On an impulse he threw the raincoat over his shoulder and began dragging McWilliams' body backwards towards a doorway. Swearing to himself, biting his lips to keep silent he winced at the pain in his foot and desperately hauled until with one last heave McWilliams rolled over with him back into the close mouth. A crowd of drunken revellers ran past, singing and laughing.

His breath regained, he pulled McWilliams back further past the stairs to the back court where a little pale light from the moon was falling onto the ground. He grappled around and found the key on McWilliams' belt and with difficulty found a way to jam it upright and turn the lock on the handcuffs around it. Eventually they clicked open softly and he sighed, slowly lifting his hands up until they wavered in front of his face like long lost friends. He smiled. Then he focussed on McWilliams' face, upside down, eyes closed, head resting unceremoniously in the dirt. A sad expression crept gently over Jakey's face for a moment.

A cat meowed somewhere and emerged from the darkness of the back court to stand in the moonlight and stop, distrustful, its huge luminous eyes glowing like fires looking up at Jakey. Its expression was cold and neutral. It seemed to be questioning him.

Jakey looked down at the dead body and then back at the cat: which nodded its head once and then slinked off into the night. Jakey swallowed hard as he felt some kind of resolution taking him over. He began unbuttoning McWilliams' clothing.

A few minutes later Jakey emerged from the close mouth in a police uniform and took the hat off and scratched his head. He picked up the raincoat that had covered McWilliams and pulled it on over his uniform. Finding the street relatively quiet again he produced his torch and ventured over to the wrecked panda car. He fished around inside until he found a sealed transparent polythene bag and took out its contents: a wallet and a set of hotel room keys stolen from an American tourist a few hours earlier. Then, hands in pockets, he walked off into the uncertain night.

*

To her horror, Stella now saw in her wing mirror that some
of the abandoned cars behind her were drawing unwelcome
interest from dubious-looking passers-by. Some young men
in tracksuits and baseball caps, shockingly young perhaps
had passed a particular vehicle several times on the pretext
of looking for a way through the closely-packed cars to
cross the road. Now looking around one last time, one of
them reached for a stone lying in the gutter and hurled
it through the driver's window as Stella watched, mouth
open, heartbeat speeding up; pulse audible inside her own
head.

An air of unreality was taking her over. How could she
watch this frozen, as if it were television, entertainment?

Hands shaking, scrambling, keys falling from her hands
she got herself out of the car, almost forgot to lock it, then
hurried off down the nearest side street, not looking back.
She moved in a curious indecisive stroll that constantly
broke in and out of an attempt to sprint.

*

In Room 613 of the Holiday Inn, the only hotel with an
emergency generator on this side of town, Jakey took off his
raincoat and uniform and ran a hot bath. He opened the blinds
and looked out over the whole city. There were patches of
light where other generators in hospitals and government
buildings were working, and a few fires billowing from shops
and warehouses. Opening the windows he could hear the
distant sounds of celebration, demonstration, criss-crossed
with occasional emergency sirens.

He was confused at first by the lack of any buttons on
the television set until, giving up, he sat down on the remote
control and the set blinked on, making him jump. Most of
the channels seemed to be down with electrical interference
although he was amused and heartened to find one station
showing late night pornography.

After his wash Jakey stood in front of the mirror and,
using his hosts' trimmer and scissors, began the slow process
of reducing his profusion of unruly hair. He laughed as his
full beard transformed into a fashionable goatee then into a
buffalo bill moustache and finally disappeared altogether.
His long hair he now also pruned mercilessly, astounded to
see his whole face and character changing, gradually

emerging as something new and strangely beautiful after years in gestation.

Finally his naked feet stood amid a pile of black hair and he gazed admiringly upon his new self. He turned his face from one side to the other, one hand held up to his cheek, exploring, noting how distinguished the lines on his face had become, how pronounced his cheekbones after years of outdoor undernourishment. He had the face of a hawk, an eagle now he thought. Not the soft ruminant eyes of one of the other millions: the defeated middle-aged Saturday-men, with their worries and wives and waistlines.

He donned his uniform with a ceremonial touch, like a toreador or a Roman gladiator. He put on his hat and looked for his new name on his lapels: he was PC Stanley McWilliams now. He stuck his jaw out stiffly, in a regimented quasi-military manner.

Touching curiously the toys on his belt, he jumped as the radio resumed its all-night commentary: ... *disturbance in Market Street, all units, Roger Charlie Mike over ...*

*

Finding a public telephone at last, Stella sighed with relief as she dialled her parents' phone number. Through the glass door she could see a crowd at the end of the street moving slowly, political banners blowing, a few people running around out in front, throwing objects at the pavement, at shop windows, until one of them broke a window and an orange glow began to emanate from within.

Molotov cocktails ... her mind was saying.

Just as this thought crystallised the tone in Stella's ear resolved itself into a computer voice, steely and cold: *I'm sorry, a temporary fault has suspended services in your area. Please try again later.*

Keeping one eye on the distant crowd, she hurriedly slipped out of the booth, hand shaking as she returned her purse to her bag, mind reeling, not entirely sure where she was heading or with what intent except back to the car.

Turning a corner back to the street near her car she collided with two teenagers in white shellsuits, the uniforms of juvenile delinquency. She cried out involuntarily, dropping her handbag to the ground and all three of them,

stunned and disconcerted for a second which seemed like
an age, stared at each other wide-eyed.

*

Walking the streets Jakey found people looked at him
differently.

A group of revellers, well-behaved outdoor drinkers
really, became astonishingly quiet as he walked by them. He
turned and saw that they had run off, so went back and
picked up one of their bottles; a good strong cider.
Continuing on his way, he took a long swig and tossed the
empty over a wall.

Turning a corner, a middle-aged couple approached him
in the dim twilight, their faces sweating and anxious: *Officer,
officer, there's LOOTING going on up there, there that way,
are there more of you coming? Thank heavens you're here ...*

He looked at them seriously and said in his most sombre
voice: *Don't worry, it's all under control. Go to your homes.*
He saw their faces relax slightly.

As he walked on, the woman called after him: *but
Officer, you're going the wrong way, they're up on the High
Street ...*

Oh be quiet Agnes, the man must know what he's doing,
her husband muttered and led her off.

Despite his best efforts to keep a low profile, Jakey soon
stepped out of an alleyway to find himself in the middle of
another disturbance, having walked in the opposite direction
from the first one.

He stopped and hesitated, about to move back into the
darkness. But the eyes of the crowd only rested on him for a
second before they all scarpered, vanishing almost magically
like melting frost. An old man dropped a crate of beer onto
the broken glass underfoot and fled empty-handed. Various
other figures disappeared with piles of leather jackets
clutched to their chests.

Jakey stepped forward into the regained silence, and
knelt in a jeweller's shop window, raking amongst the glass
and silver with his torchlight. He found a silver locket on a
chain, gold wedding rings. Things that might have meant
something to respectable people. He pocketed these, and
running his torch over the remaining debris concluded that
most of the good stuff was gone already.

Walking on he heard another crowd closing in and turned up an alleyway to escape. Suddenly his ears were filled with alien sounds: some kind of scuffle was going on. Before his eyes could adjust or he could reach for his torch somebody grabbed him by the lapels and forced him up against a wall. *What's your fuckin' game, mate? Jist keep yer fuckin' trap shut and back off right outta here ...*

Jakey could smell the guy's breath he was so close, but sensed by his voice that he was quite young, more afraid than him. He could see a knife glinting near his face and make out now that a woman was struggling on the ground and another youth had his hand over her face, was ripping at her clothes, trying to rape her.

Then the youth holding him accidentally disturbed Jakey's belt with his other hand and the distinctive sound of the police radio rang out into the guilty hush. *Jesus Fuck!* the boys were startled and the woman bit her assailant on the neck. He fell back, screaming like a child. *He's fuckin' polis man, beat it, run ya eejit ye!*

They were gone. Jakey had done nothing. He continued to stand in the darkness for a moment breathing easily as the woman wept on the cobbled pavement at his feet. Curious, he put his torch on and walked towards her. Without making any conscious action he found that she had reached out and he had helped her to her feet. She fell against him and actually embraced him for a second before stepping back, sweeping her hair out of her tearful eyes. He looked at her without any emotion, neutral.

Oh thanks ... Jesus ... thank God ... those bastards ... they'd have raped me ... My car's stuck. I'm stranded. Oh God I didn't know what to do. The whole place seems to be going to pieces tonight. Can you get me out of here, help me, just get me to somewhere safe to stay even?

You'd've been awright ... Jakey said, turning away bored now, *those wee twats probably wouldnae huv been able to get it up anyroad. Gotta go now, sorry ...*

Stella was stunned for a moment as he walked off, then coming to her senses pursued him out into the street, the moonlight. *But you must do something to help me!* she said, clattering after him in her suddenly inappropriate heels.

Irritated, he turned and looked at her: *Look at ye ... dressed like yon ...*

She looked down and saw she was wearing a black miniskirt, white stockings, torn now, her work gear.

Nae wunder they thought ye wur up fur it. He shook his head and laughed to himself and walked on.

She kept after him: *But please help me, can you take me to the station at least? Shouldn't you be doing that? Taking my name and a statement?*

Jakey stopped in front of a jeweller's shop and eyed it carefully, then without bothering to look at Stella, continued: *Miss, ah don't think you get the story here ... ah've goat a joab tae dae. Bizness like.*

Well yes I can imagine you're all overstretched tonight ... Her voice trailed off as Jakey smashed the window and the alarm began wailing. She stared down, wide-eyed, her ears hurting from the noise, but too disconcerted to move away. Jakey walked about inside, scanning with his torch, and choosing the most promising pieces for his pockets.

Moving on, Stella stepped after him, her heart hollow and tired: *Who are you? What kind of policeman are you anyway?* She was almost talking to herself now, staring at the pavement, when to her surprise Jakey walked back and faced her.

Make yersel' useful ... he said.

She thought to herself he was quite handsome really, a rough diamond, as he pushed handfuls of jewellery into both her pockets and gestured to her to follow him. When some more revellers were startled by Jakey, he picked up the pure vodka they had left and drank a good mouthful straight from the bottle and passed it back to Stella who walked behind him like a shy orphan. He had some kind of plan clearly, and anyone with any idea at all was surely worth following on a night as black as this.

The bells of St Giles rang out as they passed and she noticed that he spat on the Heart of Midlothian. Stella lifted her eyes up towards the moonlit castle and remembered that she should have been celebrating New Year tonight. Taking another swig of hard spirits she hurried on to catch up with her nameless saviour and into her first day of *Twenty Twenty*.

Valerie Thornton

ELEVENSES

I'm still shaking.

I can't believe he'd do that to me – not deliberately anyway. He wasn't that kind of a gent. And I mean gent. He walked these streets of Kenmure like they were palace gardens and he always dressed up special to do so, with a good coat – heavy, mind – and his crimson silk scarf and gold bow tie. Dandy like, but Welsh, not English.

'Ah! How lovely to behold you!' he would say in his big round voice, standing back with his arms spread wide in admiration. 'If only I were fifty years younger, my dear.'

And me outside Malik's Minimarket in that fluorescent yellow coat with a six-foot lollipop in my hand – I ask you!

'Is that you, Madame ...' he'd call me Madame, French-like, the only person who's ever called me that. 'Is that you, Madame, your young charges all ferried to the safety of the bosom of learning?'

Bosom of learning! I had to laugh, Kenmure Street Primary School! Wee souls right enough, with that first-thing-in-the-morning look – sleepy, scrubbed, and cleaner and tidier than they'd be at dinner time or home time.

He'd take out this watch – d'you know? I never knew his name – he'd take out this gold watch on a chain from a wee pocket in his waistcoat – he was a waistcoat man too – and pop open the cover.

'Nine-thirty. Overtime again today, my dear,' he'd say. 'You'll surely get your reward in heaven, Madame, but if it were up to me, I'd make sure you got it long before then.'

I'd offer him a sweet – I usually have some left after the morning crossings. The wee ones don't seem so keen on them first thing, but dinner and home time, my pockets are emptied before I've crossed them all back again.

But he would never take anything from me. Instead, he'd slip a bar of chocolate or toffee or fudge or that lovely rum truffle into my coat pocket.

He always wrapped them in a wee brown paper bag – one from Malik's Minimarket – and it was a treat for me to unwrap it for my elevenses.

'For you, my dear Madame, we have to keep your
strength up. You're doing a very important job!'

Then I'd take him over. Not that he needed taken over
by me – but I liked to do that for him, stride out and
hold up my lollipop and make all the cars stop for him –
and he'd thank me and bow courteously on the other side
and wish me a good day, 'until we meet again, dear
Madame.'

I suppose because I saw him – we all did – every day, I
didn't notice the change. And winter can give you a pale skin
anyway. And sometimes the unevenness of the pavements –
and they're dreadful round here – can make you stumble a
little.

But today, he looked ill. No other word for it. Just ill –
a funny pale yellow colour, like old ivory, and a bluish tinge
to his lips.

'Are you okay?' I asked him.

'Bearing up, Madame, bearing up! The better for seeing
you, my dear,' he said, and slipped my elevenses treat into
my pocket.

But he was swaying and looking beyond me, like to
distant towers on the horizon, and yet there's nothing but
multi-storeys rising up all around us here. I reached out my
hand to him and was about to ask him again if he was okay,
when he crumpled and fell at my feet – his legs all wrong,
his good coat bunched up on the ground and his scarlet scarf
trailing in the dust.

We do first aid as part of our training, in case a wee soul
gets knocked down, God forbid, so I checked, but he wasn't
breathing. And I put my fingers on his neck, and there was
no pulse. I slipped my hand under his waistcoat – I can still
feel his warmth and the smoothness of the silky lining on
the back of my hand – but there was no heartbeat.

And Malik, when he saw what had happened, came
rushing out with a glass of water. He's a dear soul too. Then
a nurse, a proper nurse, came by but none of us could do
anything.

Like I said, I'm still shaking. I couldn't take my elevenses
– who could? – and Malik was shocked too. He said a prayer
for him there on the pavement, in his own special language,
before the ambulance came and took him away.

He knew, though. I know that now. I've only just opened

today's elevenses gift. I have it warming here in my hand, ticking like a tiny heartbeat.

And I feel grateful that he didn't drop in front of my wee ones, he was too much of a gent for that.

And sad that I didn't get to take him over for the last time.

I see him yet, bowing to me.

In memoriam: Crispin Allen, 1928–2001

LOOKING FOR BLANCHE DUBOIS

She must have stepped here once –
Decatur, Dumaine, Bourbon, Toulouse –
quartering the French Quarter
in humid heat
for gentlemen callers
lounging below black lace balconies
dripping with watered baskets
of bright ferns and white flowers.

Magnolia-scented handkerchief
to her nostrils, her satin heels
would rise above
the smell of stale beer and worse
from a sidewalk stained
with crushed green caterpillars,
their stings as voluptuous
as their jagged fur.

And what would she make of you,
Roselyn Lionheart, busking on Royal
with cheekbones to die for,
a nose hooked sweet as Brando's
and teeth so white
behind that big black voice
raising rhythms, and blues,
above sooty, salt-frosted armpits?

Affecting disdain, she'd tiptoe
silkily past, but linger
enchanted not by the lingerie
or liquor stores on the left there,
but by your House of the Rising Sun
which sends a tingle
all the way down
her whiter than white spine.

PLAYGROUND GAMES

She could chalk beds
in a flash
on the asphalt
with straight lines
and even boxes
and numbers as neat
as her brown polished shoes
and her playpiece pair
of chocolate digestives
carefully folded
in a white paper bag
by her fat-armed mum.

Her grandpa made gravestones
and a round peever
of white marble
with gilded initials
and two full stops
which eclipsed
our Cherry Blossom tins
weighted with earth.

She could skite her peever
to the dead centre
of any box
and hop and skim
with such precision
until her dad died
and was put in a box
and folded into the earth
under a gilded stone
and her mum's arms shook
and someone brought
skipping ropes instead.

Ryan Van Winkle

IT IS SUMMER AND IN CONNECTICUT THE GRILL IS GRILLING

Grandma roasts swordfish on the grill while smoking her
  death down.
Dad brings brown bags bursting with ripe tomatoes,
  zucchini, eggplants
from his prescribed garden. They eat off a long picnic table;
the same table Grandma danced on in that impossible
  photo from the Fifties
before she broke her hip.

The table has been painted many things: argument red,
family yellow, divorce brown. Today, it's just her favourite
  blue.
I think the corn will be sweet and its green husks will wait
  in the trash
for dinner's meaty remains. Eric won't touch the fish,
  neither will dad.
Burgers must be cooked.

They do not know the time in my zone.
Ghosts are in the sockets and they write to me of food: of
  Thanksgiving dinners,
Christmas hams, summer hot dogs. I could write about the
  yellow rings on the sheets,
the teeth in the pipes, all the light bulbs which have gone
  missing, the hair of the dog,
the colours of the rain I wear, the plaque on benches, the
  voices behind walls.
I send a letter, later, about nothing.

FALLING #147

The hum of the bar fridge over there
and all the bottles under the lights.

Tonight she left him
'cause she heard about Sara.

But Sara cut north and even the bartender
has gone out back to change a keg.

In the stillness he can suck his beer
till it is warm and flat. He can hear

his heart keep beating and think
for the first time in years.

THEY WILL GO ON

The western horizon is still lightning blue.
To the east, everything is side-of-the-bridge grey.
I am patient as trees and flowers, desert cacti.

The grand-kids hide inside with swollen eyes
and I want the rain to come quick, slap
their pale necks. I've counted the summers left

and the young should take this rain beside me
as I took father's wheat, corn, and whole bloody harvest.
I roll one more September cigarette,

Summer coughs her last cough; a dribble
from which the children hide to stay dry
as the rain loosens the soil.

Greg Whelan

VIRGIN MARIA

The world's big, right? *Bingo.* Science. Nature. Religion. Philosophy. Mathematics. Language. Love. They helpin'? Nah man. Yeh dinny understand the world 'til that wan definin' point. That moment when yur standin' on wan side eh the door, ind the meanin', *nah*, the understandin', is waitin' on the ither side. Ind yur reaching fur the door haundle, fuckin' touchin' it man – it's smooth, wahrum, invitin' – blood rushin' fi wan end eh yur body ti the err, excitement explodin' through yeh, anticipation eh this wan final push – it's cummin', it's cummin'! – bit then – *ring ring!* – the door's disappearin' man, it's fuckin' fawin' awaugh fi yeh ind yur jist watchin' it go, kinnin yersel, thit that's it, yur fucked. Yeh came close son, gid try, but nae coconut. Ind in that moment, yeh've missed it. Yeh've tried ti jump in front eh the train, but yur five minutes too early, ind it's jist pooin intae Markinch. Pick yursel' up son, it's over. Yeh getting' meh it aw? Nah, yeh probably willny. No 'til summin' happens ti yeh yursel, till summin' rips that door awaugh fi yur ragged, graspin' fingers.

Lit meh pit this in context fur yeh. Twah weeks ago, ah've done it. Ah'm a future English student at Edinburgh University. Aye, me, an English student at Edinburgh Uni, yeh fuckin' believe that? Ah canny. Ah canny believe thit ah've pood ma wey oot eh the dirt ind the filth ind the grime – ah've clawed masel tiwards the sun, ind ah'm finally gaspin' in the air – ah've got the envelope in mah haunds ind it's unconditional – ah've got mah maw ind mah gran in tears ind mah fer ind mah grandad beemin' – ah've got haund shakes, pats on the back ind well wishin' aw roond – *is that no terrific, ah always kint he'd dae it* – ah've – ah've – ah've – ah've – avé Maria. The best supportin' actress in this crumblin', heart wrenchin', fuckin' poor excuse fur a HEBS advert.

Yeh'll kin the story, even afore ah tell yeh. A short story long, it's a couple eh nights efter ah got mah unconditional right, ind me ind the lads get 'invited' – friend eh a friend kind eh hing, kin? – ti this pirty oot in the middle eh naewhere up the erse end eh Glenrothes. So wan wahrum twenty-four pack litter ind we're ridin' the spirits eh the last few days across a field tiwards an awready audible mish mash eh laughin', screamin' ind shite techno music. Ind ah'm lookin' it the lads, wi the sun poundin' doon, ind even though ah hink ah'm lookin at the least likely students ah've ever laid mah sorry een on, ah canny help but hink thit it wiz meant ti happen, thit somebody wiz gonny make it through eventually – thit it wiz a natural inevitability.

Anywey, we get ti the hoose, right, ind it's the kind eh pirty yeh eyways see in films, or on the telly. Yeh kin the type. The type yeh eyways look it ind go, *'pirties are never like that'*. Ind fur the most part yeh're right, but this wiz it, ah swear. A massive hoose, wi nae neighbours as faur as the eye could see, kegs in the kitchen – afore this man, ah'd never even seen a keg afore, ah thought it wiz jist an American hing, kin? – ind enough braw fok ti have meh wonderin' just where they've aw come fi si late in the game. So, we're makin' the grand tour eh the hoose, makin' share we're takin' foo advantage eh the free booze, ind ah hink it must hiv been somewhere aroond the upstairs bathroom queue thit ah first seen hur. Noo, ah've seen photies eh hur since, ind she's no the type ah usually go fur, but it the time, the absinthe ah got in the kitchen wiz tellin' me thit she wiz. Ah remember she hid this innocent, sweet, butter-wouldny-melt look on hur face thit totally dizny suit who she really is – or the gutted bottle eh Tesco vodka she wiz cradlin' in hur airms, fur that matter – but yeh kin what it's like – first impressions an' aw that. So the minute ah saw Maria, ah kint thit that was me, ah wiz gonny be focusin' aw mah energies that wey fur the rest eh the night. The rest eh the boys had obviously aw realised that as well as they'd suddenly disappeared in a cloud eh fuckin' smoke. So, withoot gon too much intae it, we got a bit banter gon, wan hing led to anither, and an 'oor later she wiz nibblin' ma ears ind fumblin' wi the studs on ma belt ind tellin' meh she loved meh ind thit she wanted meh. Ah mean, a man kin only resist si much.

The next mornin', ah woke up in some bed – ah dinny even kin if it wiz in the same hoose man, ah never looked back – ind ah lean err the body lyin' next ti meh – *must have been hur, still sweet smellin', fuckin' searin' ma nostrils, fuellin' the hang err* − and gave her a quick peck ind got the fuck oot eh there, ma heid swirlin'. Wan twenty-four oor sleep ind a fry-up later and am speakin' ti the friend eh a friend err the internet aboot the pirty, tryin' ti fill in the gaps, ind we git talkin' aboot Maria. He says he seen meh bein' dragged aff bi hur, ind he thought he'd let meh learn fi ma ain mistakes or some shite like that. Aye, cheers mate. So anywey, he starts bangin' on aboot hur ind hoo she's kint as 'Virgin Maria' at her skill, no simply fur the fact thit she isnae, but cos hur boyfriend − *Joe or some shite* − still believes hur when she tells um that he's the only cunt she's ever been wi. *Are yeh no worried?* Nah, am no. The cunt left skill in fourth year ti gon dae joinery or summin', ah kin the type. Ah figure thit wi the track record thit a friend eh a friend's been listin', it's no the first time thit Maria's exploits hiv went er his heid. Plus, ah'll be movin' oot ti the city in four months anywey, ind there'll no be too much chance eh meh bumpin' inti thum thair.

Anywey, a few months litter, and ah'm slouchin' on the couch doonstairs, half watching Jeremy Kyle, or Springer, or some ither judgemental garbage hosted by sanctimonious hypocrites, when mah phone − *ring ring, ring ring, ring ring, ring*:

> − Hullo?
> − ... Shaun? ... Is that Shaun? ...
> − Aye ... This is Shaun ...
> − It's Maria ... fi the party ...
> *Who? Fuck. What the fuck eh yeh phonin' fur?*
> − Aw aye ... Uh, hiya ... How ... Are yeh?
> [Ma stomach draps as she starts breakin' intae loud sobs]
> − Shaun ...
> *Oh shit ... Fuckin' hell, spit it oot! Virgin fuckin' Maria!*
> − Aye, Maria, what is it? Yeh awright?
> − Nut. Ah'm no ... Ah'm pregnant ...
> *Oh shit oh shit oh shit oh shit oh*
> − What'd yeh mean pregnant? Wi what? Like, wi a bairn?
> − Aye ...
> − Bit ... bit ... yeh said yeh were on the pill ...
> − Nah Shaun ...

Lyin' fuckin' bitch.
– YEH FUCKIN' DID!
[she starts wailin' ti meh noo] – CALM DOON
SHAUN! A wiz drunk, ind anywey, ah didny see you dashin'
oot fur a condom! It might no be yours anywey.
– Then why are yeh phonin'?
– Cos it might still be yours!

Err the past few minutes, several hings hid begun ti happen
aw at wance, mah mulched brain unable ti even begin ti
comprehend a single freight train eh thought. Mah stomach
felt like it was eatin' itsell. Uni was disappearin', replaced wi
the misery eh teenage pregnancy; a baby ah could never bring
masel' ti love without grudgin' fur the rest eh mah life, mixed
wi the horrors eh fetid cooncil flats ind furever hauntin'
whatifs – ma faimly's smiles ind congratulations replaced wi
tears ind heartbreak – *is that no awful? Ah always kint he'd
fuck it up* – ind a horrible feelin' eh failure thit maybe if
they'd jist emphasized 'the talk' jist that wee bit mare, it wid
have turned oot hoo it wiz meant tae, aw sunshine ind
fuckin' lollipops.

– Aye, but it still might be his though eh?
– Well aye, of coorse.
Yeh'd get an abortion though eh?
– Right, well hiv you thought what you're gonny dae
wi it?
– 'It'? Fuckin' 'It', Shaun? It's a human bein' fur Christs
sake!
No fuckin' yit it's no.
– Aye, ah kin, but hiv yeh thought aboot ... yeh kin, it?
– Fuck off! Ah'm no havin' an ... Ah'm no, Shaun. Joe's
gonny go wi meh ti Leven the morn ti the clinic jist aff the
High Street, yeh kin the wan? Ah've got an appointment it
nine in the mornin'.
– Aye, a kin the place ... the wan thit gee's the johnnys
oot?
– Yeh fuckin' kint that ind still yeh never hid wan on
yeh it the pirty?
Tit.
– ... D'yeh want meh ti come wi yeh tae?
Please no, God no.

– Whoar?
– Yeh kin, the clinic.
[Click. Bzzzzzzzzzzzt]
Thank fuck.

Noo yur startin' ti see jist whit a wiz bangin' on aboot it
the start eh? What aw that empty philosophisin' wiz aboot?
Well it is fuckin' empty. Awhing. Jist try and say ti yersel thit
it's no. This is aw too much man. Ah need a lie doon, far
awaugh fi Jeremy Kyle's condescendin' pish. Ah bet it must
bi awfy black and white for aw the righteous cunts in the
world.

Ah get upstairs ind mah pilleh feels like a fuckin' vice,
squeezin' ma hed on bith sides. Right. It's done noo. It's aw
done. She's done. Am done. It's done. Yeh want fries wi that?
Bit where does it go fi here? Could ah face aw this? Could
ah really be the dad noo thit ah want ti be ten years doon the
line? Ah'm ah jist bein' over dramatic hinkin' ah could never
bring masel to love It's wee sonsy face? *Abortion. Abortion.
Abortion abortion abortion abortion. Get it flushed oot, yeh
kin still mak it ti Uni. Mon! What's wi the conscience noo?
Mind when yeh stood up in yer religious studies class in fourth
year, arguin' against aw the pro-life – mainly birds eh? –
cunts across the desk fi yeh?* What if she's right? Murderer?
Me? Naw. Dad? Noo? *Naw. Might no even be yours yet, stop
panickin' yersel', breathe normal.* Ah canny. Whit if it is
mine?

Ah sit the rest eh the day, no even hinkin'. Just sittin'. I
might no even have been sittin'. Ah canny mind. Jist a fuzz.
Mah maw comes back. Starts rattlin' pots ind pans. A wee
while later ah hear mah dad cloddin' his work bits aff it the
front door, eager fur the tea sittin' on the table fur him. No
a thought ti thersels. Ah couldny dae it. Ah cannae taste
anyhing, jist a few bites ti show face ind try ind fight the
taste eh bile in the back eh mah throt. Mah maw's gassin' ti
mah dad aboot somebody or ither's daughter bein' knocked
up – *terrible. Her sae smart tae* – Even if Maria is up the
duff, they'll still hae tae find oot. Everybody will. Just as bad,
it's nae option. Canny stey here … *Thump thump thump
thump thump* … Next hing ah kin ah'm upstairs, hyperventa-
latin', feelin' like ah'm gonnae spew mah fuckin' guts oot.
Ah want tae crawl up the fuckin' waughs and hing masel' fi

the light fittin' – *Easy wey oot* – Yeh hink this is easy? God. God'll save meh – *yeh hypocritical cunt* – Doon on mah knees. Repent. REPENT! Ask fur a door oot – ask thit she's no pregnant – ask thit it's no mine – ask thit it's never born – *Impossible! Natural inevability!* – ask thit she's hit by a car – fuckin' anything man. Jist fuckin' help meh! *C'mon! Dae it right! Cross yer chest! Say yeh'll be a gid boy fur the rest eh yer days! C'mon! Dae it like aw the ither atheists!* Please God! Please God! Please God!

Ah must have managed ti faw asleep sometime efter that cos the next hing ah remember ah'm sittin' on a couch in front eh a studio audience ind ah'm absolutely shittin' it. Maria's sittin' next to me, but she disny look normal. Hur stomach's fuckin' massive ind hur usual hairdresser look's been replaced wi a couple eh layers eh foundation ind a cheap shitey tracksuit. Ah'm just aboot ti comment when ah realise ah'm clad in treckies tae and ah've got it least four chakit gold rings on, ridiculously emblazoned wi the mockin' faces eh saints and holy figures. Beyond the rings, ah've got mah fingers clasped through Maria's on the haundle eh a pram, but it's empty, except for summin' thit looks like soil. Ah look oot intae the audience, squintin' ma een through the blindin' studio lights. Ah kin only see silhouettes bit somehoo ah kin that it's ma faimily and friends sittin' oot there. Ah kin literally feel their een fuckin' borin' intae meh.

– So it says here that the pair of you had sex without contraception. Now Mary is one month pregnant.

Ah look up and stare straight intae the mirror. Ah'm staundin' there in a cheap suit wi a microphone ind a stupid fuckin' mortar board on mah heid. Err the tap eh this, ah can hear a chorus eh *oooohhhs* fi the audience.

– Nah, that's no hoo it happened! We thought thit ... It wisny on purpose! Ind hur fuckin' names' Maria!
– So it says here that the pair of you had sex without contraception. Now Mary is two months pregnant.
Oooooooohhhh
– Ah swear! We didny kin! It's no like yeh read in the pippers!

– So it says here that the pair of you had sex without contraception. Now Mary is three months pregnant.
Ooooooohhhh

Ah look at Maria. Hur face is cheery and glazed, like an innocent china doll or summin'. Ah start feelin' masel wellin' up, ind it's gettin' harder ind harder tae breath. The cheap Argos necklace aroond ma neck feels like it's gettin' tighter ind tighter. Ah look inside the pram ind see tiny green stems pokin' through the darkness, pushin' up tiwards the studio lights.

– So it says here that the pair of you had sex without contraception. Now Mary is four months pregnant.
Ooooooohhhh
– This canny be! It canny!
– So it says here that the pair of you had sex without contraception. Now Mary is five months pregnant.
Ooooooohhhh
– Dinny yez look at meh like that! Yeh fuckin' judgemental hypocrites! We aw mak mistakes!
– So it says here that the pair of you had sex without contraception. Now Mary is six months pregnant.
Ooooooohhhh
– Shut it! Shut it! Shut it the lot eh yehs!

Ah canny tak it anymare. Ah feel mah cheeks burnin' wi tears, fast ind heavy. *No on telly, no on telly ...* Looking up, ah see mah friends' silhouettes gettin' up ind dissapearin' one by one. Noo there's only four folk left in the audience. Maria's started leanin' err the pram, pushin' summin' smaw doon in ti the soil wi hur thingertip.

– What eh yeh daein'?
– Ah canny furget ti tak ma pill!
– So it says here that the pair of you had sex without contraception. Now Mary is seven months pregnant.
Ooooooohhhh
– Leave meh alaine man! It's no mah fault! She said weh'd be fine! She's no fuckin' innocent! Look it hur like that is well!

– So it says here that the pair of you had sex without contraception. Now Mary is eight months pregnant.
Oooooooohhhh

Somewhere aroond the studio the low wailin' eh a weein is startin' ti rise. Ah look intae the pram again, but there's nuhing bit floors pokin' oot the dark. The wailin's getting louder, fillin' mah heid. The shrill cry risin' in pitch, piercin' mah eardrums ind pokin' mah brain. Ah look roond but naebody else seems tae notice.

– So it says here that the pair of you had sex without contraception. Now Mary is nine months pregnant.
Oooooooooooooooooooooooooohhhhhhhhhhhhhhhh cummin'! Cummin'!

Then the studio starts shakin' violently, the rumbles increasin' wi the wailin' eh the bairn, so ah grab on ti the airms eh mah chair ind hod on like it's the end eh the world. Ah look over it Maria's glazed, rosy cheeks, hur smilin' eyes still lookin' forward. Slowly she starts ti open hur legs, the wailin' getting' louder still. The lights in the studio are beginnin' ti smash as the earthquake rips through it. There's a sudden rippin' noise ind Maria's treckies begin fawin' ti bits as thick, thorned roots start pushin' their wey oot fi between hur thighs. Ah start screamin', but it's only droont oot by the wailin' fillin' mah ears. The roots are speedin' oot faster and faster, mah een transfixed, their thick barbed airms spreadin' er the waughs and roof like veins – ind ah'm screamin' louder ind louder as ah see mare eh the thorned roots burstin' oot eh the soil in the pram ind the stage aroond us. Ah look err it Maria's porcelain smile bein' speckled wi crimson – *Fuck fuck fuck ah didny mean it ah didny what the fuck is this mak it stop mak it stop mak it fuckin' stop!* – ind ah watch in terror iz the thick twisted roots work their wey aroond ind intae the audience – wrappin' thumsells aboot ma faimily's bodies, pooin' thum apert – ind ah try ti staund up bit their wrappin' thumsells around ma airms ind legs – pooin' me back – bindin' meh ti the flair – ind Maria's bloodied, battered body's climbin' on top eh meh – *ah love yeh, ah want yeh, ah need yeh Shaun!* – Ah sit up, back in mah room it the fit eh mah bed, a sweatin' shakin', greetin' mess. *Ah hiv ti go ti the clinic the morn, ah need ti kin!* Ind wi that, a faw on ti ma bed and pass oot fur the night, exhausted.

Ah wake up the next mornin' feelin' brand new. Then ah remember, ind it's like fawn doon a well in the middle eh the desert. Mah backs soakin'; ah roll oot eh the puddle eh sweat ah've been lyin' in ind go doonstairs fur a shower. Sittin' there wi the shower thunderin' doon on mah head, fillin' ma senses, ah start hinkin' aboot the next step. Should ah phone Maria? Tell hur ah'm gon? Should a jist show up, fuck hur boyfriend? Ten minutes later ind ah'm sittin' in front eh a bowl eh cereal, secretly hopin' it chokes meh. Mibbeh it'd be easier. Ah look at the clock – *Shit! Ah've only got twenty minutes ti get doon there!* Quickly, ah scrape the cereal in ti the bin, grab ma coat ind dash oot the front door, mah mind fuckin' swimmin'. Anither ten minutes litter ind ah'm fuckin' swimmin' tae. Never even thought ah might need a jacket runnin' doon through wind ind hailmary.

Efter carefully contemplatin' mah options, ah decide ti wait a wee bit doon the street, see what the crack is. It's no long bifore ah see Maria steppin' aff the bus. Hursel'. *The fuckin' cunt's jist ditched her!* But jist iz ah'm aboot ti run err, ah see some hulkin' brute steppin' aff the bus ind swingin' his lumberin' airm aroond hur. Fuck. He's huge. A fuckin' fridge. *Go fur it then tough cunt!* Ah dinny. Mah bottle draps ind ah walk hame, feelin' worse than ah did before. No the solution ah wiz lookin' for.

When ah get back, ah decide ti fire Maria a text message thit takes meh the next twah hoors ti carefully craft. Efter much debatin', editin' and rewritin' – *Canny make it too obvious incase Big Joe sees it, but canny make it too abstract in case she disny tell yeh what yeh want ti kin* – ah finally perfect it:

?

Ah hit send ind go through ti the livin' room. Efter switchin' on the telly ind bein' bombarded wi pregnancy test adverts, ah decide ti sit in the dark fur the next three oors, the only hing keepin' meh awake bein' the smell eh the new paint fi the games room next door.

Why the fuck is she no textin' back? Did she no get yir text? Diz she no care? Mibbeh it's gid news? Mibbeh Big Joe's foond oot. Mibbeh yur fucked. Ah sit up ind grab mah phone. Should ah text hur again? Too much? Beep beep. Thank fuck man! Quickly, ah scroll through the million menus eh ma phone ind finally reach hur text:

Soz bbz, havn a nitemare. Def preg bt 1 o Joes pals tld him they hrd ive bn seein other folk and he went raj in the clinic. Says he wnts me 2 dna test. Clinic said I can do sum pre natal patern test or sumthin after 12 wks. Goin 2nite. Txt later xx M xx

Shit. Definitely pregnant. Bit that wizny botherin' meh si much. There's still a chance thit It's his. Bit he kins? He hid haunds like fuckin' clubs! Aw man, if he finds oot it's me – *He probably awready kins! Yeh wereny the only two it the pirty yeh fuckin' knob. Yeh hink nae cunt else seen yehs like?* Ah curl up on the flair in front eh the couch like the pithetic piece eh shit ah am. Fuck man, he's gonny pit me in a box – six fit under man – back in the dirty groond – jist food fur the worms ind the beetles ind the earth – strippin' the deed fertiliser fi mah smashed-up bones – just anither step in the natural cycle – he's probably awready got it dug man – soft wet mound – *who could resist?* – Cunt! How could aw this hiv happened si fast?

Ah grab ma phone, hinkin' eh who ah could tell who wouldny fuckin' spread it like fire. Need ti git it aff mah chest. Ah end up geein' friend eh a friend a phone, but ti nae avail. So ah start scrollin' through ma phone book till ah settle on Big Craig, then it least if Big Joe came knockin' litter on the night ... *Fuckin' coward.* Thankfully ah manage ti get him in. We git banterin' ind he says him ind a few eh the lads would fire roond ind see meh the night. Ah try tae object but he's hivin' nin eh it, so ah figure thit since solitude's no done meh much gid, ah might as well. Ah pit the phone doon ind decide ti mak masel' summin' ti eat. Efter rakin' through the cupboards fur whit seemed like hoors, ah finally settle that eggs are aboot as far as ah kin go.

As ah start pittin' the toast on ind crackin' the eggs intae a fresh, clear glass, mah mind drifts back ti the conversation

ah'd hid wi Maria. Hid it really been si wrang eh meh ti
suppose she'd get an abortion? *Crack.* Ah mean, wur only
young ind it's a big fuckin' responsibility fur anybody, let
alone us. Should ah feel proud eh hur fur bein' si
determined? Or angry at hur naivety? Force hur ti dae it?
Crack. Wid it really hiv been si different fi the mornin' efter
pill? Or even jist the normal pill or a johnny? Are they no
unnatural tae? Ah reach intae the fridge ind grab the milk,
splashin' the creamy whiteness intae the eggs. *Whit kind eh
eggs are yeh wantin'?* Should ah poach thum? Or boil thum
slowly, carefully pickin' thum oot eh their shells when their
done? Nah, too much hassle. Ah finally jist decide tae
scramble the eggs, it's easiest efter aw. Anywey, ah realise
ah've awready cracked the eggs ind pit the milk in. Wizzny
fuckin' hinkin'. Reachin' intae the drawer, ah find a fork ind
start beatin' the eggs. Ah'm ah jist bein' a cunt expectin' that
eh hur? Is thur really a universal right or wrang? It's her
body ... Ah look doon at mah eggs ind suddenly dinny feel
sae hungry. Ah end up drappin' thum in the bin ind
discardin' thum. Whit a waste. Ah eat mah toast ind go back
upstairs fur a lie doon.

Half seven ind ah've still no heard fi her. Again, ah
canny work oot if that's a gid hing or a bad hing. *It
least Big Joe's no came knockin' yet, that's got ti count fur
summin'* – aye, especially since Big Craig's no appeared yet
either.

   – Shaun?
   – Aye Dad?
   – Yeh've got three wise men doon here waitin' ti see
yeh ind they're bearin' gifts!
   – Aye? Ah'll crack the jokes! Send thum up!

Speak eh the Devil ind he's sure tae appear – *Speak eh God
and yeh've nae chance.* Ah look at mah phone again.
Nuhing.

*Thumpthumpthumpthumpthumpthumpthumpthumpthump
thumpthumpthump.*

   – Whoar've yehs been yeh cunts? What took yehs?

    – Wi got caught behind the fuckin' Starr bus aw the wey doon fi Glenrothes man, sorry. Yeh heard fi hur yet?
    – Nah man.
    – Nae worries, yeh will. We've got summin' fur yeh.
    – Aw cheers boys.

A twenty-four pack wiz the first gid hing ti happen in what felt like furever. Ah thought ah wiz gonny greet. Well, mibbeh no, bit thur wiz definitely summin' gon on.

    – Wi thought it'd dae yeh whether it wiz gid news or bad.

Ah kint straight awaugh thit it hidny helped bein' on ma ain, ind thit ah should've jist done this fi the start. There wis nae judgement, nae cynicism, nae guilt. They kint it could hiv easily been any wan eh thaim, ah jist picked the short straw. Iz wi got banterin' it got clearer ind clearer thit it wiz a shot in the dark thit it hidny happened ti thaim tae it the pirty. Mibbeh it was fate. Mibbeh wan eh us needed it tae happen, bring us aw tae oor senses. Though dinny get me wrang, ah wiz still sare ah'd got stung ind nae cunt else hid.
    Anywey, wi tanned a few tinnies in mah room till Craig pit it forward thit wi should hae a game eh pool, tak oor minds aff the absence eh the phone call. Nae objections later ind wur headed doonstairs ti the games room. When wi get thair, wi find an empty, not un-hospitable room, void eh any recognition ti meh. The earlier whites eh the waughs hid vanished under a mare mature ind sultry deep red, the smell eh fresh paint hauntin' meh wi images ind emotions eh the blurry days before.

    – Dad! Whoar's the pool table went?
    – Eh?
    – The pool table. Whoar's it went?
    – Aw right. It got moved when weh wur decoratin'.
    – ... Ti?
    – There wis nae spare room in the hoose so the Shepherds' next door took it in their garage. Gon ask thum, ah'm sure they'd still let yeh play.

We walked oot the front door, slowly makin' oor wey ti

the Shepherds', enjoyin' the comfort eh the wahrum summer air, the memories eh that night in the field driftin' back on the gentle zephyrs – *the night before life wiz complicated.* It aw seemed si different. Ah seemed si different, ah felt different, ah hink ah'm even hinkin' different. Even lookin' it the boys around meh, ah felt the urge ti blurt oot summin' definin', summin' ti pin it doon, bit ah'm startin' ti use a bit eh restraint, discipline, ah realise noo thit the world's no that easy and it never will be. Reachin' the hoose, we see Mr Shepherd in his girdin ind he tells us jist ti feel free ti help oorsells, ind no ti mind the clutter aw aboot us.

So thair we wur, me ind the three wise men waitin' in the Shepherds' garage fur a text fi Maria, or a beatin' fi Big Joe, when the phone finally goes:

Hi Shaun, srry this took so lng. Testing took 4 eva. Jst 2 let you no, got results and its no urs. Joes 4got aboot b4, says he cnt believe it, hes a dad! Were keeping it and he says hell mrry me in the summer. Enjoy uni. M

... Jesus fucking Christ.

Ian Nimmo White

A QUEEN AND I
(at Lochleven Castle)

*Queen Elizabeth the First imprisoned her cousin Mary, Queen
of Scots, for nineteen years before signing her death warrant.
In all that time she couldn't pluck up the courage to visit her
fellow queen. It remains to this day the one stain on the
reputation of a woman widely regarded as the greatest
monarch England ever had.*

> Lang afore the watter wis laiched,
> she hud nae trees nor gress
> tae saunter in ootside the waas.
>
> And three missin flairs abune ma heid,
> she'd dowped, for the weir o time,
> tae the chackin o her wyvin wires.
>
> Leastweys she hud a vizzy.
> Oor English freends wid caa it
> panoramic – braw, aa roond.
>
> The wund seuched and birled itsel
> up and atoor the shell o stane.
> Ah luiked thru the glessliss windae
>
> the lenth o Burleigh Saunds
> whaur she wis oared, wan week o scowth
> and nineteen years o jile aheid.

Long before the water was lowered,
she had no trees or grass
to wander in outside the walls.

And three missing floors above my head,
she'd bent, to pass the time,
to the clicking of her knitting needles.

At least she had a view.
Our English friends would call it
panoramic – beautiful, all round.

The wind soughed and wound itself
up and around the shell of stone.
I looked through the glassless window

as far as Burleigh Sands
where she was rowed, one week of freedom
and nineteen years of jail ahead.

Jane Whiteford

SLIPPAGE

I am losing my grip. Winching me up, my brother-in-law
heaves me over the side of the bath, straining against gravity
as he deposits me under the shower. Clambering in, he
switches on the water and gathers me up to the spray. I lean
against him, breathe in the damp skin of his neck, and watch
glass drops fly. He smells of stale tobacco, offering a luxurious
memory of suck and burn. Attached, conjoined, we waltz to
get soap and cloth. He holds me with one arm around my
waist while using the free hand to soap me down; I hang on
to the side rail to take some weight. Bony as a barstool, he
sets to work on me. Beads of water accumulate at the edge of
his fringe, trickle down his nose and, after a brief pause, leap
off in single file. I know the large purple vein at the side of
his forehead; it snakes sideways around his temple, and
upwards to nest in a thicket of hair: I have stared at it for
years. A whiff of fish slips under the door.

There are compulsory requirements when we congregate:
the constitutional walk, copious amounts of red wine, pizza
for those not yet come of age, and, well, fish. When the kids
were little they sat at the table while I prepared the food.
Waiting until they were settled and ready for 'the game', I
would pick up the fish, bring it close and let its jaw drop
open. Usually they took off with scream-studded statements
of disgust and hilarity: 'Yeuch, they're disgusting!' Or, more
blatantly, 'That stuff's minging!'; but sometimes they would
wait for me to act the poor ventriloquist, watching with
wide-eyed blinks as the fish shouted for help, and then sheer
mayhem would break out: shrieking as they scattered to
different rooms. Sauntering in to the kitchen, a cigarette
dangling from his lip, Mr Bony Man would chastise me for
upsetting the kids, and hand me a large drink. He would lean
against the counter with one arm outstretched, and give me
a full account of why we were in the grand state we were in:
the world at war; environmental devastation; globalisation
and the social disintegration of local communities. His glass
waved about wildly without a drop being spilt. During all of
this the slate-grey corpse lay there with its mouth gaping
open as if it had something to say.

'Can you put your arms around my neck?' says my brother-in-law.

Over his shoulder, there is a picture of my father smiling as he presents a large salmon. I am not born; I am waiting in the wings for a night when my father wants to laugh with my mother, instead of at her.

The rare times I saw the old man animated was after he had been walking in the hills. My father adored a run-down old tourist resort in the north. I thought this was something to do with the similarities between them: empty, abandoned, with visitors rarely wanting to stay and, when they did, leaving early with an agreement not to return. This remained relatively unchanged. I rarely thought a visit worth the effort, even in the passing. On the rare occasions I saw him the hours stretched out to extend the pain. He would have a lunch during the day consisting of mince and potatoes. Before cooking he would ask how many potatoes I would eat. I can remember standing at the bleak oak fireplace trying to fathom whether it was one, two or three and what would be the problem, really, if I miscalculated. He had one photograph on a side table of the two of us at the caravan. I might have been four or five and this was the only visible relic of our time together.

At the caravan he would go off for the day as I sat at the window, breathing on the glass, drawing faces in the moisture, and waiting for him to come back. One day, he tapped the window, beckoning me to come outside. I ran to the door, stuck my feet in my wellies, and flung myself onto the tiny green garden patch. He stood with a rod in each hand and declared he was taking me fishing.

I walked beside him breathing in soap and hair cream and trees. Standing to attention at the side of the river, I watched carefully as he attached the metal lure, unleashed some of the wire and cast the line as far as he could manage. Linking his arms with mine, we held the rod together as he whipped the line back and it arched through the air, landing in the water with a plop. Side by side we stared into the distance and momentarily caught each other's eye. He smiled. 'I think it'll be a big one today, lad.' I nodded furiously as I held my rod slightly above my shoulders to avoid snagging. I turned to see him shuffling back and forwards, arms up and down in some weird dance with the pole. He had caught a fish, like the ones I had seen in tanks, only bigger and less colourful, leaping in and out of the water.

'It's alive!' I shouted.

He picked up a small net and moved towards the shore. On a short lead, he ladled it out of the water and flung it towards a grassy patch away from the river. Dropping my rod I ran to it. After a few seconds of flipping from side to side the fish was motionless apart from the mouth. I lay down beside it. My father was nearby. 'Get a stick and thump it, if you want,' he said. With my cheek pressed against gravel, I watched the mouth open and close. 'Breathe,' I whispered. 'Breathe,' I said again. It stared out with forced grimace and glass eye. I stroked its slimy skin and saw a rainbow dance on its back.

'A trout, lad. We've just caught a trout.'

'It's dead,' I said.

'Well of course it's dead.'

'I want it to live.'

'Fish can't breathe out of water.'

'Why not?'

'You know why not. They can't breathe air; they take in water. If you take them out of the water they can't get the oxygen.'

'But there's oxygen in the air!'

'They can't use their gills out of water. Take them out of their own environment and they can't survive. It's that simple, son.'

On the way home I carried the fish in a plastic bag. It swung from side to side, batting against my leg to remind me of what I had done. As my dad put the kettle on I went to the woods at the back of the park and dug a small hole with my hands. I slipped the fish in the dirt, said sorry and covered it in mossy soil.

We sat eating jam pieces and drinking sweet tea.

'Where's the fish?' he said, steam from the cup fogging his glasses.

'I don't know.'

'Yes you do.'

'No I don't.'

'Yes you do.'

'No I don't!' I said, thinking that I was doing well to keep up.

'We don't need any melodramatics in this family. We've got enough of that from your mother.'

'What does that mean?'

'What?'

'Melodramatics.'

'Never mind that, where's the fish?'

'Heaven.'

'Don't be daft. Tell me where it is!'

'I don't know where it is.'

'You're lying.'

'I'm not.' He caught my eye and I looked away.

'You can tell a man's lying because he can't look you in the eye.'

I concentrated on the window, thinking of the fish lying in the dirt where it does not belong, keeping it in a place it cannot breathe.

The trips to the caravan faded after a few years, as did my father. Coming home from work, he would sit by the fire and, and within minutes, he would be gone: a thin ghost above his head. For a long time I would not open the windows or the door for fear his spirit would flee out of the house and never be found. I envisaged it silently floating over streets and houses and fields. Of course I knew I would raise the alarm, and a search party would trawl the faraway hills. And he would keep drifting through the mist and the clouds and air, making sure he would never come back to the place where he was supposed to live: with me.

My mother used to say, not long before she left (and came back again), she had seen him muttering away to himself just like the folk who get out of the mental hospital too soon. She said he needed a doctor because when he was in company you could not get a word out of him, yet put him in the middle of nowhere with a wild wind going and he would chunter for hours as if the mountains had ears. On hearing this, my father smirked at her, not insulted on this occasion by my mother's remarks. 'That's right,' he had said, 'blah, blah, blah. Your hot air gets in to everybody's ears and that's why people know our business; but you go to the hills, try it, go there: one, they listen better than any of the half-wits you spend your time with, and two, it stops there. You don't get a man's opinion on something you don't want his opinion about.'

I would have listened. But to my father everyone was sent to irritate or disappoint.

Oddly enough my mother followed the advice after her return. I had asked her where she had been and she replied that it was for her to know and for me to find out. This confused me because I was trying to find out by asking her. I was told that she ran off with Mr Alexander from the newsagent – which was also a poodle parlour on Wednesday afternoons as the shop shut early – and that they returned three months later. The matter was never discussed in the house again: the relentless silence a lead weight of incrimination. Over the years, my mother's change was surreptitious and so slow that I struggle to remember what she was like before Mr Alexander. Day after day I thought there was little change and then, when I stopped to look, I barely recognised the silent woman with the slip dangling below her skirt and tartan legs splayed at the fire. Retrospect, always helpful and always, inherently, too late, taught me that I had lost my mother because she came back, and my father because he stayed.

I bet they have overcooked it. It is easy to do and utterly avoidable. A simple task: keep the heat down and the time in the oven short. Everything should be prepared and ready when the fish goes in. And, when the minutes have passed, unwrap it from the foil to see steam rising from skin and bunches of charred thyme sticking out a gashed gullet. It is ready.

There is a constant thump behind my right eye as if my heart has relocated itself. In the not too distant future, when they open up my chest, to their surprise they will realise it has moved. No doubt, after the irreconcilable job of autopsy, the elusive muscle will be finally found parked in front of my brain. And with everything accounted for, the redundant items packed away, they will go for lunch: everybody starting the afternoon with a full stomach.

Now the hands and feet are numb. I pull on him to increase movement without losing balance and allow blood to flow, fingers and toes to be resuscitated. Mr Bony Man does not say as much these days. I am sure a war pretending

not to be a war is still going on, and that the monarchy
continues to live off our taxes, but he has become reticent in
his global dissention; instead he tells me about homoeopathy
and reiki massage and meditation. I want to kiss his brow
with the protection I offered my newborns. I think better of
it. In a momentary flash I can see a dire twist of fate when
he turns to face me and my lips are pursed at the ready. I
would apologise extensively and suggest the puckering up
was an aberration, stating the drugs addled my brain. The
moment is gone. I pull back to see his clenched jaw.

'You're standing on my toes,' he says.

'Sorry.'

I do not know where to place my feet when we are
locked together, embracing in a bath with the available foot
space of a doormat.

'Are you okay?' he says.

'Yes, make it hotter.'

'We won't be doing this for a while,' he says, wiping
the dripping fringe from his eyes.

'You might not but I'll be surrounded by a gaggle of
nurses the next time I'm in a bath.'

'Aren't you the lucky one?'

'You've got to be kidding. It's like being encircled by a
soap opera. You don't want to interrupt the TV ladies or
they'll take a wire brush to you and they won't use it on
your neck.' It's good to see him laugh.

'Pass the shampoo,' he says.

'No.'

'The shampoo or the wire brush!'

'The brush. You never know, I might like it.'

'Please ...' The water jumps around his shoulders and he
looks like a rag doll with his wet stringy hair and puckered
skin. I pass the shampoo, hunching down, holding on to the
taps as he starts to massage my scalp in gentle, rhythmic
motions. My eyes are shut tight as sheets of water slide round
the side of my face and the rest spews over the top of my head.
I open my mouth, breathe in, search for air, and find chunks
of water. I'm choking and gagging. I inhale the chemical
liquid, gasping. He tilts my head up as I cough and splutter.

'Come on, spit it out,' he says, as if I am chewing gum
in class.

'I can't breathe!'

'Cough it up.'

'I'm trying to breathe!' He wipes his face as I splutter, and I glower at him.

'You're spitting on me,' he says.

'No I'm not, the bloody shower is spitting on you.'

'Time for us to go.'

'Us? Go? Go where? You're not going anywhere.'

'I didn't mean that.'

He leans back to face me. 'I don't know what to say.'

'You don't have to say anything.' I push up against the tiles and slip down again. He moves to me. 'Leave me alone, I can do it myself.' I start hitching myself up again and he catches me on the slide down to the taps.

'You're cold,' he says.

I nod. 'Time to get out, I'm tired.'

We reach for the railing and I slip: my head bangs off the metal pole, an elbow hits cold stone with a crack and knees buckle. I shout in pain as one leg goes from under me and thin, brittle hands attempt to break the fall.

Familiar and fresh pain teases my assessment of location and type of injury. The throb behind the eye is working to full capacity while an involuntary tremor takes over my right hand. I contemplate moving although staying still feels the safer option. I check him for collateral damage. He is waxen and holding one hand out in an open gesture, almost in explanation, while the other tugs at a small piece of hair above his ear.

'I dropped you. I couldn't hold on. I ... I let you go.'

'You didn't drop me. I slipped.'

'But I'm meant to look after you.'

'You are not *meant* to do anything.'

'You know what I mean.'

'You do look after me.'

'Sorry,' he says.

'Don't apologise.'

'Sorry.'

I narrow my eyes in admonishment and see he is tempted to say it again.

'It's not your fault,' I say, trying not to blame him.

'What if you're really hurt?'

'You mean what if it's serious?' I look up at him, smiling. 'I think we could cope, don't you?'

'I nearly stopped breathing,' he says.

Lying there, wedged in, I'm back in a cot, arms outstretched, ready to be picked up and carried out. I draw myself on to one knee. 'Give me a hand up.' I nod at the open arm, '– before I disappear down the bloody plughole.' Wincing, struggling to control the shaking, I grip both the man and the shower rail. He eases me out with raspy reassurances that it will be all right. I look at him and he looks away.

Christopher Whyte

GU BÀRD ÒG ALBANNACH, A SGRÌOBH GUR E SUIDHEACHADH ÀRAID A TH' ANN NUAIR A BHIOS NEACH EÒLACH AIR A' CHÀNAIN ÀS A THA E EADAR-THEANGACHADH

Nach mìorbhaileach a bhiodh e, bha thu sgrìobhadh,
ach ùine gu leòr a bhith aig sgrìobhadair
cumanta, stuama mar thu fhèin, airson
a' chànain ionnsachadh, a chleachd am bàrd
a b' àill leat a dhàintean eadar-theangachadh!

Ach chan e sodalan no flath a th' annad,
chan eil thu neo-thruacant', do-lùbtha, sgrìobh thu,
mar a tha mise, 's tu nad dhuine maoth,
strìochdach. A bharrachd air sin, tha uimhir
a ghnothaichean agad, le do bhàrdachd fhèin,

is leis an rannsachadh as feumail rithe...
Cha tuig thu idir carson a nì mi casaid
ma bhios tu, no fear dhed cho-oibrichean,
fear nach eil' aig', an truaghan! ach dà chànain,
sealladh mun cuairt air, feuch an lorg e tionndadh

rinneadh mar thà gu Frangach, no gu Beurla,
as urrainn dhà Bheurla shnog fhèin a chur air.
Bha mi smaoineachadh air na coin sa chèidse,
a' sìor ruith timcheall 's a' dèanamh comhartaich
ùpraidich, ach an uair a thèid an doras

fhosgladh, nach mhosgail bhon an àite, 's fios
aca gum faigh iad pailteas bìdh co-dhiù.
No air a' chaileig mhàlda, is làn-mheadhrach,
a ràinig, gun lorg dhe ruadhadh air a gruaidh,
obair-lann nan eadar-theangaichear

gun aon teanga fhileant' aic' ach Beurla,
is i 'na suidhe gu socair ri taobh bàird
a bha cur Beurla siùbhlaich, air a son,
air a chuid ranntan fhèin, a sgrìobh i sìos
's an dèidh sin bhiodh i toiseachadh ag obair.

Dè 'n obair a bh' aice? Cur Beurla air Beurla.
Am faod sinn ràdh gur eadar-theangachadh
a bha i trang leis? Shaoil mi air na h-uairean,
na làithean, seachdainean a chur mi seachad
's mi crom air gràmairean is faclairean,

a' lorg facail seach facal, 'g ionnsachadh
òrdugh ùr nan litir ann an cànain
aig a bheil aibidil as diofaraicht'.
Thàinig gum chuimhne bùth an Sarajevo
le dà leabhair a fhuair mi ann, ach nach

do cheannaich, chionns gu robh mo chompanach
cho imisgeach mun deidhinn. Faclair Laitbhis
gu Ruiseanais a bh' anns a' chiad fhear dhiubh,
is bha 'm fear eile a' toirt mìneachaidh
air gach dòigh-labhairt Thurcaich bha ga cleachdadh

sna dùthchannan sin ris a chanadh neach
uaireigin Iugoslàbhia. (Cheannaich mi
'n ath-bhliadhna, ann an Zagreb e). B' e faclan
Arabaich no Pearsaich bh' anns a' mhòr-
chuid dhiubh, is iad air astar fada, sgìtheil

a choilionadh mus an do ràinig iad
na beòil 's na bilean Eòrpaich bhiodh gan cumadh.
Bha iad mar shiubhlaichean a ruigeas ceann
an ùidh', 's a thoisicheas a' fuireachd ann,
ach tuigidh neach bhon gluasadan, bhon dòigh

a th' ac' air coiseachd ann an aodach ùr,
neo-àbhaisteach, agus bhon fhàileadh ghallda
tha ga liubhairt air fad an craicinn-san,
nach ann an seo a tharmaicheadh 's a chinn iad.
Chuimhnich mi leabhar sònraicht' eile cuideachd,

a thachair mi ris ann an Kosova
's e sgrìobht' an cainnt nan Albàinianach,
a bha toirt làn-fhios air ainmeannan
nam planntaichean a gheibhear anns a' cheàirn ud,
chan ann a-mhàin an Laidinn, ach anns gach

cànain Bhàlcanaich a mhaireas fhathast.
'S mi smaointinn air an aighear uil', an luathghair
a thugadh dhomh le faclan 's cànainean,
cha b' fharmad a bh' agam ris a' chaileig
mhàlda, air neo riut is ri do chòmhlan,

gu dè an t-ainm a bhios oirbh, an Ràibeart,
Ailean no Teàrlach, Uilleam, Dàibhidh, Seònaid
no Mairead. Bha mi duilich air ùr sgàth,
is sibh gu diorrasach a' dèanamh brochain
nas tain' dhe bhrochan bha tana mar thà,

toirt ruaig air sgàile sgàil', 's an neach a thilg e
siubhal ann an làinnireachd a dheòntais,
an àite eile, dol an seòladh eile,
fhad 's a tha sibh, no feadhainn dhibh co-dhiù,
ceumnachadh sìos is suas an cèids' a' Bheurla,

a' leigeil oirbh, agus math dh'fhaoit' a' creidsinn,
gu bheil an saoghal uil' agaibh fo smachd.
Cha b' urrainn dhomh aithreachas dùrachdach
fhaireachdainn air sgàth mo shaothrach cruaidhe
no m' dhìchill ann an ionnsachadh nan cànain.

'Nam bheachd fhìn b' ann mar gu robh sibh a' dèanamh
shìnteagan gu cabhagach air fad
trannsa, 's a ballachan gan còmhdachadh
le leabhraichean bha sgrìobhte anns gach cànain
a tha ga cleachdadh anns an t-saoghal, ach cha

do stad sibh, b' ann mar nach robh sibh gam faicinn
gus na ràinig sibh na leabhraichean
a sgrìobhadh ann am Beurla, no a chaidh
eadar-theangachadh gus a' chànain sin.
Ach 's mi sealltainn air ais, nach fhacas leam

iomadh pearsa clis, beag, dìcheallach,
fàraidhean ac', is iad dol suas is sìos orr',
trang leis na leabhraichean a dhearmaid sibh!
Thuig mi gur iad na daoine a bhios eòlas
nan cànain ac', is ged nach bi an obair

a' faighinn luach no luaidh no aithneachaidh,
gu bheil gach oidhirp a nithear leibh, gu ruig
na dàintean a sgrìobhas sibh nur cànain fhèin,
an aon chànain a th' agaibh, is a bhios,
an eisimeil air a' chuid a tha dol thairis

air iomallan nan cànain, is a tha
cur facail làimh ri facal eile, nach
do choinnich e ris fhathast, gus an tomhas
air meidh na cèill; a' chuid a rannsaicheas
gu dàna cogaiseach gach uile crìoch

a th' aig an do-thuigsinneachd, is a thig
air ais le stòr a ghabhas pàirteachadh.
Nam b' urrainn dhomh bhith air mo ainmeachadh
'nam measg, bhithinn-sa sàsaichte gu leòr!
Ma leughas tu na ranntan seo, is dòcha

gum fàs thu dìreach cho feargach 's a bhà
an uair a sgrìobh thu litir thugam. Ach
cha bu chòir dragh a bhith orm, 's e mòran
nas coltaiche nach leugh thu iad a-chaoidh.
Bhiodh feum agad air eadar-theangaichear.

TO A YOUNG SCOTTISH POET WHO WROTE THAT IT IS AN UNUSUAL SITUATION WHEN SOMEONE UNDERSTANDS THE LANGUAGE THEY ARE TRANSLATING FROM

Wouldn't it be splendid, you said, if an ordinary,
unassuming writer like yourself had time to learn the
language used by the poet you want to translate!

You, however, are not a snob or an élitist, not rigid and
inflexible like me, but accommodating, easy-going.
Moreover, your own poetry, and the research required for
it,

take up so much of your time you cannot understand why
I should make a fuss if you, or one of your colleagues,
some poor guy who only knows two languages, looks
around for an already existing

translation into English or French, then puts this into his
fine English. I was reminded of dogs in a cage, running
back and forth, barking uproariously, who nevertheless stay
put

when the door is opened. They know that they will get
their fill of food without moving. And of the thoroughly
likeable young woman who arrived at a translation
workshop with no trace of a blush on her cheek,

though the only language she spoke was English, sitting
calmly next to a poet putting his own work into English
for her sake, after which she could get busy.

What work was she doing? Turning English into English?
Can that be called translation? I thought of the hours, the
days, the weeks spent bent over grammars and
dictionaries,

hunting down one word after another, getting used to the
different order of the letters in languages which use a
different alphabet. Or of a shop in Sarajevo, where I came
upon two books I failed to buy

because my fellow traveller was so scathing: one was a
Latvian to Russian dictionary, the other listed all the
Turkish expressions used

in what used to be called Yugoslavia. I bought it in Zagreb
the following year. Most were Arabian and Persian words,
which had made a long, exhausting journey

before reaching the lips in Europe that would utter them.
They were like emigrants who settle down upon reaching
their destination, but you can tell they did not originate
here

from the way they move, their gait in unfamiliar clothes,
the alien fragrance of their skin. Another book came into
mind,

bought in Kosovo, written in Albanian. It listed the names
of all the plants found there, not just in Latin, but in every

Balkan language spoken today. Reflecting on all the joy, the
exultation I derived from words and languages, I could not
envy the young woman, you or your friends,

whatever your names, Robert, Alan, Charlie, William,
David, Jane or Margaret! I pitied you, diligently making
watery soup from soup that was watery to start with,

chasing the shadow of a shadow. The one who casts it
moves forward in all the brilliance of his spontaneity, in
another place, heading in another direction, while you, or
some of you at any rate, pace up and down inside the cage
of English,

pretending, and maybe believing as well, the whole world is
at your fingertips. I could not bring myself to regret the
sheer hard work of learning languages.

You might all have been rushing without stopping down a
corridor whose walls were lined with books written in
every language in the world,

behaving as if these were invisible till you reached the
books written, or translated, into English. Looking back,
though, what did I see

but a host of small, nimble, figures running up and down
ladders, working on the books you had ignored! They were
the people who learn languages. Even if

their work is not recognised, praised, or rewarded, every
task you undertake, even the poems you write in your
mother tongue, depends on them. They cross

the frontiers between languages, placing a word on the
scales of meaning next to another it has never met before.
Boldly, responsibly, they explore the limits

of what can be understood, returning with a treasure that
can be shared. It would be sufficient satisfaction for me to
have my name appear alongside theirs. If you should read
these lines,

you will get just as furious as you were when you wrote
that letter. But I shouldn't worry overmuch. You will still
be depending upon a translator.

(prose translation by the author)

Hamish Whyte

OTIS

I'd like to see you in my dreams,
old cat, nose pushing at the door
in welcome; warming your snowy
underside at the fire; ginger hovis
on my lap. Instead, I can't help
seeing you in your last minutes
staring at us with blind open eyes,
wheezing as your lungs shut down,
as all of you shut down,
your chin coming to rest
on the table as the drugs took
hold, put you to dreamless sleep.

Fiona Wilson

MAGPIE

On the cut-glass *if* of the day,
this chancer, then, already in deep,
head-first among the holly leaves,

and pleasing herself and tricky as a die,
that tips and birls and drops,
she lands, lands in sharp relief,

a chatter of berries, red in her beak.

BIOGRAPHIES

Keith Aitchison lives and works in Inverness. He writes chiefly during winter, when darkness and poor weather bring the urge to make stories. These usually have their beginning in something seen or heard, and may finish as mostly recollection, or mostly fiction, so long as they entertain.

Edinburgh based, **Ruth Aylett** researches computer-based interactive narrative. She writes stories about the impact of technology, emotion and politics on people's lives; dreams about possible and impossible futures.

Colin Begg, 35, is a paediatrician from Ayrshire. His poetry has appeared in various magazines and anthologies including *New Writing Scotland* 24. Colin has practised medicine from Govan to Gundegai, while also studying Creative Writing at UTS (Sydney) and Glasgow University. Between poems he works at Yorkhill hospital and is finishing a novel.

Liam Murray Bell was born in Orkney. He is writing for the MLitt in Creative Writing at Glasgow University. He has previously been published in *New Writing Scotland* 21, and will be published in the upcoming MLitt anthology *(in)fidelity*. He is currently working on a novel based in the Orkney Islands.

Tom Bryan was born in Canada in 1950. Long resident in Scotland, he lives in Kelso, and is a widely published and broadcast poet and fiction writer. He has appeared in previous *New Writing Scotland* anthologies.

Eliza Chan is teaching in an island in Japan with mixed but amusing results. She studied English Literature and History at the University of Glasgow where she developed 'Subtext' from the apparent madness of most feminist literary critics. She is a member of the Glasgow Science Fiction Writers' Circle.

Ian Crockatt is currently translating Rainer Maria Rilke's *Neue Gedichte* (*New Poems*) written between 1904 and 1908. 'Washing the Corpse' gives a sense of the power and originality of Rilke's imagination and technique, although it is very much a 'Crockatt' interpretation and update of the original.

Tracey Emerson started writing fiction in 2003 and in 2004 was a runner-up in the Scotsman and Orange Short Story Award. Her short fiction has been published in anthologies and magazines. She is currently studying for an MSc in Creative Writing at Edinburgh University and writing her first novel.

Graham Fulton has been widely published in the UK and USA. His collections include *Humouring the Iron Bar Man* (Polygon), *This* (Rebel Inc.), *Knights of the Lower Floors* (Polygon), *Ritual Soup and other liquids* (Mariscat). Two new collections, *Upside Down Heart* and *Black Motel*, are due to be published by Dreadful Night Press.

Mark Gallacher was born in 1967 in Girvan. Since 1999 he has lived in Denmark. He is married and has two young sons. Poems, prose, short stories have appeared regularly in many quality UK literary magazines, and in Italy and the USA.

Alan Gay: *The Boy Who Came Ashore* (Dreadful Night Press) is his latest publication of prose and poetry. It pays tribute to the courage and endurance of east-coast fishermen caught at sea in the great storm of 1881. He lives in East Lothian and sails all summer with his wife in their five-ton cutter.

Diana Hendry's poetry collections include *Making Blue*, *Borderers* (Peterloo), *Twelve Lilts: Psalms & Responses* and, with Tom Pow, *Sparks!* (Mariscat). Her junior novel, *Harvey Angell*, won a Whitbread Award. She's worked as a journalist, creative writing tutor, writer-in-residence and currently is a Royal Literary Fund fellow at Edinburgh University.

Kate Hendry teaches in Barlinnie prison and for the Open University. She has had short stories published in *New Writing Scotland*, *Mslexia*, and *Harpers* amongst others. She lives in Ayrshire with her partner and two children. 'When Gordon Ran Away' is from a novel-in-progress.

Angela Howard's short stories and poetry are published in UK and US presses including *Orbis*, *Chapman*, *New Writing Scotland*, *Poetry Monthly*, *Poetry Scotland*, *Paris-Atlantic*, *Littoral*. Her poetry collection *Jostled by Ghosts* was published in 2006 (Poetry Monthly Press). She has broadcast literary programmes for the BBC, and lives in France.

Ian Hunter writes children's novels, short stories and poems. His poem, 'Grey Baby', appeared in a previous *New Writing Scotland*. He is the Chair of the Michty Johnstone Writers Group and a member of the Glasgow Science Fiction Writers' Circle who 'crittered' this story into shape for him.

David Hutchison was brought up in Assynt, Sutherland. He draws upon his Highland roots to mix Scottish myths and legends with contemporary culture. For more information see **www.davidhutchison.co.uk**.

Linda Jackson works as a creative writing tutor in Strathclyde and at a Glasgow College. A writer and musician, she is working on her second novel, and has had many short stories published in various magazines. She has edited a book of critical essays on Janice Galloway, *Exchanges*, and is about to launch her third album in June. Sometimes she does rest.

Paula Jennings lives in Cellardyke, Fife. She was awarded SAC Writers' Bursaries in 1999 and 2002, a Hawthornden Writing Fellowship in 2003, and was a featured poet at Stanza Poetry Festival 2005. She has published a poetry collection, *Singing Lucifer* (Onlywomen Press). A new collection will be published this year.

Vivien Jones lives on the north Solway shore dividing her time between writing prose, drama and poetry and devising reading events, often with music. A short chapbook, *Something in the Blood*, was published in February 2008

(Selkirk Lapwing Press) and another longer one, *Hare* (Erbacce Press) is due later this year.

Alex Laird spent his working life in the building industry, and in the Architects' department of a large local authority. On retiring, he joined his local writers' group under the tutelage of James Robertson. Previously published in *New Writing Scotland* and many others.

Helen Lamb has published a poetry collection, *Strange Fish*, and a short story collection, *Superior Bedsits* (Polygon). Her work has also been widely published in literary journals and anthologies. Many of her stories have been broadcast on radio. She is currently a Royal Literary Fund fellow.

William Letford lives and works in Stirling and is currently working on his first collection of short stories.

Rowena M. Love lives in Troon and has many published poems and articles to her credit. She has one solo collection, *The Chameleon of Happiness*, and one joint one, *Running Threads* (both published by Makar Press). She is also an accomplished speaker, performer and workshop leader.

Peter Maclaren taught English in Glasgow schools between 1971 and 2005. Wrote a regular column in *TESS* until a new editor spiked his copy. Has had poems in *Lines Review*, *Akros*, *Teaching English*, *Glasgow Review*, *Glasgow English Magazine* and *Cencrastus*. (How come so many of these magazines are defunct?)

Lois McEwan is a sub-editor on *The Sunday Times*. She won second prize in the 2007 Asham short story award and is published in their collection *Is This What You Want?* Her poetry appears in Virago's *New Poets* anthology and has been broadcast by Australia's ABC. She is from Edinburgh.

James McGonigal has combined writing with teaching since the early 1970s. His poetry has been published in various Scottish anthologies and in *Driven Home* (1998) and *Passage/An Pasaíste* (2004), both from Mariscat Press. He co-edits the critical series SCROLL (Scottish Cultural Review of Language and Literature) from Rodopi.

David McVey is a lecturer at the University of the West of Scotland. He has published nearly 100 short stories and also writes non-fiction. He would like to write a novel and live to see Kirkintilloch Rob Roy win the Scottish Junior Cup.

Michael Malone, from Ayr, is well-published in the literary press and has two collections available from Makar Press. With his fellow Makar Press Poets he has performed at over 50 venues throughout the country. He was awarded the Dorothy Dunbar Poetry Prize 2008 by the Scottish Association of Writers.

Greg Michaelson lives and works in Edinburgh. His writing has appeared in *Scottish Book Collector, Textualities Online* and *Science and Intuition* 1. His first novel, *The Wave Singer*, will be publised by Argyll Publishing in the summer of 2008.

Jason Monios is an Australian writer resident in Scotland. He completed his PhD in 2001, investigating the concept of the vortex in the poetry of Ezra Pound. His writing has appeared in *Void, Softblow, Dogmatika, Umbrella, Flutter, Nuvein, La Fenêtre, The Dogwood Journal, Subtle Tea, Sidewalk* and *Bluepepper.*

Richard Mosses runs a medical device company in central Scotland. He has been writing since he can remember. He is an active participant of the GSFWC and the WordDogs spoken word group. He is currently working on his second novel, *Adocentyn*, set in a street beneath Glasgow's Central Station.

Anne B. Murray was born in Glasgow where she now lives. She facilitates writing and reminiscence workshops and organises poetry sharing sessions with carers and other community groups. She has had poems published in various magazines and has three collections of her poetry published by Terra Firma Press.

Alison Napier lives in Sutherland where she is employed as a part-time social worker. Her short stories and occasional non-fiction have appeared in anthologies, national newspapers and magazines and her first novel (featuring the characters in 'Invisible Mending') will be completed by the end of 2008.

Liz Niven is a poet and creative writing tutor. Originally from Glasgow, she's based in Dumfries. She has published several poetry collections in English and in Scots and has participated in a range of International Literary events. **www.lizniven.com**

Helen Parker loves language – reading, writing, teaching English as a second language: she's even passionate about grammar. At present she is trying to learn Modern Greek. She belongs to a book club and a writing group, and gets her ideas while swimming. Her best critics are her husband and her young adult 'children'.

Vix Parker lives in Inverness and is a founding member of the Random Acts of Writing Collective, producers of *R.A.W.*, the Highland-based short story magazine. She previously appeared in *New Writing Scotland* 24, and in 2006 she wrote a novel with the help of a Scottish Arts Council bursary.

Allan Radcliffe was born in Perth and now lives in Edinburgh. His articles, short stories and poems have appeared in *The Sunday Times*, the *Scotsman*, *Scotland on Sunday*, the *Sunday Herald*, *Celtic View*, *The List*, *Metro* and *The Big Issue*. He is currently working on a novel.

Alan Riach holds the Chair of Scottish Literature at Glasgow University, is the general editor of the *Collected Works* of Hugh MacDiarmid and the author of *Representing Scotland in Literature, Popular Culture and Iconography* (Palgrave Macmillan, 2005). His fourth book of poems, *Clearances* (2001), follows *First & Last Songs* (1995), *An Open Return* (1991) and *This Folding Map* (1990). His radio series *The Good of the Arts*, first broadcast in New Zealand in 2001, may be visited at **www.southwest.org.nz**

BIOGRAPHIES 259

R. J. Ritchie, an anagram of Erotic Rebirth, this year celebrates/grieves 15 years of running Stirling Writers' Group. Recently described in the *Scotsman* as one of Scotland's best wits and central Scotland pun-meister. Poems have appeared in *New Writing Scotland*, *Chapman*, *Poetry Scotland* and other poetry-based products.

Nancy Somerville is a Glaswegian now living in Edinburgh. Her poems have appeared in various magazines and anthologies. In 2004, with Stewart Conn, she co-edited *Goldfish Suppers*, an illustrated poetry anthology for children. She is currently working on her first collection for Red Squirrel Press.

Kenneth Steven lives in Dunkeld in Perthshire but travels widely to give readings and to run writing workshops. In December of 2007 a volume of his selected poems was published by Peterloo in Cornwall. 'Lemon Ice Cream' was broadcast on BBC Radio 4 in the same month.

Jim Taylor was born in Glasgow in 1962. As well as prolonged stints as a benefits claimant, he has had jobs in Glasgow, Shetland, the West Highlands, China and Australia, and stories in *Chapman*, *New Shetlander*, *West Coast*, *Rebel Inc.* and *Edinburgh Review*.

Douglas Thompson won the Grolsch/Glasgow Herald 'Question of Style' Award in 1989, and won second prize in the Neil Gunn Writing Competition in 2007. Has published short stories in *The Herald*, *West Coast Magazine*, *Northwords*, *Chapman*, *The Drouth*, *Bad Idea*, *Dreamcatcher*, *Random Acts Of Writing*, *Ambit*, and the *Subtle Edens* slipstream anthology. **www.glasgowsurrealist.com/douglas**

Valerie Thornton is a writer, an editor and a creative writing tutor. She has held two Royal Literary Fund Writing Fellowships at Glasgow University. Her tutoring embraces mainstream and specialist groups, and the Open University. Her latest creative-writing textbooks are *The Writer's Craft*, and *The Young Writer's Craft* (Hodder Gibson).

Ryan Van Winkle lives in Scotland. He is a member of

The Forest, a non-profit arts collective based in Edinburgh. In 2007 he placed third in the Ver Poets competition and was featured in *The Golden Hour Book*. His work has also appeared in *New Leaf* (Bremen) and *FuseLit* (London).

Greg Whelan is twenty years old and hails from Methil, on the coast of Fife. He is currently in his third year of English Literature at Edinburgh University and writes in his free time. His short story 'Virgin Maria' won the University's 2007 Sloan Prize for writings in the Scots vernacular.

Ian Nimmo White is a prolifically published poet who was a youth and community worker with Fife Council for 35 years. He writes in both English and Scots and has produced three collections of poetry: *Memory and Imagination* (Scottish Book Trust 1998), *Standing Back* (Petrel 2002) and *Symmetry* (Trafford 2007).

Jane Whiteford teaches in social work part-time. In 2003 she co-authored a report on young people's experiences of being in care. Last year she was runner up in the Orange Broadband Short Story Competition. She has recently finished her first novel, *The Foundation*. She lives in Edinburgh and is a member of Scottish PEN.

Brian Whittingham is a poet, fiction writer, playwright and editor. Born in, lives in and teaches creative writing in further education, in Glasgow. Has held various writing fellowships with the most recent award being a RLS fellowship in Grez in 2008. **www.brianwhittingham.co.uk**

Hamish Whyte is a poet, editor and publisher. His latest poetry publication is *Window on the Garden* (Essence/ Botanic), a Shoestring Press collection forthcoming. He has edited many anthologies and runs Mariscat Press. He is an Honorary Research Fellow, Department of Scottish Literature, Glasgow University, and lives in Edinburgh.

Fiona Wilson grew up near Aberdeen and now lives in New York City. Her work has appeared most recently in *Markings*; *Poetry Review*; *Painted, spoken*; and *Pequod*. She is currently completing her first book of poetry.